OH, GEMINI!

Riley Angulo

OH, GEMINI!

~~~~~

Riley Angulo
~~~~~

Published by Riley Angulo
Salt Lake City, Utah, USA
ISBN: 979-8-90030-244-7
Cover design by Love Lee Creative
Printed in the United States of America
10 9 8 7 6 5 4 3 2 1
First Edition

F*or those brave enough to chase the story others have doomed from the start. This story is for you.*

Playlist for *Oh, Gemini!*

"There She Goes" – The La's
"Moves" – Suki Waterhouse
"State Of Grace" – Taylor Swift
"Peaches" – In The Valley Below
"Time Shrinks" – Arcy Drive
"Sometimes" – Goth Babe
"Ode to a Conversation Stuck in Your Throat" – Del Water Gap
"Call It What You Want" – Taylor Swift
"Trouble" – Cage The Elephant
"Supercut" – Lorde
"When the Sun Hits" – Souvlaki
"Kiss Me" – Sixpence None The Richer
"Blue Honey" – Lunar Vacation
"Chiquitita" – ABBA
"invisible string" – Taylor Swift

chapter one

Welcome to Saltmere, where love always washes ashore!

The faded wooden sign at the edge of Saltmere, North Carolina swishes back and forth on its hinges, waving at me as I enter into a town that believes the concept of love is as steady and promising as the tide.

I want to believe that too; I want to smile at the thought of finding a soulmate being as easy and relaxing as the ocean waves just outside my car window. But right now, it feels as if both the tide and my own trust in love, of all kinds, are slipping away from me.

My phone pings in my cupholder, and a message pops up onto the screen of my car. It's from Jenny, my boss.

`You got this, Holland. Call me if you need anything. Please don't hesitate to let me know if it gets too hard being there.`

Tingles sprinkle down my throat, stinging it as tears line my eyelids. Even if it does get hard being in this town that I got to dream in my sleep about after my mom's bedtime stories, I won't give up. I won't leave and go back to my empty, lonely apartment in New York that doesn't feel like home. I won't let anything ruin this second chance. Not just because my mom loved this small, beach town on the East Coast and couldn't stop talking about it before she passed last November, but because if I don't at least try to love it the way she did, it feels like losing her all over again. And maybe, if I can find some kind of spark here, I can finally write again, before my editor runs out of patience and I lose the only thing I love that I have left.

I blink away the salty liquid because I refuse to cry today and shift my focus to the wide stretch of the North Carolina sky, soft and endless outside my window. My mission here is to *save the town* by writing a portfolio of articles that will attract our magazine's readers and others to visit Saltmere. Jenny has family from here, but she can't leave our New York office as our editor-in-chief, so she wants me to travel down the East Coast's edge to the town that, according to the pictures I've seen online *and* what I am looking at through my rolled down window of my Toyota Prius, might be in more desperate need than I thought.

Not even the town's residents walk along the streets of the tiny town as my car rolls into it. I slow down to a reasonable speed to observe the businesses, watching in the windows as the reflection of my car drives right along with me. The flower shop, Petal Parade, has a paper sign taped to the glass door that reads: **TEMPORARILY CLOSED**. Next door, The Book Burrow, sits in darkness. So does the hardware store.

The sight matches what I already knew: Saltmere, my mom's and North Carolina's "hidden treasure", is struggling. Jenny's cousin, the town sheriff, said so himself. Gift shops, rental services, food shacks, and beachwear stores lining the main street are threatening to shut down or have already. Even the annual Sea Glass Festival, once famous along the boardwalk, has dwindled to too many rides and not enough people to make them worth running.

There is, however, human interaction at the grocery store, Green Basket. The parking lot is half full, and I can see people walking in and out of the sliding doors. Women pushing shopping carts with small children in the front seat, men carrying reusable sacks in one hand and a case of beer in the other. Pleasant smiles on each of their faces, even the babies.

Behind the buildings, on my right-hand side, the ocean is endless. Once I drive further down the main street and the buildings begin to clear out, I can see some folks on the sand leading up to the sea's edge. Some sailboats are in the water, drifting along the calm waves. The cooler ocean breeze outside makes the bangs of my shoulder-length brown hair fly over my eyes and nose, and all I can smell is salt. It brings a smile to my face. A real, genuine, hopeful smile.

The GPS directs me to turn right five minutes out of town. My tires crunch against the uneven road as I enter a neighborhood of houses with sandy backyards that open into the sea. The movement jolts the unfinished painting of my mom's I secretly took from her abandoned art room in our childhood home in the back seat, sliding it against the upholstery. For a moment, my chest aches, like even her art is reminding me of everything I've lost. I grip the steering wheel tighter, mentally shake it off, and focus on the road ahead. Mabel, the homeowner of the cottage I'm renting for the month, said in her email that her place is at the very end of the street. And when the blush-pink, two-story cottage finally comes into view, my smile resurfaces.

I pull into the driveway, against the edge of the perfectly cut green grass. Palm tree leaves hang down from the branches, caving in towards the bright blue front door. My sandals slap against the pavement as I step out of my car and walk up the steps to the house, my eyes wandering around the property with each stride. The wraparound porch is draped in string lights that cast a warm glow over the potted hydrangeas and buckets of seashells near the front door, and it has a wooden swing hanging in the left corner. The two windows on either side of the door are surrounded by white trim and yellow paint chipped shutters, with flower window boxes full of petunias underneath.

I form my hand into a fist and knock three times. Only a matter of seconds pass before the front door whips open. An older woman with black curly hair thrown up in a messy bun stands in the doorway, wearing a bright green blouse and white capris. She gives me a wide smile. "Hiya! Are you Holland Anderson?"

"Yes, I am," I say with relief. It's the right house. "You must be Mabel."

"I sure am!"

"It's so good to finally meet you. This place is beautiful," I respond, stretching my hand out in front of me.

She glances at it, then shakes her head. "Sorry, I'm a hugger."

Then she throws her arms around me, squeezing me in the embrace. She smells like cinnamon and coconut. I giggle as she lets go of me, then she waves her hand for me to follow her inside.

"This beauty is my pride and joy, but she hasn't seen any visitors in a while. Not many come around here anymore, you know?" She's not asking me the question. My gaze roams around the open, airy, and sun-drenched space. The inside is full of bright pastel colors and whitewashed wood-paneled walls. The living room has a white oversized sectional that sits in front of the large windows with light pink curtains pushed to the sides to exhibit the ocean view. A soft, tan and pink patterned rug lays on the dark hardwood floors underneath, and the mantle against the far wall has a large flatscreen television resting on it, along with colorful books and frames full of pictures of seashells and the horizon at sunset.

The kitchen to the left is open concept, with seafoam green cabinets and white countertops. The scent of fresh coffee and driftwood filters and floats through the space. Some of the open shelves have hand painted mugs of all shapes and colors and pots with tulips resting on them. A wooden table is placed in between the kitchen and living room, with a vase of bright yellow and red flowers in the center.

Mabel begins explaining the history of the home, detailing how the house was built in 1964 and has been in her family's care for over thirty years. She offers me insight on some of the neighbors–how I need to be aware of Patty Corrington, the older woman who owns a cozy bed and breakfast and has a half-blind chihuahua that likes to munch on the plants on the front porch. Patty, apparently, purposefully lets the small dog wander across the street to the house because of an argument Mabel and Patty had over *fifty* years ago. Mabel doesn't even remember what the fight was about, but Patty hasn't forgotten, and therefore lets her *demon dog*–Mabel's words– loose on the streets to ruin Mabel's lovely yard.

I snicker as she moves on to inform me of the neighbor directly next door, Atlas Richens, the mysterious boatbuilder of the town that doesn't say much to anyone.

"If you can get that man to talk, or maybe to move his boat from the dock right outside, let me know," Mabel says. "He's been living next door for only a couple of years, and not one person in the town knows much about him. Just that he builds boats and would occasionally make an appearance at The Book Burrow before they shut down a few weeks ago."

Interesting. "I'll let you know if I make friends with the guy," I say, huffing a laugh. Silence falls over the two of us as I peer out the window. "So is it really true that the town doesn't get too many tourists?"

Mabel nods. "Sadly, yes. You're my first renter in over a year. I was about to put either this house or my condo up for sale right before you emailed me."

"Why is that? I would assume that coastal towns like this one does great with tourists."

"We did, once upon a time. Back when Gemini Development didn't sweep in and buy most of the shops down main. The construction company promised the owners that they would be able to still run their shops, but, of course, they lied. Tricked the owners, right under their noses. Most of the stores that have been here for decades will be torn down in the next few months so they can build a strip mall and more apartment buildings."

I should be taking notes. "Damn," I confess. "That's horrible. Who runs Gemini Development? Are they local?"

"Kurt Gemini and his two sons, and no. Kurt claims to have visited Saltmere multiple times, but no one in the town remembers him or his family. I think all that comes out of his mouth is bullshit." My eyebrows rise on my forehead. "I have a feeling that you are probably telling the truth, Mabel." I look around the living room once again. "I'm glad that I found this place before it wasn't available to rent anymore. The house is so cute."

I take a step closer to the large windows, shoving my hands in my jean pockets. Sure enough, a small skiff boat drifts in the marshy water outside, next to the wooden dock. But before the shore, the open deck attached to the house has two rocking chairs with faded cushions propped up in front of the railing. The grass is perfectly trimmed and a mix of bushes and flowers line the yard like a makeshift fence. A few wooden chairs circle around a small fire pit in the far-right corner, with string lights that attach all the way to the ceiling of the house hanging overhead. The sun is sinking lower towards the line of the sea, the water now reflecting an array of oranges and pinks and purples. Seagulls swarm high in the air. I can hear the waves of the ocean all the way up to the glass of the window, the sound comforting and reminiscent.

"Have you ever been to North Carolina before?" Mabel asks from behind me.

I shake my head. "No. My mom has been to this town, though. It's another reason why I'm here. She would tell me and my siblings how much she loved it here. She used to spend so much time painting beaches of the Outer Banks before her attorney career took off and her cancer made her too ill to paint."

Mabel places a hand on my forearm. "You should check out the art gallery next to the boardwalk. I think you would find something you'll love. Or something she would've loved."

Her words sink into my skin, warming it instantly. I give her a watery smile, and she nods, clicks her tongue, then saunters off to the front door. "I have to head out, but I'll be back tomorrow morning to get some things from the shop in the back. I left my number on a Post-it on the fridge. Call me if you have any issues!"

She exits out the door, shutting it gently behind her. I slouch down onto the couch, resting my head against the soft cushion behind me. I exhale into the lavender and salt scented air, closing my eyelids for a moment to breathe it all back in.

Mabel's words float around in my head. *Gemini Development.* I should interview Kurt, get the rundown of his plans. Or maybe one of his sons. Any information I receive could help the town's businesses from disappearing.

The full day of traveling from New York to Saltmere is getting to me. My body loosens up against the cushions, and I tuck my legs under me. My stomach grumbles unhappily, clearly not satisfied with the Nature Valley granola bars and Mott's fruit snacks I snacked on the entire nine-hour drive, but I let my eyes flutter shut.

I jolt awake when I hear a door slam outside. A car door. Or a truck. I blink rapidly to force my eyes to adjust to where I am, sitting up straighter to glance out the window. The full moon stares at me back, glistening against the water just a few yards away from the house. *Right. I'm in Saltmere.* My bare feet land on the soft rug on the floor after I wrap a blanket from the basket next to the couch, and I pad my way towards the front of the house. My fingers spread the blinds farther apart so I can peek through them. Thanks to the moon above and the few houses in the neighborhood that have their porch lights on, I can see a large Chevy truck connected to a long trailer with a white boat on it right in front of the house. The boat appears to be another skiff boat, but this one has the word *Richens* written in red lettering on the side.

I watch as a tall man appears from the other side of the trailer, rubbing his hands together before he raises to his toes to peer into the boat. He's wearing a blue ball cap and a black t-shirt. My eyes, surely against my will, travel over the man's tight denim jeans that perfectly shape his–

Stop.

It's clearly been too long since my breakup with my ex, Gordon.

I blink twice and shake my head, flicking on my own porch lights to help him see better, but the man doesn't seem to notice. My eyes continue watching the man outside lower to his knees on the rocky pavement of the road. The sleeves of his shirt crawl up, revealing his toned upper arms and an array of inky designs that I can't see clearly from where I stand like a stalker inside of the house.

He continues peering under the trailer, his hands digging for something, so I slip my sandals back on my feet and exit through the front door. The strands of grass of the yard tickle the sides of my feet as I walk straight to the end of the trailer.

"Hi," I say.

The man startles and inhales sharply at the sound of my voice. His body freezes in the position he's in, one hand holding him up and the other tucked under the trailer, but his head turns and looks directly at my bare legs. As slow as a snail, his gaze travels up my entire body, probably internally judging my bright purple running shorts and the *Easily Distracted by Peckers* t-shirt I have on that has a cartoon chicken on the front of it under my blanket. I stole the shirt from my sister, Corinne, years ago and will never return it.

Finally, the man's eyes meet mine. His irises are a dark shade of brown in this lighting, and the tanned skin of his face appears to be smooth and licked with a coat of sweat. He rises to his feet, brushing his hands on the fronts of his perfectly fitted denim jeans.

"Hi," he says, his voice rough. "Who are you?"

"Ah, so he does talk," I mutter, tilting my head to the side. I look at the name written on the boat next to him. "I'm assuming you are Atlas Richens?"

"Who's asking?" His dark eyebrows frown on his forehead.

"Me?" My voice accidentally shoots up into a question. I stick my arm out for him to shake it, and my blanket slips off of my arms and falls onto the pavement. The man, most likely Atlas, watches it all the way until it rests like a puddle at his boots.

With his hands on his hips, he scoffs. "And you are?"

I snatch the blanket up and bundle it in my arms. "Who's asking?" When he gives me a pointed look, I relent. "Holland Anderson. Your new neighbor for the month."

"You don't know that I'm Atlas Richens."

"Given that you decided to park a big truck and an even bigger boat that has your last name written on the side in front of my house, I can only believe that you are, in fact, Atlas Richens. The mystery guy of Saltmere whose name would piss off a Flat Earther."

He grunts. "Mystery guy? Flat Earther?"

"Uh huh. Mabel told me that no one in this town knows much about you. Only that you build boats and choose to leave them right behind Mabel's house." I narrow my eyes. "Do you even know that Mabel is your neighbor?"

He rolls his eyes. "I have seen her around, yes. I know that she rents her house out."

I hum and look back at the boat. "So you think it's fine leaving your humongous truck and shiny new boat in front of *my* house?"

Atlas takes another step forward, and I am impaled with his pine and cedar scent. My chin rises so I can meet his gaze, and I don't back down when he lowers his neck several inches, so his lips hover right above my ear. Quietly, he says, "If Mabel has a problem with me leaving my truck and boat in front of *her* house, she can be the one to bring it up to me." He straightens, his cedar-pine scent crowding me, and his voice drops lower. "But you? You're just here for a month. A tourist with opinions. You'll be gone before anyone bothers remembering your name."

He doesn't wait for me to answer, just turns back to his truck, keys jingling in his hand. A second later, he locks it with a loud *beep* that makes my shoulders jump.

Atlas, or Flat Earth's Nemesis, saunters past me, the wind he carries knocking my hair across my face. He climbs his porch steps and places his hand on the doorknob, then glances back at me.

"I like the sound of being the mystery guy, Holly. Do yourself a favor: take a note from the rest of this town and don't bother trying to figure me out. We both know you'll have better things to write about."

Anger boils in my veins as he shuts himself inside. I stomp my foot like a child and yell, "My name is Holland!"

chapter two

I'm woken up the next morning by the sound of pounding over and over again. I crack one eye open, but I am met with a single ray of the sun's that pokes through the slits of the blinds of the bedroom's window. I sit up and rake a hand through my knotted hair as the pounding continues outside of the bedroom. With a pair of black running shorts on and another one of Corinne's shirts that I stole hanging off of one of my shoulders, I trudge to where the pounding is coming from. The front door.

It's Mabel standing on the porch, looking extra happy to see me. "Hi, dear! Did I wake you?"

"No," I lie, then look down at my attire. "Okay, maybe. But come on in." I move to the side as she steps inside the house, and I shut the door behind her. "Don't you have a key to this place? You could've just come in. I wouldn't have minded."

"I do, but I once walked in on a couple…you know. Having fun." She winks before faking a gag. "They were my first renters, and I happened to forget my cell phone on the table as I was heading out. I will never make that mistake again."

I stifle a laugh under my palm. "I'm sure that was horrible for you." I pad to the kitchen. "Do you want some coffee?"

"No, I'm alright. Already had some at the cafe. I just need to head back to the shed to grab some things." Mabel digs through a drawer next to the kitchen sink. She pulls out a set of keys and tucks them into her pocket. Then she turns back to me. "So, what exactly are you here for? I mean, I know you're a journalist. The town already knows all about you coming here. But why Saltmere?"

"I'm a travel journalist. My boss, Jenny, has a cousin that lives here. Sam, I think? He was telling her how the town is losing tourists and businesses are shutting down. Jenny sent me here to write some content for our magazine to try and help bring some people down here."

Mabel looks like she either wants to cry or throw her arms around me in excitement. She's bouncing, *bouncing*, on her toes, and she's got her hands covering her mouth. Her shoulders crunch into her neck as she smiles at me. "That's the kindest gesture I've ever heard, Holland. I don't even really know you that well, but I fully believe in you. I think you'll do so much good here. I know that once everyone knows what you're doing here, everyone will shower you with gratitude for saving this town."

Yeah, no pressure at all. Thanks, Mabel. I smile back. "I hope I can write a collection of articles that will hopefully help."

"Wait, did you say Sam?" When I nod, she tilts her head to the side, a smirk crawling over her lips. "He's the sheriff here. I'm sure he would love to meet up with you. He can give you more of the town's history."

"Yeah, that was my plan. I have a meeting with him tomorrow morning, actually."

Mabel winks, and not at all smoothly. "He's single, too."

My cheeks get rosy, but I roll my eyes, smiling. "You rent this house *and* are a matchmaker? Wow, maybe I should write about that first. I can already see the headline: *"Head on down to Saltmere, NC, full of beautiful rental homes and single folks"*."

Mabel disregards my words. Her face lights up. "Oh my god, you are a genius!"

"I was just joki–"

"You should write about the festival!"

"What?" I rear my head back. "How does that have anything to do with you being a matchmaker?"

"The Sea Glass Festival happens on the boardwalk every year, and this year we are having a kissing booth for the adults. It was my idea, but most people on the board think it won't do anything to help bring people down here. But if you write about it, it could attract your readers!"

"A kissing booth?" I mutter. "That would make headlines. People will want to click on that." I reach for my notebook in my purse that's hanging on the doorknob of the pantry. I take a seat at the table and flip open to an open page. With my favorite pen, I tap against my chin and look at Mabel. "So you really could be a matchmaker," I say, scribbling notes. "This could be what my first article could be about. When's the festival again?"

"It's this weekend. In three days. On Friday."

"That might be a little soon, but it can work," I mutter, my hand jotting down on the lines of the paper with my notes. I'd have to finish a draft by the end of tomorrow. Doable, but tight. I'd done it with the Acadia piece back in August. "I'll still meet with Sam to get some history and background of the town, but could I meet with you to talk about the festival? Like maybe tomorrow?"

"Of course. I can stop by here tomorrow afternoon."

"Great." I nod, and a wave of excitement flutters down my skin. This always happens when I feel the urge to write about something I deeply care about. When ideas rush through me and I can't get to my laptop fast enough to begin flushing them all out on a fresh document. "Is there anyone else on the festival board that would be willing to talk as well? The more people I can interview, the better it is for the article."

"I can bring over Ed and Gill. Both of them are as old as the town's stoplights, but they love being on the festival's board. They know a lot, and they would be delighted to talk about the different rides and contests going on during the festival. Both of them would back up the kissing booth, too." She blows some hair up to her hair. "They are the only ones that ever support my ideas."

"I think it's a great idea. After I meet with you all, I'll get straight to writing. I can get the article done as soon as possible, and I'll make sure my editor is quick to put it out before the festival starts."

Mabel takes a seat next to me, then places a smooth palm over my forearm. The action makes me look up from my notebook and peer into her dark brown eyes. She gives me another one of her warm smiles. "Seriously, thank you, Holland. I can already see just how much you care about saving this town." She swallows, and her lips quiver. "I really can't thank you enough. Is there anything else I can do to help you in the meantime?"

I have to look away from here because emotion is rising–*crawling*–up my throat from her sincerity. I stare straight out the large windows that exhibit the sparkling ocean behind the house. But my eyes catch on someone walking down the narrow dock. A man. *Atlas Richens.* His words from last night flash in my mind. *You'll be gone before anyone bothers remembering your name. Take a note from the rest of the town and don't bother trying to get to know me.* His cocky attitude makes me want to vomit. His stupid map-like name makes me want to roll my eyes and flip him off. His perfectly toned body makes me want to press my thighs together.

An evil idea pops into my head like a floating thought bubble in a comic book. "Actually, there is something you can do before I meet with you tomorrow." I give Mabel a big, evil grin. "Do whatever you can to make Atlas Richens work the kissing booth."

chapter three

The late May sun beats down my back on Wednesday morning as I walk to the cafe, Velvet Bean. I bypass other residents of the town, smiling genuinely at the customers walking in and out of the small cafe. A jingle above the glass door hums as soon as I step into the building. Inside, the wooden floors creak underfoot, and mismatched vintage chairs surround small, round tables. The brick walls are adorned with local art, paintings of the mountains and the ocean, as well as abstract collages of all colors. Near the windows, plants of all shapes and sizes spill from pots that hang from the ceiling. I walk a few steps to the counter and peer up at the chalkboard menu, then order a medium vanilla latte with oat milk to the barista, Cierra.

I feel a tap on my shoulder, and I turn my head. I stare straight into dark green eyes.

"Hi, are you Holland Anderson?"

The man before me has dark blond hair that is perfectly combed over to the side, and a light brown mustache. He is wearing black pants with a tan collared shirt, and he has a sheriff's badge pinned to the material, right under another badge that reads *S. Kelley*.

"Yes, I am." I stretch my hand out in front of me. "Sam, right?"

The corners of his mouth tick up as he shakes my hand. "That's right." He puts his hands on his hips as he turns to Cierra. "I'll have whatever she ordered," he says, then reaches into his back pocket to pull out his wallet. In a blink of an eye, he gives Cierra his card after she tells him the total.

"Thank you," I tell Sam, and he leads me to a table in the corner of the cafe. He helps me in my chair, then sits across from me.

Sam leans his elbows onto the top of the table, resting his chin on his hands. He gives me a big grin, exposing the dimples on either side of his cheeks. "So, how are you liking Saltmere so far?"

I take my recorder out from my bag and press the button. "I love it. I haven't done much exploring yet, but it's beautiful here."

"It *is* beautiful. But it only will be for a few more months."

"Because of Gemini Development?" When he nods, my shoulders slump. "Is there anything you can do to stop them from tearing the businesses down?"

He exhales. "No. And I've tried everything. Even the folks here are starting to think I'm on Kurt Gemini's side because technically, everything I know of what he's doing is legal, and I can't do anything to stop him. Unless he does something illegal, I can open up an investigation."

I take out my notebook from my bag that hangs on the back of my chair. I flip it open and undo the lid of my favorite pen. "But he lied to the owners of the shops, didn't he?"

"Yep, but he didn't make them sign any contracts or anything, just made friends with them in the beginning to gain their trust." He shakes his head. "We all were misled by that man."

"That's horrible." Cierra comes to deliver our drinks, and the two of us take a few sips before resuming our conversation. "Do you have Kurt's number? Or his sons' numbers? I would love to set up an interview with them, if they will allow it."

"Oh yeah, I have all three of their numbers because they can't stop reaching out to me. They want me to partner with them." He sighs, eyes finding the ceiling before he leans forward in his seat. "I don't know how, since I clearly have a job already as the sheriff of the town."

"It seems like they just want to get on your good side," I point out.

"You're probably right. I can forward their contacts to you. I can't promise that they will interact with you, unless you tell them that what you are writing will benefit them somehow. If you need someone to go with you over to their headquarters, I can."

Sam is genuine. He's passionate about the wellbeing of the town, and for that, I nod and smile. "That would be great." I take another drink of my mug. "So, I'm not sure if Jenny already told you my agenda, but I am writing a collection of articles while I am here for the month. I was talking to Mabel about the Sea Glass Festival, and I'm thinking of having an issue of the event being the topic of my first article. But I would love for you to give me some background information of the town, if you don't mind."

"Yes, of course." He cracks his knuckles like he is preparing for a punching battle. "I like to think of Saltmere being the state's hidden gem. It was founded by a group of shipwreck survivors in 1792. According to the legends, their ship was bound for Charleston, but a crazy storm ruined not just their plans, but also their only way of travel. They found shelter in the dunes and fresh water in a nearby salt marsh–

hence the name *Saltmere*. Early on, Saltmere was nothing but a cluster of shingled cottages and a wharf built from driftwood and salvaged timber. The town grew slowly, mostly centered around fishing and trading. But Saltmere really became known for its sea glass coves that only us locals know about."

"Only locals know about the coves?" I ask to clarify as I write down all of this information in my notebook.

"Yes. I can take you to them, if you want. They are close to the lighthouse that everyone thinks is haunted, and I'm pretty sure all of the local shop owners would tell the tourists we did have that the coves were haunted too, and thus the reason why no newcomers go to them or even ask exactly where they are. But those coves are where the gift shop would get their sea glass souvenirs, and they sold like crazy."

"I would love to visit the coves. They already sound amazing."

He huffs a laugh. "Yeah, well, it would be great if you could write about them. Our town needs the revenue. The more people that come to visit, the more we can fight against Kurt."

I love a challenge. I love that this job makes me look at other perspectives, to understand the full picture. It forces me to formulate knowledge into power, creativity into opportunity. It challenges me to overcome obstacles in all shapes and forms just to attract a reader interested in what I have to say, what I value as important. I have worked with Wanderlight Journeys for almost three years, and each year I have the opportunity to write something that is out of my comfort zone, something that forces me to jump into the shoes of someone who has experienced a completely different life than mine.

Pressure, though, is a different story. Sam's words and what Mabel has been telling me float around in my head and drag me down like the flowy skirt I'm wearing. The fate of this town feels like it is in my hands. That pressure feels gooey and hot, like molten lava seeping through my skin and burning every tissue in my palms. It feels as heavy as the boats that sway in the ocean, as loud as the busy streets outside my New York office and the seagulls chirping outside the window. It feels unbearable. It feels like if I fail, I might never bounce back. I might disappoint my mom, the only person that ever believed in me.

But I put on my brave face and say to Sam, "Then I will go to these places only locals of Saltmere know to gather as much information as possible for my articles. And I'll try to interview Kurt to figure out more of his plans, and I'll write what I learn." Sam gives me a determined nod and a reassuring smile, and the two of us continue talking about how long he's lived here and more details of the town that come to mind. He informs me to stay clear of Peter Ivins, the older man that lives in a rundown beach cottage not far from the *haunted* lighthouse. Apparently Peter has taken on the job to be the watchdog for the lighthouse, and his *actual* dogs will chase anyone that dares to step near it.

But then Sam also informs me not to interact too much with Atlas Richens, and suddenly I am more intrigued in our conversation than I was before.

"Why? Does Captain Cartography have a criminal history?"

He snorts a laugh. Then he gets serious, his brows furrowing on his forehead. "Funny nicknames aside, all I can say is that Atlas isn't who he says he is. He hasn't done anything to get in trouble, necessarily, but…just be careful."

And just like that, Atlas Richens is on my interview list.

Even though I know he probably won't agree.

Sam and I talk for another thirty minutes before he has to go back to work. He gently shakes my hand in farewell, and as I say goodbye to Cierra and step out of the door, my phone vibrates in my bag.

It's Mabel. I press my phone to my ear. "Hello?"

"Hi, dear. Are you free to talk right now? I have Ed and Gill with me, but they won't talk nicely until they have food in their stomachs. Do you want to meet us at the diner on Main called Heart and Honey?"

I laugh. "Yes, I'm actually right across the street. I'll be there in a second."

I slide my phone back in my bag and walk to the crosswalk at the intersection, then walk straight into the diner. The air carries the scents of sizzling bacon and fresh coffee once I step inside. Warn booth tables line the walls, under the black-and-white photos of what I assume are details of the town's past–high school football team, tobacco harvests, and local heroes in firefighter and police uniforms.

The owner, Phoebe, a sweet elderly woman who wears her long gray hair in two hanging braids and gives me the tightest hug for visiting this town, guides me to where Mabel and the others are sitting, and they each greet me with a tight embrace that squeezes every last breath out of my lungs. Apparently, they are also huggers.

"It's so good to put a face to a name, Miss Holland," Ed says, running a hand through his light gray hair as we all sit down. I take the free seat next to Gill. The booth we are sitting in has four menus laying on the tabletop, so I push the extra one to the side.

"I'm just glad you all were willing to meet with me about the festival," I respond, giving them all a smile.

"Of course," Gill says, chuckling. "Let's order first and then we can talk all about it."

"Wait!" Mabel exclaims, her palms straight up in front of her. "We have to wait for–"

Someone clears their throat outside of the booth, and all of our heads whip up towards the sound, at the man that stands before the table.

Atlas Richens.

chapter four

He's giving me a glare that would probably make anyone else cower down onto their knees at his mercy. But I'd like to think that I know better, so the corners of my lips tip up even more. I rest my hand on my propped up elbow. "To what do we owe the pleasure today, Captain Coordinates?"

Atlas rolls his eyes, then holds out a folded piece of paper and waves it in the air. "What did I tell you last night?"

"You said a lot of things," I say with a shrug.

"What about the detail of taking a hint from the rest of the town and *not* bothering me?"

We all watch as he unfolds the piece of paper and slides it to me. My eyes scan over the scratchy handwriting that reads:

I'll tell Sam about the warehouse you illegally store your boats and parts in at the end of town if you don't help me and Mabel at the festival. Maybe I'll even inform Kurt Gemini as well, given that Mr. Gemini would love to take over that

field of work, too. Meet us at the diner at noon tomorrow.

–H

My eyes flick back up to meet Atlas's. "I literally have no idea what this is."

Mabel's fingers curl over the edge of the paper in my hands. "Oh," she says cheerfully, "I wrote that."

All eight of our eyes land on Mabel, but she is only looking up at Atlas. The sincere look on her face makes me question just how truly kind she can be, given that she pulled the *mystery man of Saltmere* out of his shell and into a very public place with a simple piece of blackmail. Mabel's a wicked, creative woman.

"Oooh, I love this," Gill says, clapping his hands together. He extends a hand out in front of him. "I don't think we have formally met, Mr. Richens. I'm Gill Colthorpe, owner of said warehouse."

I gasp. Atlas's face is as red as the curtains hanging on the diner's windows. He opens his mouth to speak, but Gill cuts him off. "Don't worry, you're not in trouble." Gill rubs his belly as he chuckles. "I like what you've done with the place."

"He sure is in trouble!" Mabel exclaims. Then she stands from the worn table cushion and leans towards the empty table next to the booth. Her hands wrap around a chair, and the legs of it scratch and shriek against the diner's sticky floors. She places the chair right behind Atlas. "Take a seat. We have a lot to discuss."

With an annoyed grunt and a moment of hesitation, Atlas slowly sits down. Ed slides a menu to him, but Atlas only gives me another glare. "So, if I'm not in trouble for using the warehouse, why do you need me to work the festival?"

"Because," Mabel begins, eyes skimming over the menu like she is unbothered by Atlas's attitude, "we need more hands. A bigger crew."

"And more lips," Ed says, snickering. I stifle a laugh and fail to hide it under my palm. Atlas's brows furrow, and Ed waves a hand in front of him. "We need more people for the kissing booth."

Atlas's hand raises, and he slams his eyes shut for a moment. "Let me stop you right there." He scoffs. "I am not helping with the festival, and I am, a hundred percent, not helping with a *kissing booth*. What even is that?"

I snatch out my notebook again, flipping to a new page. I look at Mabel and say, "Go ahead and inform both me and Mr. Directions about the festival details, please." Mabel gets right to it, eyes gleaming as she speaks. "Ten different rides. *Real* ones this time," she says, giving Ed a pointed expression. "Not any of those inflatable things that collapse if someone breathes too hard in its general direction." She smiles at me. "There's going to be a Ferris wheel right at the entrance, at the edge of the boardwalk. You'll be able to see the whole town from the top. Perfect for watching the sunset or throwing slushies and popcorn down to the people at the bottom. I don't judge." She shrugs.

"There's also going to be a carousel, a scrambler, and a ride that will spin you so fast you will think you're drunk for the rest of the night. There will be a huge rollercoaster that's dragon themed, and food stalls every twenty feet. Funnel cakes, saltwater taffy, burgers, and hot dogs. And anything deep-fried."

Her arms fly around beside and in front of her as she speaks, and she only stops when a waitress comes to take our order. She proceeds as soon as the girl leaves.

"This kissing booth will have ten contestants, you included," she directs at Atlas. He grunts, like that's still up for debate.

Five girls and five boys will take turns at the two podiums with blindfolds covering their eyes, and they will rotate after every kiss so those who are in line won't know exactly who they will kiss. People who want to participate will have to sign a consent form and confirm that they are over the age of twenty-one and completely healthy, and they will each pay one dollar for a peck on the lips or on the cheek.

"How is this even legal?" Atlas interjects, a line forming in between his eyebrows. If he lowers them more his forehead, they might sink into his eyesockets. "Like, how can we actually make sure people don't have diseases before kissing them?"

Ed waves a hand in the air. "Son, this is Saltmere. We still let Shirley Abbot run the town raffle every year and she draws the same five names for over a decade. Nothing's ever that serious here. Plus, everyone is very healthy."

Atlas blinks. "That's not very comforting."

For once, I agree with him.

Mabel barrels on. "Everyone wanting to participate will sign the form before doing anything, and we will have a nurse on standby. Well, retired nurse. But nurse knowledge doesn't expire. She mostly treats cats now, but she still has her stethoscope, so it feels official."

I've stopped scribbling notes because none of this information needs to be in the article. I'm not sure any of it *should* be in the article. I glance over at Atlas, who looks like he's mentally trying to come up with reasons to argue. Reasons to back away from the idea.

"You don't have to kiss anyone if you don't want to," I say, fighting a grin. "Unless you want Sam to find out where your precious boats reside."

He narrows his eyes. "So you really are blackmailing me into helping you?" he asks, voice low in a taunting tone.

I shrug. "I mean, I think Sam would love to know about this, if he doesn't already. It also could be vital information for someone who," I pause to point at myself, "has the authority to make any information spread like wildfire to the public in a couple of words and buttons pressed on a keyboard."

"You wouldn't." His jaw works.

And maybe I wouldn't if he hadn't gone out of his way yesterday to remind me I was temporary, forgettable, just another outsider pretending to know what she's doing, someone who'd be gone before anyone bothered learning my name. The words had stuck like burrs when he said them last night, and part of me wants him to feel at least a fraction of how small he made me feel.

"I would," I say sweetly. "It's only fair for how *nice* you were to me when I first arrived here."

Ed chuckles, clearly enjoying this interaction between the two of us far too much. "You're doing the Lord's work, darling."

Atlas sighs, angling his head to the ceiling. "I live in a town full of lunatics," he mumbles under his breath.

Mabel claps, shoulders crouching to her neck in excitement. "I'm taking that as a yes for participation, Atlas!" Her smile widens, and she leans forward, putting a hand on Atlas's wrist, shaking it gently. "We've already written your name in blue glitter on our contestant board!"

Shooting me another glare, Atlas stands from his chair. He nods to the rest of the group, muttering, "Let me know what time I have to show up," before stalking out of the building.

chapter five

I'm typing my fingers away on my laptop out on the back porch, overlooking the marshy ocean and the afternoon sun that casts streaks of glowy light onto the water's surface. Seagulls fly and call from above as they soar and circle high in the air, only descending to the sand on the other side of the back yard to pick at shells and rocks.

The view is peaceful, and I am almost finished with the first article about the Sea Glass Festival because of the natural sounds of the ocean. The environment is so different from writing in my New York office that overlooks thousands of people walking the streets and is an eruption of sirens and car horns and people shouting below the building. Instead, the only thing distracting me right now is how beautiful and calming the view is.

I can see why my mom loved this place. I wish I got to hear even more stories of her time visiting North Carolina. I wish I got to hear more of her stories about *anything*. While we were eating dinner every night–some takeout my dad would relent and buy for the five of us–she would tell us stories of her days at work, but my eyes always would travel down the hall to where her painting studio sat empty and lifeless, except for that painting of the ocean she never finished. I wish I asked her more about why she never let herself find time to do what she actually loved.

I miss her. Every day that passes since her death in November doesn't get any easier. She loved that I was a writer, loved that I let my thoughts and beliefs and dreams live and build with every word I put down on the paper. She would encourage me to never stop learning, to never stay in my comfort zone.

If she were here, she would've wanted me to explore everything in this town. She would want me to write about every little shop, about every hidden nook, because everything is monumental and a piece of history in a town like this. We lived in Chicago and only knew the city itself, never vacationing to beachy areas or where people go on spring break because my parents were too busy with work. But occasionally, my mom would reminisce on the past or on a dream she had about living in a place where the ocean is your neighbor, your best friend, an escape destination for reasons beyond recreational relaxation.

I feel like I can hear her voice in the waves that crash serenely against the sandy shore, in the laughter of the children building sandcastles along the beach. In the breeze that ruffles the leaves of the trees.

I go back to typing with misty eyes, but the sound of a door shutting makes me jump in my chair.

And suddenly, the view isn't as calming. Still beautiful, though, but for completely different reasons.

Atlas doesn't notice me right away. He saunters straight to the dock, trudging through his yard to where his boat still is floating. He kneels down to the front of the boat, leaning over the edge of the dock. I quietly shut my laptop and stand from my rocking chair, then make my way to him. He still doesn't hear me as my sandals slap against the wood of the dock.

"Hi," I say.

And he jolts. Again, like the first time we met.

I watch his shoulders rise and fall as he sucks in a deep breath, then turns his head up at me. His eyes narrow as he looks directly into mine. "Why do you have to do that?"

"Do what?" I ask with faux naivety.

Slowly, he rises to his feet, swiping his hands together. "You know what."

He's close to me now, and I crank my neck up to keep his gaze. His irises look more green in this lighting, just around the pupils of his eyes. Up this close, I can smell his cedar and pine scent and the smell of his sandalwood mixed with vanilla aftershave. His dark brown hair curls at the base of his neck, and he's wearing the same ballcap once again. The Carhart t-shirt hugs his upper arms tightly, exposing his brawny biceps and the veins that coarse their way down his skin. He's wearing jeans again, paired with brown cowboy boots.

"Can I help you?" he asks raspily.

I clear my throat, shaking my head internally to stop checking him out. "Uh, yes. I would like to ask you a few questions about the town."

"I don't think I can help you there. I've only lived here officially for two years."

"Maybe, but that's longer than me." I stand straighter. "I want you to take me somewhere."

There's a glimmer in his eyes, an infinitesimal exposure of curiosity at my statement. His dark eyebrow raises, creating a couple creases in his forehead under the brim of his hat. "You are forcing me to work that booth at the festival and you still want more from me?"

"Technically, Mabel is forcing you." He doesn't need to know that I asked her to rope him into this. But I give him a sweet smile. "Please? I would like to go to the art gallery by the boardwalk, and I figured the two of us need to get along since we will be both working the festival and will be living next to one another for the rest of the month."

"You're working the kissing booth too?"

"No, I'm going to be running around every booth and ride to take pictures for our magazine's website. Then maybe pitch in physically wherever Mabel needs me to."

He looks disappointed, but only for a second before he's back to scowling at me. He turns and walks down the dock a few more steps, and I follow him. "I was just thinking that we should spend some time together, maybe learn to be friends," I attempt instead. "I don't like that we already don't like each other."

"I'm busy," he says over his shoulder. I come to a halt when he kneels at the end of the boat and leans forward over the dock.

"I can see that. But it won't take long, I'm sure."

He looks up at me, his face stuck in its usual glowering expression. "We don't have to get along, Holland."

His voice is rough and deep, and the way he drawls out my name definitely shouldn't make chills crawl down my skin.

He keeps going. "I can't take you to the art gallery."

"Why?"

"God, you talk a lot," he mutters under his breath, but I pretend not to hear him. He stays silent for many moments that pass by leisurely, and I feel tempted to walk away, to leave him alone. Clearly, he wants nothing to do with me. I let my smile crack when I inhale and turn around to walk back to my house.

"Why the art gallery?"

I stop in my tracks and turn back to face him. He's standing again, looking at me differently than he has each time we've interacted. With a sense of regret covering every feature of his. I take a step back towards him. "My mom liked to paint before she passed. I want to see more paintings like the one she left behind."

He tilts his head to the side, and his lips loosen from the frown that I think permanently resides on his face. They curl up slightly in the corners, and he nods. "Alright. Let's go to the art gallery."

chapter six

Altas drives us to the other end of town where I haven't been yet. This side of town feels completely different than the other side, as it includes more luxury homes with the ocean lining behind them. Each house is decorated with white picket fences and rows of tulips and small trees up the walkways to the wrap around porches. Each house is either white or yellow in color and at least three floors tall, and every single one screams elegance and charm.

"These homes are beautiful," I mumble in awe as my forehead presses against the window of Atlas's truck.

He doesn't answer me, but a few minutes later, the truck pulls off to a parking lot of a small building that looks like an older cottage with the name The Gilded Frame. We park and get out, then walk up the broken sidewalk to the wooden door. Atlas opens it for me, and when I walk inside, my lungs expand and my jaw drops.

It's like my eyes can't focus on anything at all as my head swivels in every direction. Painting after painting is hung up on the walls, completely covering them. Most pieces of art are of the ocean or boats floating on the surface of rough waters in gold and brown frames. I stop in front of each one with Atlas following my every move, but I only stay at the paintings for seconds at a time before my eyes catch on another one just as breathtaking.

"Are you two looking for something in particular?"

I turn my head to a young woman standing next to us, her bright blond hair slicked back in a low ponytail. She's wearing a white blouse and khaki pants and has those naturally beautiful features that I would kill for. High cheekbones, curled eyelashes, freckles scattering over her rosy cheeks and slightly pointed nose.

"Yeah," Atlas says next to me. "Do you have anything by Lila Voss?"

The woman's face lights up, smiling wide and showing her pretty white teeth. "Yes, we do. Follow me."

"Who's Lila Voss?" I ask Atlas, but I don't think he hears me. The woman turns around and begins walking through the narrow walkways towards the back of the cottage, and Atlas rests his hand on the small of my back and gently nudges me forward. But my body straightens at his touch, at the warmth of his palm. He stays close behind me as we walk, but I don't want to move in case he moves his hand away. Bolts of something electric slide through my veins, burn on the skin of my back under the flowy shirt I'm wearing that has material far too thin.

I've only known Atlas for such a short amount of time. I shouldn't be this affected by a simple gesture.

His hand disappears when we enter after the woman into a different room. Atlas takes a step forward to one of the two paintings in the room that rests on propped up, metal easels.

"These paintings aren't for sale, technically, because they are pieces of history to this art gallery. The women that painted these were natives to this town and were great friends with our store owner, Esme, before she passed away."

The painting in front of Atlas is a landscape of a brown wooden barn with willow trees in the background. A tree stump with an axe stuck on the top of it sits next to a dirt trail caused by an off-road vehicle. The edge of a glimmering pond with lily pads is painted in the right corner of the canvas, and birds are flying high in the cloudy sky. In the left corner, the initials *CLV* are written in sloped, cursive writing.

"Are you sure this one isn't for sale?" Atlas finally says, his voice hoarse and choked up. My eyebrows frown as I watch him stare at the painting like it is going to disappear at any second. His knuckles are white at his sides, and a vein is pulsing on the side of his neck.

"I'm sorry, it's not. But you can come by anytime to look at it."

Atlas finally looks up at the woman. "What about the one next to it?"

The three of us turn our heads to the painting next to the first one. I take a step closer to the detailed artwork, standing in awe at the way the canvas displays the backside of two people holding onto one another as they walk down a bricked path towards a shadow of darkness. To their sides, large oak trees and the bases of skyscrapers and glowing yellow streetlights reside. The path has reflections of the dark, cloudy sky, like rain had just finished falling. The painting is like a city quiet in the night, undisturbed from other pedestrians and life itself. It is just the couple holding onto one another, walking towards whatever lies ahead of them. It's beautiful. In the corner of this painting, the initials *VMC* are imprinted in disheveled writing.

Atlas extends his hand out to the initials, and both of us women are stunned into silence as we watch his pointer finger trace over the letters, then over the couple in the painting. His face is paler in color, and his lips are curled in.

"Neither are for sale. I'm sorry," the woman finally says, clearing her throat. Atlas and I both turn back to her. She looks directly at me, squinting her eyes slightly. "Wait, are you Holland?"

"Yes," I say with a nod.

Her shoulders crouch to her neck, and her face displays an excited expression. "I've read some of your work. You're an incredible writer. That article about your experience in Paris and demonstrating the French lifestyle for two months? I was obsessed with it."

"Oh," I huff a laugh, "thank you. What's your name?"

"I'm Grace Bennett. I was supposed to swing by and meet you yesterday, but Kurt Gemini stopped by the gallery, and there was no way I was going to leave with that evil man lurking around."

Atlas stiffens at my side, but I can't focus on anything besides Grace's words. "Wait, do you think that Kurt is going to try to buy this place?"

Grace folds her arms. "Oh yeah. He's already tried talking to our new owner."

"Who is the new owner?"

Grace smiles and winks. She swipes the hair of her ponytail off her shoulders. "Me." Then she rolls her eyes and lets a new ounce of anger take over her demeanor. "That man will *never* take over this place. I won't be deceived by his words. I care about this gallery too much to let it crumble in the hands of Gemini Development."

"Good," Atlas mumbles. "Don't let that man do anything to this place. He can't be trusted for shit."

Grace's eyes narrow in curiosity. "I don't think we've formally met, Mr. Richens." Her hand sticks out in front of her for him to shake. He does, and a sliver of jealousy licks my skin for reasons I don't want to admit to. I should *not* care about the way that Grace is looking up at the man next to me and how her smile is wider than it was before.

"It's great to meet you. But we have to head out," Atlas says. He puts his hand back on my back, and I fight a shiver. Grace nods and we follow her back out the room. She waves us goodbye before we step out into the salty air.

My neck cranks up to look at Atlas. I can't stop the question, "Why does Grace get niceties and I only get your snarls and grunts?" from escaping my lips the second we exit the gallery.

"She doesn't make me do things I don't want to do."

I roll my eyes. "You didn't have to agree to anything."

"Mabel made that difficult. She was going to rat out my boats' location."

"I don't think she really was going to say anything to Sam, and definitely not to Kurt. Just from all of the things she's told me, I don't think she can stand fifty feet away from him without blowing a gasket."

Surprisingly, Atlas chuckles. The sound sounds so foreign coming from someone like him that I can't help but gasp. I point at him and ask, "Did you just laugh at something I said?"

"I've *been* laughing at *everything* you've said, Holly. Internally."

I scoff as he opens the passenger door of his truck for me. I look up at him with a frown.

"What?" he asks.

"I'm just shocked you have a nice bone in your body," I tease. "No one's opened a car door for me before."

"Not even your boyfriend?"

I fold my arms against my chest and cock my head to the side, studying him. He still has a hand extended and holding the door open, but I don't make an effort to get in yet. "I don't have a boyfriend."

"But your work profile–" He stops himself. Clears his throat. Stares at the ground like he has been caught. And *yes*, he's been caught.

I laugh, then arch a brow up. "What about my work profile, Mr. Directions?"

"Your nicknames for me are horrible."

"Don't change the subject. Have you looked me up online?"

"I had to see if my new neighbor was a criminal of any kind." He kicks at a rock on the pavement, refusing to meet my gaze. "I saw that you used to write and work with a guy named Gordon. The two of you were holding hands at some award thing just a few months ago."

Any other man telling me all of this information and confessing that he has stalked the profile the magazine has for me probably should scare me and make me run to the nearest police station. But Atlas intrigues me. Sam's words about him ring in my head, but he doesn't seem like he would hurt anyone, even if his impolite exterior would convince you otherwise. I've seen how he treated Mabel and the others this morning, even when she threatened him and his career. And for some reason, my body and mind feel pulled to him, somehow. I can't stop my brain from wanting to get to know him better, to understand why he has the attitude of a hungry toddler.

Gordon and I did date. For two years. I've worked with the magazine for almost three years now, but Gordon has worked at Wanderlight for seven, accepting a job as an editor as soon as he graduated from Columbia, the same university I attended. As a travel journalist, I work closely with editors with every project I complete, and Gordon specifically found interest in my work as soon as I was hired. We started out as friends, staying at the office late together when I would return from trips so he could personally get all of the details out of me and help me organize further key points in my articles. He was always dating around, never interested in staying in a relationship–until I went out on a date with another one of our coworkers, Aaron.

Two years ago, Gordon's protective behavior over me when he found out about me and Aaron charmed me. After all, it made Gordon realize he did have feelings for me. But now, I know just how demeaning Gordon was to me. Jenny assigned him to be my editor for every project. He would tear me down, shred everything I wrote into pieces–literally. He would get extremely protective over me at every work party and event, and would cuss out Aaron if he even just breathed in my direction. Aaron was another journalist like me, so Gordon pleaded to Jenny to become his editor as well. Jenny complied, unknowing to Gordon's hatred for him–and Aaron didn't last another month at Wanderlight.

Gordon left me a few weeks after my mom passed away last November. *You aren't the same anymore*, he said. *I can't be with you while you are in Chicago and I'm in New York*. I took a month off of work to attend the funeral and visit my dad with my siblings to figure out the logistics of my mom's will. I stayed even longer for my dad, becoming a strong shield for my dad's mourning, taking care of him in every way. But when the month had passed and my dad was still struggling, I took until the end of February off. Jenny was understanding and let me as long as I kept writing some type of material. Gordon was still my editor, and I sent him work as often as I could, and he declined everything I wrote, saying that it wasn't publishable material.

I don't mourn Gordon and the loss of our relationship. I just mourn my mom.

This is the first project Jenny has sent me on since my mom's passing. She trusts me to get back into my usual routine, but in a way that is sympathetic and considerate. She knows I probably never will be the same again since my mom died, but she also believes in my success as a writer. She knows I can do this, and this time, Gordon won't be my editor. He won't ruin this for me.

"Are you okay?"

I shake my head, not to answer Atlas's question, but to mentally force myself out of my thoughts. Atlas is looking at me with concern etched in his frown and in the creases of his temples. I nod rapidly. "Yep!" I inhale sharply. "Gordon and I ended long ago. I'm as single as a sock without its pair in the laundry."

Without looking at him, I get in the truck. I can feel Atlas watching my every move, and after a moment of hesitation, he shuts the door and walks around the vehicle. He gets in and starts up the engine, then pulls out of the parking lot. I keep my eyes glued to the art gallery that I already know I love so much. Watching it leave my line of sight feels like a punch to the gut, as if I shouldn't go. As if the gallery itself won't stand against the determination of Kurt Gemini, a man I have heard so much about but have yet to meet. It feels as if the little cottage full of so many beautiful paintings is pulling me towards it somehow, and for some reason, tears spring their way up to my eyelids.

Atlas drives back towards our houses, both of us silent the entire way. When he pulls into my driveway, I hurriedly open the door before the truck is even in park. "Thanks!" I shout way too loudly over the noise of the engine. But Atlas's hand wraps around my wrist, halting me still.

"Holland."

I slowly turn to face him. "Yes?"

His hand is warm around mine, and my fingers itch to touch his. *Am I actually crazy? I've only known him for three days.* But the way he is looking at me would fool anyone. He looks worried, uneased. Uncomfortable. "I'm…sorry about your mom."

I study him, letting my eyes trace over every centimeter of his face. We are close, only inches apart, and his hand is still around mine. But I pull it away and step out of the truck, because he brought up my mom, and suddenly all I want to do is cry. I clear my throat as soon as my sandals hit the cement. "It's fine, Atlas. Thanks for taking me. I'll see you at the festival."

chapter seven

An hour after Atlas drops me off, I finish the article and send it to my new editor, Ariana. Then I drift off on the couch in the living room.

I dream of my mom, of course, like I have every night since she died. This time, I'm back in my childhood kitchen, sunlight slanting through the glass of the window above the sink. Everything is exactly the same; the loud, humming fridge tucked in the corner next to the pantry, the chipped tile behind the old blender, the faint smell of my mom's cinnamon candle on the counter.

My mom is standing in front of the stove, stirring something in a pot, wearing her favorite blue sweater with ruffles at the sleeves. She doesn't look sick. Her cheeks are full and flushed with warmth, her smile real and beautiful. When she turns to look at me, her eyes crinkle the same way they always do when she laughs.

"You're late, dear," she says, teasing gently. "You always are."

"I brought you more paint," I hear myself say, but my hands are empty and the words taste like regret.

My mom pauses, setting down the spoon. "You don't have to bring me anything, honey. Just being here is enough. Just being *you* is enough."

I want to run to her, wrap my arms around and embrace her, but my legs are heavy, and the air is as thick as water. The closer I try to get to her, the further away my mom seems, like the two of us are on opposite sides of a memory that refuses to line up.

"I miss you," I say, flinching at the cracking in my throat.

My mom smiles. "I know, dear. But you're doing okay. Better than you give yourself credit for."

Then the kitchen windows blow open suddenly, scattering loose papers and pulling the scent of the candle away. My hair whips around widely on the top of my head. I shift the strands away from my face, and when I glance back at where my mom was standing, she's gone. Only the bowl is warm on the stovetop, and the wooden spoon is gently spinning inside of it.

"Just being here is enough. You are enough" chants through the air, the voice of my mom in my ears sounding like my own personal anthem.

I wake up in the middle of the night with tears streaming down my face to my phone ringing. I blink to clear my cloudy vision and the dream that caused it, swipe at my damp face, then reach for my phone on the coffee table and bring it to my ear.

"Hello?"

"Holland, hi," Jenny says on the other line. "I'm so sorry it's so late. Ariana has edited your article, and it's already posted on our website. I just wanted to let you know that it already has hundreds of views."

I feel an immediate sense of relief. "That's amazing!"

"It really is. I know that this process is a little different than what you normally do since we wanted to release the article in such a short notice, but I read what you wrote after it was edited." I know what she is trying to say. *I trust Ariana with your work. She isn't like Gordon.* "It's really great. I wish I could make it down this weekend to go to the festival. How are you settling in? Was Sam nice?"

"Everything's great so far, and yes, he was. All of the people here are so kind–" *Maybe except for my neighbor, but I'll keep that to myself for now.* "–and there seem to be so many hidden gems that I am determined to find and write about."

"My family used to go to the tulip garden about a half hour out of the town. You could write about that as well. Oh, and the lighthouse! I think our readers would love to read about that old thing. People say that it's haunted, so just please don't die if you visit it. And don't go alone."

I scribble all of that down in my notebook and laugh. "I'll try. Sam did tell me about the lighthouse, so maybe I'll have him take me."

"That'd be great!" she exclaims. Then the line goes silent for many long seconds that I think she hung up. But then I hear her exhale. "How are *you* doing, Holland? I know being where your mom has visited once and loved can't be easy."

I swallow. "I'm hanging in there." I think I've cried more today than I have the entire month combined, but I refuse to admit that to anyone besides myself. "Really, I'm doing okay."

"Please don't hesitate to tell me if it gets too hard, okay?"

Jenny is the sole reason why I am still trying to bounce back at the magazine because of her empathy and passion for the field. "I will. Thanks, Jenny."

"Of course. I can't wait to read more about the town. It's like I'm living through your words. We'll talk soon!" She hangs up, and I slide my phone back onto the table. I fold up the blanket I was using and put it back into the basket, then pad towards the bedroom. I crash onto the bed, letting exhaustion wash over my limbs. I fall back asleep to the sound of the ocean's waves with a new hope for my purpose here flowing through me.

chapter eight

On Thursday morning, I stroll down the boardwalk to take pictures of the festival being set up so I can send them to our social media manager, Selena, so she can post them to our socials. I get to know more of the board of the festival, including an elderly gentleman named Vance and his oldest son, Jessie. I also meet some of the crew setting up the motorized rides, Aiden, Dez, and Sebastian, after I get lost in conversation about Mabel's excitement with her and Grace.

I then walk down the quiet main street of Saltmere. Since I already finished my first article, I figure I need to explore the town and observe the lifestyle of the residents. Visit the rest of the shops that are open, dine at the local and historical restaurants, stop by the town's museum and library.

After lunch at Heart and Honey– where the owner, Phoebe, spent my entire meal wanting to get to know me and question what exactly a travel journalist does–I rent a bike and pedal my way towards the residential areas of the town, where the schools and city government buildings are. With my headphones hanging onto my ears and ABBA's "Chiquitita" acting as my own personal soundtrack, I ride in bliss on the sidewalk, my eyes wandering over to the line of the ocean in the distance. My bangs blow widely and the straps of my yellow tank top under my denim overalls slide down my shoulders, but I don't care. All that matters right now is how at peace I feel at this moment. The late May afternoon sun is definitely burning the top of my head and the skin of my arms, but I haven't felt this calm, this serene, since before my mom died.

I turn into the library parking lot, then rest the bike against the side of the old building. The library is tucked away behind large red maple trees. A wrought-iron gate, slightly rusted, leads to a stone pathway bordered by overgrown flower beds. The stone facade of the library is graying with age, ivy creeping up the walls, its green tendrils winding around the windows like old friends embracing. The large, arched wooden door is a worn shade of brown with brass handles. The parking lot is empty except for three vehicles parked in the employee lot.

Inside, I am transported through a tunnel straight to the past. The air is thick with the scent of aged paper and leather bindings, the smells of pure elation for a person with a need for knowledge like me. The young woman at the front desk has curly black hair and tawny skin, and she wears black trousers and a pink blouse. The rims of her glasses slide down the slope of her nose as she stares down at her computer screen, clearly not noticing me yet.

The floorboards creak under me as I step up towards her. Her head raises, and bright blue eyes beam into mine as she smiles. Her shoulders crouch into her neck as I read her name plate that says *Charlotte*. "Hello! How can I help ya?"

"Hi," I say, smiling in return. "I would like to get a library card."

"*Here*?" Her mouth opens in shock. "Are you sure? Will you use it?"

"Uh, yeah." I tilt my head to the side, looking at her with confusion. "Does no one have a library card anymore?"

She recovers her initial shock by brushing her hair off her shoulders and typing quickly on her keyboard in front of her. Her upper body sways side to side as her features light up, and not just because of the dancing white screen before her face. "Not really, but I can get you all set up right now!" she shouts, excitement laced in her tone. "Just give me a second, I haven't had to do this in a long time."

"No worries, I'm in no rush." I look around at the open space, soaking in the silence. I haven't stepped foot in a library since before I had to go back to Chicago, but all of the others I've been to don't measure up to the appeal this one has.

Dust particles float lazily in the slivers of sunlight that filter through tall, arched windows, their glass slightly fogged from age. A set of stairs leading to the second floor splits the open room in half, but to the sides of the railing, there's a colorful rug next to smaller shelves full of children's books–graphic novels, board books, and picture books. On the wall, a mural is painted of a tree with apples with letters of the alphabet printed on them. At the corner of the rug, there's a reading nook with an overstuffed armchair, its purple and brown fabric faded slightly. A small, dim lamp casts a warm glow over the pages of a book resting on the arm of the chair.

On the other side of the room, dozens of shelves stretch towards the ceiling, hundreds of books stacked and arranged on the wooden boards. I can't tell what genre they are, but my fingers itch to run over them, to feel the cracked spines and flip through the yellowed pages.

"Okay, sorry about that! I just need some information from you." Charlotte's words pull me back into the moment, and after I answer all of her questions and give her the information she needs, she hands me a personalized library card.

"Okay!" she exclaims. "You're all set. Nonfiction and children's on the first floor, fiction upstairs. Let me know if I can help you find anything in particular. This is so exciting!"

I thank her and begin towards the neverending rows of books, my smile permanent and expanding with each step I take to the second floor.

I can't see another person in sight, so I start with the first aisle to my left and begin to browse through the thriller and mystery sections. I put my earbuds back in and hum to Harry Styles's "Satellite". I lose track of time reading the titles and opening each book that interests me as I walk through aisle after aisle, and I end up in the romance section. Six different books of the thriller, fantasy, and romance genres are tightly tucked in my arms like someone will pry them away from me, but I can't help it. Excitement flows through me with the thought of reading out on the porch of the house, listening to the ocean waves and breathing in the salty breeze at sunset.

A flash of dark hair makes me gasp when I turn the corner of the horror aisle. I pluck my earbuds out one by one as I look straight at the side profile of Atlas Richens.

He doesn't notice me right away because he has his own earbuds in. He has his head lowered to the open book in his hands. He flips over the pages one by one, and I watch his eyes scan the pages. I take a step closer to him and tap his shoulder. He jumps, once again.

"God, Holland!" he yells, far too loudly, clutching a hand over his chest. "You *need* to stop doing that to me."

His shoulders rise and fall, but the scared look on his face is priceless. I laugh and he takes out his earbuds.

"What are you doing here?" I ask.

"What does it look like?"

"I just mean," I say, blinking rapidly, "I didn't think I would see you here."

"You don't know me."

"I know that. But what I meant was that I figured you would be in the atlas or travel guide section downstairs, given your name." I shrug. "But it honestly makes sense why you are in this section instead. *Horror.* It suits you."

He rolls his eyes at me. "Funny." Then he goes back to flipping through the pages of the book in his hand again. Curiosity boils in my veins, tickles my skin, so I use my pointer finger to poke at the cover of the book, but I accidentally close it on him. He exhales, but I'm too busy observing the cover. It's *The Omen* by David Seltzer. The cover is black and red and has a small child with the shadow of a cross on it. But before I can even blink, Atlas snatches the book away from me and tucks it under his arm. Then he walks back down the aisle, leaving me behind.

But I follow. "Wait!" I whispershout.

"I'm leaving," he says.

"Why? You don't have to leave just because I'm here."

"I know," he says over his shoulder as he heads towards the staircase. I'm walking so fast to catch up with his long strides that I fumble with the books in my hands. Atlas notices. He comes to a stop at the top step and grabs all of them out of my slippery, failing grasp before the books clatter onto the floor. Then he proceeds down the stairs without another blink in my direction.

I trail behind, but once our feet land on the first floor, Atlas walks straight to Charlotte's desk and begins checking out his book. Then he turns to me with his hand out in front of him, and I mistake it as a high five. I slap his hand and grin, and he looks at me like I have three heads and no brain.

"Your card, Holland."

Oh. Duh. My cheeks redden, but I hand it to him. Charlotte checks out my stack of books. Atlas grabs my books and places them in a stack with his, then picks them up. Charlotte waves us goodbye as Atlas and I both exit the building, and I squint my eyes up to him as soon as the door shuts behind us.

"What if I wasn't done browsing in there?"

"You're the one that followed me out." He walks to his truck parked against the curb of the street dozens of yards away, in front of the city hall building. I walk straight past my bike, but I keep trailing next to him because he is still carrying my books in his hands.

We get to the truck, and he finally turns to me. "How'd you get here? Do you need a ride?"

I put my hands on my hips. I struggle to catch my breath, and I pant into the air like a crazy person. "Was the parking lot not close enough for you?" I ask him, swiping the thin layer of sweat on my forehead.

"I had to come to city hall for something. I walked to the library after."

Well, that's humbling. He can walk for long lengths at a time without even breaking a sweat, unlike me. "Oh."

"Do you need a ride home, Holland?"

The way my name sounds coming out of his mouth should *not* make my stomach flip. He's said it three times in a matter of minutes, and it is like my heart is jumping over a bridge. "I rented a bike." I toss a thumb back to the library, and he looks around me. I watch the second he recognizes the single bike next to the building in his eyes because the next second after, he's rolling them again. The expression on his face and the vein pulsing in his neck are clearly telling me that I'm a complication for him.

He turns, then opens the passenger door of the truck. "Get in," he demands.

"No, it's fine. I just need my books, and I'll get out of your hair." I trail an *X* over my chest. "I swear."

"I don't want you to do that. I just want you to get inside the truck so I can pick your bike up and take you home."

I swallow, then nod. "O-okay."

I get inside, and he shuts the door behind me. He opens the door right behind me and carefully puts our books on the seat, then walks around the vehicle to the driver's side. Once he clicks his seatbelt against him, he starts up the engine.

"I didn't think you'd be the reader type," I say, just to break the silence as he drives towards the parking lot.

"Once again, you don't know me."

"Mabel told me that you used to shop at the bookstore before they shut down."

He side-eyes me. "Yeah, I did. But I also get my books here, too." He pulls up to the curb of the library, and he gets back out to put the bike in the back of his truck, and then he's back inside in a matter of seconds. "Did you rent the bike from Megan's bike shop?"

I nod, and he heads back to the opposite end of town. It's another silent drive, and I can feel his frustration, his annoyance, he has for me swarming in the limited space between us. After today, I internally vow to leave him alone. I don't like being someone that others dislike, and I'd rather not bother him anymore if he doesn't want to get along and be friends while I'm here. I'd rather not see how much he would probably like to not have me as a neighbor, even if we have only known one another for four days.

I've been unwanted before, and I don't want to make that mistake again. This time, I'll take the signs I'm given and not make a fool of myself.

chapter nine

When he's on the route towards our neighborhood, Atlas turns his head to me. "Did you finish your first article?" I'm still shocked he even knows what I do. Or cares. "Uh, y-yeah," I stutter. "Yes, I did."

He nods. "That's great. I'll read it when I get home."

"You will?"

He frowns and glances at me again. "Of course."

"Why?"

"Because I think what you are doing here is great. The town is really grateful."

I lean my elbow down on the middle console. "And how would you know? Mabel also told me that you aren't very social here. No one in the town really knows you."

His mouth twitches. "Maybe that's why I notice you so much. You're… loud." I blink. "Loud?"

"In the way you ask questions. In the way you look at everything like you're going to turn it into a headline. It's hard to ignore."

I gape at him. "So what you're saying is that you're stalking me."

He smirks, eyes back on the road. "Don't flatter yourself, Holly."

I cross my arms. "Well, thanks for the compliment. Most women would kill to be described as loud."

He actually chuckles now, low and raspy, and for some reason, I want to savor the sound. He gives me a bigger grin now, and my heart is now doing flips off of that bridge. "Mabel felt bad after I left the diner. She said she would never tell anyone about the warehouse where I keep my boats."

"So does everyone just keep your secret, then? Why would they do that if you don't really talk to anyone?"

"Lots of questions," he mumbles. "The people in this town are different from anyone else I've met in my life. I don't need to go out of my way to talk to everyone and everything in order to be liked." He swallows. "I don't have to be someone I'm not, and they don't pressure me to become friends with them. At least to my face, anyway."

But why are you so reserved? The question is on the tip of my tongue, but I don't want to push him. He's still a stranger, for the most part. And he's made it clear that I don't know him.

Sam's words come back to my head. *Atlas isn't who he says he is.* Is Sam protecting Atlas too? *Why?* "Does Sam know about the warehouse?"

He tenses. "You've met Sam?"

"Yes. I asked him to meet me at the cafe the other day so he could tell me the history of Saltmere. He also offered to take me to the coves and the lighthouse so I can write about them."

"Don't go with him," Atlas says, his brown eyes flicking over to me. We are stopped at a stoplight, one of the only ones in Saltmere. Atlas turns his upper body to face me, his eyebrows bunched together like he is in pain. Or like he can't believe those words just exited out of his mouth. I'm in shock, too.

"Why?"

He sighs and curls his lips in. He doesn't seem to care whether or not the light turns green anymore because he leans his elbow on the console right next to mine, his brushing against my skin. Just from the simple touch, goosebumps skyrocket down my bare arms, causing the hair on them to point to the roof of the truck.

"Because," he says, "I can take you."

"*What*?" I blink. "Why? You hate me."

"I do?"

"It sure seems like it." I straighten in my seat. "I know we've only known each other for four whole days, but each interaction we've had hasn't been great."

"That's not true. We went to the art gallery yesterday, and it was fine."

"You looked like you were in pain the entire time."

He turns his head back to the windshield. I watch his nose scrunch up and his lips press together. He runs a hand down his chin and the stubble that resides there. His voice is lower when he finally says, "Me acting like that had nothing to do with you, trust me."

I watch him with open curiosity. "What do you mean?"

He finally presses on the gas pedal once the light turns green, and without answering me, he pulls into the neighborhood. I look back out my window and stare at the ocean, at the sandy beach, until the truck is in my driveway. Atlas surprises me by shutting off his truck and opening his door. "What are you doing?"

He opens the door behind his seat. "I'm helping you bring your books inside."

My sandals slap on the pavement as I walk around the truck to him. I try reaching for my books out of his hand, but he pulls them away and frowns. "I can take them now," I say. "I appreciate you helping me, but I think I can manage walking the few steps to the door while carrying six books."

"I have reason to believe that you cannot do that, given the fact that you almost tripped down the stairs at the library." He turns and saunters up the steps to the front porch of my house. I, of course, trail behind and basically jog to catch up to him. I exhale as I dig for my keys in my overall's pocket and open the front door.

Atlas walks right in and places the books down on the kitchen table before I can even lock the door behind us. I watch him take in the place, his head swiveling in every direction.

I'm an overall clean person, but because of my need to get that first article completed in such a hurry, I've left a mess behind. All of the blankets from the basket next to the couch are unfolded and lying everywhere. My laptop charger is in a tangled knot on the floor next to the TV stand, and ripped up pages of my notebook are scattered like leftover candy from a piñata. I got the munchies as I was writing yesterday, too, so wrappers of Reese's chocolate are discarded on the coffee table, as well as a half empty container of Sour Patch Watermelon, an empty bag of Lay's salt and vinegar chips, and a half eaten Twix bar.

I haven't done any of the dishes that sit in the sink, and I also left the garbage from my takeout food from the diner on the counter.

I go to pick up all of the trash in the living room. "I'm sorry about the mess. I wasn't exactly expecting anyone to come over here."

"Holland, stop."

I freeze and look at him. He's still next to the kitchen table, but he's looking at me with a hint of longing, or maybe pity. "What?" I ask, with maybe too much annoyance laced in my tone. I don't like him looking at me like this. It's making butterflies perform flips in my stomach.

He takes a step closer. "Do you want to have dinner with me?"

My eyes widen, and my eyebrows shoot up to my hair line. Then I laugh. My neck falls back, and all of the trash I did pick up falls at my bare feet. "I'm sorry," I wheeze. "I think my brain is pulling tricks on me. I thought you asked me out."

"I did."

My smile falls, and my laugh fizzles out. "You quite literally give me whiplash." I roll my eyes as I bend down and pick the trash up once again. Atlas's shadow casts over me in the limited lighting of the dining area when he stands even closer now, and he crouches to his knees right in front of me.

His hand latches around my wrist to halt my movements. With his other hand, his fingers land on my chin, and he pulls my head up to look him in the eyes. "Go out with me," he says in a whisper. It makes chills fling themselves down my arms.

Our eyes search one another's, but I'm only trying to find why he suddenly is being nice to me. "Why the sudden change? At the library, it was like you couldn't get away from me fast enough."

His hand on my chin lowers to his side. "I offered to take you home, didn't I?"

I scoff. "Barely. You wouldn't give me back my books." I sound incredibly ungrateful, but I just don't understand him. At all. I'm feeling angry and confused. "The first day we met, you made it extremely clear that I shouldn't bother you."

"That was before I knew who you were."

"And you suddenly know me now?" I straighten, my apparently weak knees cracking in the process. "Let me quote you. *You don't know me.*"

I blow past him and toss the garbage in my hands in the waste bin in the kitchen. Of course, he follows me, putting his hands on his hips.

"Fine," he says, "if you won't go out with me, at least let me take you wherever you need to go in this town. I'll go with you to the places you want to write about in your articles."

"I'd rather ask an actual local. Like Sam."

His jaw works. "Don't–" He exhales. "Don't go with Sam. Please."

"What's your problem with him?" I shrug. "He's nice." I turn to the dishes in the sink and flip on the faucet. Cold water splashes up on my clothes as it hits my discarded mugs and pans. "He doesn't act like he would rather be somewhere else when he's around me."

"You've only met up with him once."

I whip around with a dish soap covered frying pan in my hand. Drops of water pellet down onto the hardwood floor and the rug at my feet. "It doesn't matter, Atlas. You aren't helping your case. Can you blame me for being confused at your proposition?"

"It's not a proposition. It's just one date. Give me a chance, please."

He still intrigues me, even when I wish he didn't. There's something about him I can't look away from–why he keeps himself apart from the rest of the town, why he asked Grace for paintings by Lila Voss, why he acted so strangely at the gallery. I want to understand him, but the thought of letting myself care again terrifies me. My heart's still in pieces, and I can't risk it being torn into smaller ones. He's not Gordon, I know that, but he hasn't exactly been kind to me, either. I don't know if I can trust him, but parts of me can't help but want to.

On the other hand, I'd love for someone to take me to the places I want to write about. Exploring the town on my own, especially the spots my mom must have visited, only makes the ache in my chest sharper. If I had company, maybe it wouldn't hurt so much. And beyond that, I want to finally see the places I've only ever imagined, the ones she loved so dearly. I turn back around to the sink with another deep sigh and resume doing the dishes. My voice is quieter when I say, "Fine, you can take me to where I want to go in this town. But I don't think I am ready for an actual date yet."

I hear his footsteps get closer. He leans his hip on the edge of the counter next to the sink, one hand propped up on the counter and the other softly tracing circles on my elbow. I slowly turn my head up at him, and he's giving me a warm smile that I haven't seen before from him in the short amount of time we have known one another existed.

"I can do that." He swallows, his eyes zeroed in on my lips for a split second before they flick back up to meet mine again. "I know I haven't been the nicest, and I'm sorry. But you can trust me, Holland."

He brings my wet, soapy hand to his mouth and presses a soft kiss on the back of my palm. Parts of me wish I could tattoo his touch permanently there, but I shake those thoughts away. He winks at me before he walks back to the front door, and in a matter of seconds, it shuts behind him and he's gone.

chapter ten

"This is fucking awesome!" Grace shouts over the booming pop music blasting from the overhead speakers that scatter around the boardwalk. She picked me up from my house, determined to stick next to me the entire day, and now she's skipping a little ahead of me with cotton candy in her hand like she's the one visiting for the first time.

I can't help but laugh. Somewhere between her dramatic storytelling, her obsession with fried dough, and the way she refuses to let me feel like an awkward outsider, I've started to really like her. She's relentless in the best way, warm where I'm hesitant, bold where I'm quiet, and it's impossible not to get pulled along in her current. For the first time since coming here, I feel like maybe I won't have to carry all of this alone.

Young children sprint past us, ruffling my long violet skirt up in different directions. I watch as they head straight to the line of the Ferris wheel, jumping up and down as their parents catch up to them. Elderly couples are holding hands with popsicles hanging in their mouths, humming and smiling to one another as they stroll past. Teenagers joke and laugh as they stand in line for the rollercoaster, *Fire Dragon.*

It *is* awesome, how perfect day one of the festival has turned out. I obviously haven't been here in previous years, but based on what I have seen in pictures of how the festival did before, I *know* we have more visitors today. I don't know if it was because of my article or just a sheer amount of luck, but I'm grateful, and a slight amount of pressure that buried itself in my chest lightens.

Grace and I go on all the rides together, waiting in line next to the other residents of the town and those Grace swears she has never met before. We chat with a woman named Andi and her daughter Blake, who are visiting from Oregon. Andi owns a bookstore and was at a bookstore conference on the East Coast before she read my article and stopped here before their flight home tomorrow. My heart swells and threatens to explode as Andi tells me and Grace this, and the hug my new friend in Saltmere gives me makes me experience a funnel of happiness that I haven't felt since November.

"Come on, let's go see how the kissing booth is doing." I drag Grace behind me as we maneuver around the crowd until the end of the boardwalk when the sun is setting on the ocean water next to us. The booth is *packed*–I can't even see Mabel or Ed or Gill. Or Atlas. We gently push through everyone waiting in line for their turn and those who only want to watch, and I can finally see a familiar face on the stage.

Mabel is standing in the middle of the lines at the center of the booth, announcing in a microphone at her own podium. The booth itself is a wooden structure, painted red and white with a flowy curtain hanging at the back of it. The flashy sign that I know Gill made is centered at the top of the structure, reading Kissing Booth in bold, whimsical lettering, with shapes of hearts and lips on both sides. The other two podiums are low enough that people can lean over them, and on the corner of the stage, there is a painted pink wooden sign that reads: **$1 Kisses–Today Only!**

The woman contestant at the female podium right now has dark curly hair flowing out from the band of the blindfold. "Is that Charlotte?" I ask Grace in shock. I didn't know the town's librarian would be one of the women with the blindfolds.

Grace laughs next to me. "Oh my god, go Char!" Grace jumps up and down.

The kissing booth is only open for another thirty minutes, and Grace purchases a ticket and gets at the back of the line. I wait with her, but there is no way I'm kissing anyone tonight. Or for a good while. At the male podium, Brady, one of the younger members of the board that I haven't technically met yet, is in the middle of kissing a pretty woman with bright red hair. Gill declares to the crowd that no more tickets can be purchased for the booth, meaning that Grace will be the final participant.

Grace ends up having to first kiss Jeremy, Ed's oldest nephew, then her ex-boyfriend from high school, Zander. But she doesn't seem phased at all; she only shrugs as Zander meets her with a blindfold covering half of his face at the podium. They break the rules and kiss longer than a peck, receiving a bundle of cheers and shouts from the crowd, and Mabel has to shoo them off the stage. They both go willingly, and I laugh to myself under my hand.

I'm still waiting at the base of the stage when Atlas walks out with a blindfold on. I peer over at Mabel in confusion, since Jeremy was supposed to be the final contestant for the night, but Mabel only winks at me. The rest of the crowd has dispersed back towards the rest of the festival, and Ed and Gill and some other members of the board chat to one another as they begin to clean up the area where the participants were standing in line.

Mabel saunters down the steps two at a time until she is right in front of me. She puts her hands on my shoulders.

"I know you don't have a ticket, but I told Atlas he has one more kiss tonight."

"What? Why?"

She only shrugs and begins to pull me towards the steps of the stage. But my feet drag against the pebbled dirt. "Hold up," I whisper, so Atlas doesn't hear me. "I'm not kissing anyone tonight. Or ever. I don't really want to play your matchmaker game. Sorry."

Mabel has the audacity to look hurt at my words. "So you are just going to leave him up there? After you made me blackmail him into this?"

I swipe the air. "You could go tell him that he doesn't have to kiss anyone else. I'm sure he'll be relieved."

"The two of us are finally becoming friends, I think. If I tell him that he's done for the night right after I told him he has one more, and after I saw him mentally prepare for something I know he hates doing, what does that make me?" She clenches a fist at her chest. "A bad friend. And a liar. Please?"

I roll my eyes at her words, and I can't help but huff a laugh. I glance back at Atlas. His hands lower down to the top of the podium, as if he doesn't know that he doesn't have to kiss anyone anymore. His lips are in a line, and his fingers tap against the wood like he is impatient as I inhale a deep breath and walk up the steps of the stage. I take a quick glance back at Mabel, who is now standing next to Ed, Gill, Brady, and Charlotte at the side of the stage.

Great. We will have an audience for this.

Charlotte must read my mind, because she turns around and forces everyone behind the red curtain that I know they will probably peek out of once they all are behind it. But I look back up at Atlas, who appears not at all nervous, like me. I don't know what I'm doing. I shouldn't be here, shouldn't be in front of him and about to kiss him.

But I can't get his words from last night out of my head. *You can trust me, Holland.* With a deep, shaky exhale, I clutch at the sides of the podium now in front of me. My finger gently grazes over Atlas's, and I watch his entire body tense. He swallows, his Adam's apple bobbing up and down twice.

Here goes nothing. Or everything. I rise to my toes and lean in, my hands now cupping the sides of his neck to slowly pull him down to me.

"Hi, Holland," he whispers before his lips crash onto mine.

He swallows my gasp with his mouth. My eyes flutter shut when his own hands extend above the podium and pull at my sides, like he wants to get even closer. Our lips brush together and this kiss becomes its own rhythm that I don't want to end. The feeling soaring through my body makes me feel like flying into the air or launching into space because this kiss is like a taste of ecstasy, a tang of rhapsody. When our tongues clash, a groan escapes from inside the curvature of his throat.

His hands find my hair and his fingers press into the back of my neck. It's the electricity flowing through my limbs that makes me rip the blindfold off of his face. The air suddenly feels hot, stifling, but it doesn't matter. Nothing does, not the tightness I am clenching at the sides of his collared shirt, not the pace my heart is beating, not the squeals or snickers of those watching us. Our kiss quickens, like we can't get enough of one another, can't stop the rush that courses through our veins. But it becomes so overwhelming, the way my body is *humming* to the song his body is singing, so I pull away.

Our pants mix together in the limited space between us. He's staring at my eyes, searching back and forth between them. Everything around us blurs and fades into nothingness as intense silence engulfs the two of us, swarming us into a state of confusion and shock. More seconds pass with me lost in his gaze before my voice finds me once again. "D-did Mabel tell you it was me?"

He shakes his head once. "No."

"How did you know?"

He runs a finger down my jaw. "I just did." He then walks around the podium and grabs my hand. "Come on, we're leaving."

He pulls me down the stage steps, and I glance back at the curtain, where everyone has their heads poking through the opening. They are all grinning at me, especially Mabel, and Charlotte is giving me a thumbs up.

I turn back around and giggle under my hand, tracing over my swollen lips. I look back up at Atlas as he leads me back through the chaos of the festival. He notices me peering at him, so he glances down at me and smiles, then presses a kiss to my forehead like it's the most casual act in the world for the two of us.

"Where are we going?" I ask him.

"You'll see" is all he says.

chapter eleven

We walk towards the crowded parking lot of the boardwalk, away from the noise and the colorful lights of the festival. My hand is warm wrapped up in Atlas's. The material of my skirt swishes behind me as my legs try to keep up with his pace, but as soon as we get to his truck, he comes to an immediate stop.

A tall man with dark hair and a sharp jawline like Atlas's is leaning against the exterior of the vehicle, his dress shirt half untucked and the belt around his dress pants hanging undone. He has his arms crossed against his chest, where a gold chain with a pendant with the letter *G* dangling from the center rests right below his neckline. Next to the man's untied shoes, two empty bottles of whiskey are lying on the rocky gravel.

Atlas lets go of my hand. "What do you want?" he demands to the stranger, taking a step forward.

The man tilts his head. His lips twist into a smile, and when he rubs one hand over the stubble on his chin, purple and blue blemishes dance over his knuckles. He flicks his eyes to me, then back to Atlas. "No need for your protectiveness, Atlas. Who's the g-girl?"

"Doesn't matter," Atlas grinds. "What do you want, Roman?"

The man, Roman, takes a lousy step forward, kicking one of the bottles at his feet in the process. He places a hand over Atlas's shoulder. Atlas stiffens next to me. His jaw is clenched so tight I swear I can hear his teeth grinding. A vein pulses in his neck, and I watch him resist the urge to shove Roman's hand off of him.

Roman chuckles, head tipping back like he's the only one in on a joke no one else can hear. "R-relax, man. I just saw you and thought, why not say hello?" His words stumble, but his smile is crooked, almost boyish. He glances at me, blinking too slowly. "D-didn't realize you would have company. You always did keep the g-good things close to the chest."

"Roman," Atlas says, voice low and edged with warning.

Roman lifts his hands, swaying on his feet. "What? I'm being nice. Look at me, practicing m-manners." His eyes flicker between us before settling back on me. "I've been meaning to call you," he mumbles. "Found s-something about Da–"

"Roman." Atlas's interruption is sharp, final.

Roman blinks, as if the cut-off sobers him for a moment. Then he shakes his head and laughs under his breath. "Figures. Still playing it safe." He presses a hand to his temple, like he's trying to rub away the night. "Secrets never did us much good, huh?"

There's no malice in the words, just a weary resignation.

Atlas takes a step forward, shoulders squared. "Go home, Roman."

For a moment, Roman studies him, studies us, like he wants to say more. His mouth opens, then shuts again, the words swallowed by something heavier than whiskey.

Finally, he tips two fingers against his brow in a sloppy salute. "Another time, then."

Atlas latches onto my hand, gentle but firm, and pulls me back toward his truck in silence, leaving Roman hunched against the streetlight glow.

chapter twelve

Atlas is tense while he drives us towards the opposite side of town. I don't know whether to talk or not, or if I should touch his hand lying in the middle console in between us. His other hand is clenched around the steering wheel, and even in the darkness, I can see how white his knuckles are.

I don't know what to make of that interaction with Roman. *Secrets never did us much good.* What secrets? What is Atlas hiding?

I don't know what any of it means, or why Atlas looked like he'd rather swallow a piece of glass than speak another word to him.

I want to ask. The questions are right there, stacked at the tip of my tongue. But something about the way Atlas is sitting, coiled like a wire pulled too tight with his back straight and arms stiff, makes me hold back.

I turn my head to look at him, but he's already glancing over at me with dark eyes that match the night sky. The lights of the town passing by get lost in his irises as we drive on the street, and they look like the stars glistening above us. His lips are rolled together. He's tucked them in so tight in a line that his cheek dimples still show. But then he looks away, back to the road, not looking at me again.

The silence stretches, thick with words unsaid. I boldly inch my fingers towards his, hovering just over the space between us. I don't touch him, not yet. I just let my hand rest near his. It's like an offering, a quiet gesture as if to say *I'm here.* I may not understand, but I'm here.

He doesn't take it, but I see his hand flex as if he's noticed, as if it matters. And that's enough.

We pull into an empty parking lot full of potholes in front of a large warehouse. I gasp and clutch my fingers around the seatbelt resting against my chest, desperate to shift the mood back to excitement. "Did you take me to see your boats?"

The corners of his lips tilt up at my excitement. "I figured we could take one out on the water. I want to take you somewhere."

"For my articles?"

A rush of excitement trickles through me, a feeling I haven't touched in over a year. Atlas taking me on the water ignites a sense of longing for the career I almost let drift away from me, but I can feel it coming back to me, piece by piece. I can already picture it: the night sky draped above, the town's lights scattering across the water like fireflies, the lighthouse on the ledge of the rocks acting like a personal bodyguard for the town. Through my camera lens, it won't just look magical, it'll tell a story. One that might finally let people see Saltmere the way I'm already starting to.

He looks down, then opens his mouth to say something, but clamps it shut. He hops out of the truck. I unclick my seatbelt and go to open my door, but Atlas is already opening it for me. I thank him as my shoes hit the rocky pavement, and he places his hand on the small of my back as he leads me towards the building.

There's a dim hanging light above the single door on the left side of two large garage doors, but the cone of light only shines bright enough on the door itself and a few inches before it. I lean more into Atlas's hand as crickets croak and sing into the darkness surrounding us, and I keep my eyes glued to my feet so I don't lose my footing and trip into a pothole.

Atlas is still just as tense as he was when we left the festival when he unlocks the door of the warehouse and pushes it open. He lets me step inside first, and in a matter of seconds, the lights flick on, illuminating a large room full of machinery and flat trailers with enormous boats on them. On the walls, wooden beams and sheets of plywood are stacked on top of one another, next to shelves and shelves of tools and appliances. Four boats are arranged before us, two still in a wooden form, and the other two are shiny and polished, as if they are ready to be on the water.

It's an organized chaos in here, but I can't stop looking at the boats before me. I walk a few steps to one of the polished boats, a light gray skiff boat with the word *Candace* written in blue lettering on the side. The interior includes one white swivel chair next to the steering wheel, and another at the bow of the boat.

I look back at Atlas. "Why building boats? Did you always want to do this?"

He pauses running his hand over the word on the side of the exterior, lost in thought. He stares down at his fingers, like at any second, they could disappear. He swallows, and after what feels like a long minute, he finally utters, "No, I didn't."

"What did you want to do?"

He still doesn't look up. "I…I was supposed to become the second chain of command for my dad's company."

"That doesn't really answer my question."

His head rises, and his brown eyes beat into mine. There's a shadow of a smile on his lips. "Are you trying to interview me?"

"Sorry," I say, glancing down to the floor. I drag the toe of my shoe against it. "I can't help it. It's the journalist in me. I'm not good at small talk." An idea pops in my head, like a string of a lightbulb being pulled, and it fizzles out any other thoughts in my brain. "I could, though. Interview you, I mean. I could write about what you do. Maybe it could help you get more business from people besides those who live here."

He shakes his head. "I don't know–"

"It wouldn't be a hassle, I swear. I have so many things I want to write about for this town, and I would love to highlight your company. It would be so fun to learn about what you do. Do you have a boat you are in the process of building right now? I could observe you work on it one day, and then I could–"

"No."

His answer is so curt, so final that I smack my mouth shut. I blink up at him.

"I don't want you to write about or interview me." He rubs a hand over his chin, the stubble there. He doesn't look at me as he finishes, "I don't want to be involved in your articles."

I swallow down the lump that forms in my throat. It's an emotional one, but I don't feel like crying. No, I feel like *hiding*. I've felt like this before, when my siblings Corinne or Emmett or my dad tell me that what I do isn't a job that's plausible. Isn't financially stable or long lasting. My siblings both followed my mom's footprints in graduating from Harvard and becoming attorneys. My dad has never technically vocalized his opinions of my choice of career, but

I saw the disappointment in his eyes when I said goodbye to him at the airport before my flight back to New York just a few months ago. He saw just how affected I was from Gordon's words and feedback on my work, and even though he was drowning in his own grief, I could tell that he wished I did something else for a living.

I can feel my cheeks redden, but I nod. "Okay."

He exhales hard. "It's not because I don't care, Holland. What you are doing for the town is great, I told you that. I just…can't. I'm sorry."

I swipe at the air in front of me. "I get it!" I exclaim, probably too eagerly. "I promise, it's not even a big deal."

I turn my head back to the boat next to us when he takes a step closer to me and extends his hand out in front of him for me to grab. I do, after a moment of hesitation, and he leads me to the opposite end of the open room. We walk past other boats on trailers, then walk to a workstation tucked away in the corner. Power and hand tools lay scattered on the large workbench, and behind it, a bulletin board full of pinned blueprints and hand drawn drafts of boats displays just how much time Atlas spends in here. Even his drawings are ridiculously amazing, the way each detail is perfectly placed like he's spent hours and hours on them. He's incredibly talented.

I wish I could observe this place for longer, but he grabs onto a ring of keys that hang from a knob of a keyholder nailed into the wall. He then leads us back to the entrance of the building, where he lets go of my hand to open one of the garage doors. It rattles loudly as it rises, letting in the cooler night air.

I shiver to myself, bringing my hands to cover my bare arms. Atlas steps onto the trailer with the boat on it and fiddles with something inside for a moment before he hops back down. He holds out two blankets and a puffy coat for me.

I look at him, then at the items, then back at him. "Are we going on a boat ride right now?"

He frowns. "Is that alright?"

"Are you kidding?" It's *not* an ideal time for photos for an article, but I'll cross that bridge later. He's letting me in and I'm not about to shut that door. I smile and grab onto the blankets and coat. "Of course that's alright! I've never been on a boat before."

"This one isn't super fancy. It's meant for fishing, but I figured we could take it out on the water and look at the stars. They always shine better away from the town."

My mom and I loved looking at the stars together. If I didn't already kiss him tonight, I think I would right now.

chapter thirteen

The water folds over itself, ruffling up the moon's reflection on the surface. We are at least a mile away from the shore, and Atlas has shut down the motor of the boat so we can drift in the silence of the ocean engulfing us. He sits behind the steering wheel while I sit on the seat in front of the boat, my neck cranked up towards the sky.

It's scary, the way the edge of the night sky and the ocean line blend together, like two beings intertwining at the depths of the earth, merging into one expanse and never having to experience complete solitude because they share the same echoing heartbeat and dance to the same rhythm. It's significant, like a couple holding hands, like two opposing villains working together–the powerful combination of blissfulness and unfamiliarity. Both brink on the edge of the unknown, full of life's greatest mysteries, and I imagine them both wanting to be understood, to be wanted, the same way we as humans do.

It's a quiet reassurance to not be the only outcasted thing in existence.

My mom loved stargazing, so she would take me and my siblings out to towns near the Wisconsin border after her long days of work so we could see a night full of stars instead of our usual light polluted, cloudy sky. Corinne and Emmett didn't seem to enjoy those late-night trips as much as I did, and with my mom's help, I learned a textbook's worth of constellations.

I shoot my pointer finger into the air. "Look, there's Centaurus."

"What?" Atlas asks, and I point out the stars in the constellation. I think he pretends to see what I am seeing after a five-minute explanation, and I snicker to myself afterwards as I get more comfortable in my seat. The coat I have on is three sizes too big, but it acts like a shield against the crawling, chilly wind. So do the two blankets I have around me. I keep my eyes glued to the sky above, letting the tranquility of the night wash over me.

"It's so peaceful out here," I say quietly. "I sometimes don't think it's real."

"What's not real?"

"The silence."

I hear, and feel, him stand up from his chair. The boat rocks side to side faintly before he sits down on the floor, just a few inches away from my chair. He rests the back of his head against the backside of the helm console, then pats at the free space next to him.

I, carefully, at the speed of a snail, stand up from my seat and lower down on the floor. The blankets around me fall from my shoulders, so I lean my head back on the console after I place the blankets over both of our legs.

This feels weirdly comfortable, being this close together, in the middle of the ocean. Both of us focus on the stillness of the atmosphere and water as we search the sky. I don't know what time it is, it's late, and the events of these past few days– staying up late and writing until I physically felt my brain melting, prepping for the festival all morning, spending all evening with Grace, then ending by kissing the man next to me– begins to weigh down on me. My eyelids slip shut, and I exhale an exhausted breath.

But I jolt when I feel the side of my cheek land on something hard, something angular. *Atlas's shoulder.* "Sorry," I say, wincing.

"It's fine, Holland." He pauses. "If you're tired, we can go back–"

"No!" I exclaim. "I love it out here. I think it's just all getting to me."

"That makes sense. You've been staying up late every night, yeah?"

My eyebrows crunch together. "How'd you know?"

"Your music is very loud at night."

I wince. "Sorry about that." I look over at him, squinting my eyes to see him better in the dark. "Do you want to talk about it?"

"About your music?"

"About Roman."

He scoffs. "No."

I fully turn to him now. "Why? Why did he say all those things to you? Were the two of you friends at one point?"

"It feels like you are interviewing me again." His fingers rub against one another, and he doesn't make eye contact with me.

I bump my shoulder into his. "Sue me for wanting to get to know you better. You were the one that wanted to go out, remember?"

"So is this a date?" The corners of his lips rise, and the simple act makes the butterflies in my stomach flutter against their cage.

"No," I say quickly. "I was just reminding you of what you said. But I'm not just going to agree to go on a date with someone that won't tell me anything about themself."

He shrugs. "Makes sense." Slowly, to not shift the boat, he turns his body so he is facing me. His knees are propped up, and his arms hang loosely over them. "Let's play twenty questions. You start."

"Okay, but you can't make fun and avoid anything I ask because you think I'm trying to interview you." I tilt my head to the side as a million questions rise to the surface of my brain and form on the tip of my tongue. "Where did you grow up?"

"I was born here, but my mom and I moved to Charlston not long after."

"Just you and your mom? What happened to your dad?"

Atlas turns to look at the water, and I see his Adam's apple bobble. In the limited light of the moonshine, his jawline is coated with stubble, but appears even sharper from the shadows casting over his features. My eyes travel up to the curve of his nose, and the tip twitches when his tongue swipes over his lips. His dark eyebrow slants downward as his eye squints, as if he is searching for something in the darkness of the sea. He sucks in a deep breath and lets it out slowly. "I'm not close with him." He looks back at me. "That was three questions in a row. It's my turn."

I scoff. "That's not–"

"Why did you choose to be a writer?"

My mouth clamps shut. The notion to only reveal a sliver of the truth, the only parts of the truth that aren't embarrassing, flickers with light, but I might as well be real with him if I want him to tell me everything about him. I exhale.

"I have dyslexia," I say carefully. Then I take another deep breath and rip off the band-aid. "I really struggled in school growing up. I used to think that I was adopted or something because my older siblings, Emmett and Corinne, are perfect prodigies. They graduated with a perfect GPA, with perfect test scores in every subject." I huff a laugh. "Me, on the other hand, I couldn't even spell my own name. I struggled processing anything my teachers would explain to the class, and I couldn't remember anything that I would try to read. It showed in my test scores and homework assignments. Gradually, over the years, I was becoming the least smart member of the family."

"Having dyslexia doesn't make you not smart, Holland."

"I know that now. But growing up, I couldn't stand the fact that I was so different from my peers. From my siblings." I fidget with the edge of the blanket draped over us. "Even at a young age, I could see the disappointment in my dad's face. I still can."

"Over your reading disability?"

"No. Because of my choice of career." I swallow. "He would see my grades and automatically assume that I just didn't care to learn, to be better, to be like Emmett and Corinne. He didn't, and still doesn't, know about my dyslexia. I made it a personal goal to overcome all of my challenges with reading and writing without anyone knowing, and the only person that knew about my struggles, besides my teachers, was my mom. I begged her not to tell the rest of our family because I didn't want them to think of me any less. My mom signed me up to talk to an educational psychologist every other day so I could practice reading and writing, and eventually, the appointments worked." I grin and look off to the ocean. "I grew a love for writing, to capture different stories and write them in a variety of ways. Ever since my last appointment with the psychologist in sixth grade, I knew I wanted to be a writer when I grew up."

"That's amazing, Holland." Atlas gives me a warm smile that makes my insides squirm with elation. But his smile falls slightly when he asks, "So is your relationship with your dad strained, then?"

I shrug. "Sometimes, he and I can talk for hours on end, and I get this feeling that he actually *likes* me. Like, in that moment, he doesn't remember what I have chosen to do with my life, and the two of us can just be father and daughter. Good friends. But other times, our bond is as frozen over as a lake in the dead of winter. It's like we can't agree on anything, and when our relationship is like that, he likes to, subtly, belittle journalism. Especially what I do–traveling from city to city and never settling down. He thinks it's a waste of time."

"Why is that?" Atlas asks. "What you do acknowledges even the smallest towns on a map, making them even with the famous ones on this planet. You explore the places most people don't and write about what makes them special and worthy of attention. And not everyone can do what you do. It takes an incredibly large amount of skill to be able to write and publish an article, let alone dozens and dozens of them in a time crunch."

Atlas's words make me feel warm. His arms are still wrapped around his knees, but it feels as if his words are wrapped around my shoulders, soothing me against the years of pent-up doubt and frustration and disappointment.

"Thank you," I whisper, then swallow down the slightest amount of emotion that is crawling up my throat. "I don't really care what he thinks anymore. It helped to have my mom around, because even though I didn't follow her footsteps like my siblings did, she was still proud of me."

Atlas is silent for a long moment. I glance back up at the stars sparkling above us, and I smile, knowing she is probably one of those twinkling lights, watching us. "My turn," I say to Atlas. "Why boatbuilding?"

"The story of my career isn't as moving as yours is."

"That is probably not true, Human GPS."

His laughter cuts through the air. "I should've lied and said my name was something else. I have a feeling that these nicknames aren't going to stop anytime soon."

"Oh, I have lots. Don't worry." I give him a pointed look. "You're avoiding my question."

His shoulders drop, and he adjusts how he is sitting. His long legs extend out in front of him, and his head falls back. "My mom's dad loved to fish in the Outer Banks, and my grandfather had five different fishing boats. Before he passed away when I was six, he would bring me to his shop, where all the boats were stored, and tell me all about them. What they are all made of, what it takes to make them, and way too many stories that a young child probably didn't need to hear. But it made him happy, and since I knew that I wasn't going to follow through with the position my dad wanted me to fulfill for his company, I decided to do something I knew I would love. So I started building boats."

"And you're dang good at it, given that this one we are on hasn't sunk to the bottom of the ocean."

"Yet," he responds, smirking. I pretend to gasp, and he laughs again. "I'm kidding."

I roll my eyes and scoff. A gust of wind swooshes through the air, sending chills down every inch of my body and my hair flying in different directions. I bring the blankets up and tuck them under my chin, but Atlas shifts more to me, and our thighs bump into one another. The touch feels hot, but neither one of us moves as we get comfortable.

When the wind dies down slightly, I glance back up at Atlas, but he's already looking down at me. "Why do you push away the people of this town?" I ask in a whisper.

One of his fingers trails over the top of my skirt under the blanket, and I fight a shiver. He looks down at the blankets. "Sometimes that seems easier than them learning more about me."

"But you're a nice person." My words are so sudden that they rush together, and I wince. "I just think you would get along with everyone here. I mean, look at how well the festival went today. I know I've only been here a little less than a week, but you did great with all of the board members at the kissing booth."

"I *did* do great at the kissing booth," he replies, his eyebrows wagging up and down. I roll my eyes again, and he snickers. "I know what you mean. It's just hard for me to trust people."

I nod, because I agree. It is hard to trust people. But that doesn't mean he should shy himself away from caring about others. I almost say so, but Atlas rests his head back on the console behind us. We both look back up at the stars, our necks cranked back and our eyes wandering over the speckles of light. We don't finish the rest of our twenty questions game, but that's fine with me. I feel like I know Atlas better now, and I feel a shred of gratitude to be one of the only people that Atlas does trust.

chapter fourteen

Atlas brought me home a little after midnight after stargazing. I spent all day Saturday with Charlotte and Grace at the festival, and since the kissing booth was a one-day-event only, the rest of the festival board–Mabel, Gill, Ed, Jeremy, and Brady– decided to tag along with us. The entire day flew by, full of all of us stuffing our faces with more funnel cakes coated with powdered sugar and screaming to our vocal chords' capacity through the swirls of the rollercoaster, but I had the most fun I've had in what feels like years with my new friends.

The day was amazing, full of laughter and zero stress, until I stepped back through the front door of my house and glanced at my buzzing phone in my hand.

The contact that flashed across the screen read: *Emmett*

I haven't talked to my brother since a few days after the funeral back in November. He was too big in a hurry to return back to Los Angeles for work to stay long in Chicago, which I understood. Neither of my siblings have jobs that could easily transition to being remote like mine.

Mine and Emmett's relationship has always been tricky. He's only fifteen months older than me, and there once was a time in our lives where we shared everything– laughs, jokes, friends, clothes, school lunches, extracurricular activities, and music taste. We were once inseparable, until I started falling behind in school and he couldn't stand to help explain basic math or reading knowledge to me when we had to do homework together before he could go to his soccer practices. He was a grade ahead of me, and once he entered ninth grade in a new school and I was still in eighth, he met new friends. He gained popularity. He excelled in his classes, entered the high school principal's honor roll program, destined for students who withheld a 4.0 GPA and were on track for academic scholarships to the best universities around the country.

In other words, he became my complete opposite.

He had followed our older sister's footsteps. Corinne is four years older than Emmett, and when she graduated as the valedictorian of the academy we all attended for high school, he had no other dreams but to be just like her, or even better, because he was amazing at soccer. Scouts attended every game of his, even when he was a freshman. Not only was he one of the smartest students our academy had ever taught, but he had athletic abilities that most kids dream of having. There once was a time where he dreamed of playing professionally, but that dream ended as soon as my father said so.

"Playing a sport professionally doesn't determine a reliable future, Emmett. What if you don't make it? You would waste your entire college years focusing only on soccer, not on figuring out a successful career for your future family. What if you get hurt? You would waste your entire life training just to have it stripped away from you in a single second. What would you do then?"

Our dad's doubt implanted in my brother's brain, and he snapped out of the dream faster than he could run down the soccer field. He switched his mindset towards what Corinne had achieved, and she only wanted the same thing as my mom wanted, to be an attorney–and the best one. The three of them became a pact of geniuses, bonding over the scores of their bar exams and the ridiculousness of some of the cases they had to represent.

Emmett and I were basically strangers the days leading up to the funeral. Thankfully, he was the only one able to mentally and physically deal with all the logistics because my dad was a complete and total wreck. But when I tried to speak to Emmett, to console and grieve with my brother for the loss of our mom, he dragged me to the janitor's closet of the mortuary with a strained expression plastered on his features.

I'll never forget what he told me that day. His dirty blond hair was combed over to the side perfectly, and his face was perfectly clear of any tears or emotion, besides anger. His dark brows here caved in on his forehead and his lips were tight in a line. "You have to keep it together, Holland," he had said to me in the darkness of that closet. "You can't cry the entire time while you speak in that microphone. Come on, can't you see how many important people are here for Mom? Wouldn't you think it'd be disappointing to them to see how much of a wreck her youngest daughter is today? How would Mom want you to act today?"

And boy, was I a wreck that day. Emmett wasn't wrong with his words, but just with his delivery. I didn't need to hear his demeaning phrases, and I didn't care about what the *important people* thought about me then. I still believe that crying over the loss of my mother at her funeral was a completely justifiable response for her daughter. It's a shame that my brother doesn't possess the same emotional bone that I have–a shame for either me or him, I don't know.

I sigh and place the phone to my ear. "Hello?"

"Holland?"

"Yes, that's who you called, Emmett."

"Oh, yes. Right." I don't think I've ever heard him this frantic, this lost before. "Were…were you busy or something? It took you a while to answer. Did I interrupt anything?"

I frown. "No, you didn't. I was just getting home." I pause for him to answer, but he doesn't. "What's up?"

Emmett and I rarely talked in person, let alone on the phone. I could feel a bundle of nerves swirl in my stomach at the thought of something else happening, something bad, because the last I knew about my brother's whereabouts–thanks to the limited texts my dad would send me–Emmett was spending a week with our dad.

Wait. "Is Dad okay?" I ask, my chest caving in.

"Uh, yeah." Emmett clears his throat. "He's fine. Everything's fine."

His voice is still shaky, like he's nervous, but his words do bring a slight amount of relief. "Okay," I say, "why are you calling, then? Did something else happen? Is Corinne okay?"

"That's the thing," he responds. "I haven't spoken to her since we both left Chicago. Since November."

What? It's the end of May. I mean, I don't talk to my sister regularly. Or at all, for that matter. I think the last time I messaged Corinne was months before the funeral. She had congratulated me when I returned from a two-week assignment in Paris last August, after I completed a round of articles that focused on the lives of the residents of the city as they continued their daily routines with a focal point as large as the madness of the Olympics happening around them. I had researched and written about how such a large event with a large amount of attention could impact the attitudes, behaviors, routines, and even relationships of the people in Paris. Corinne loves the city and multiple clients of hers have moved there, so she, *surprisingly*, expressed her appreciation for bringing light on the matter.

"What do you mean you haven't talked to her? It's been months since the funeral, Emmett. Both of you live in California and work for the same firm. How could you have possibly not heard from her since November?"

I hear my brother sigh. "We don't work *together* every day. I hardly see her at the firm. But her assistant, Lori, came to me last night as I was leaving the office and said that Corinne's been MIA since the beginning of this month, and when I try calling her or Mac, the line goes straight to voicemail."

"Okay, well, maybe she's just busy," I remark, but that's not a justifiable excuse for my sister. She's always busy. "Or maybe she and Mac finally took a vacation. Did Lori say anything else about where Corinne could be?"

"Only that she came into the office on the last day of April and told her that she was going to take the next day off, which she *never* does, and that Lori didn't need to come in. But the day after, when Lori came in and Corinne's office chair sat empty all day long and she couldn't get a hold of Corinne, she got a bad feeling." Emmett releases an audible shaky breath. "Maybe it's nothing, but I know Corinne. She never takes a day off. She's always on a strict schedule, and if she was going to take a vacation, she would've told me. When was the last time you talked to her?"

I press the speaker button and go to my messages app. "August 29th was the last time we texted, and the last time we called was…January 3rd of last year."

"*What?*" Emmett sucks in a breath. "You're telling me that the two of you hardly talk?"

"Why are you shocked? We've never been close."

"Well, maybe," Emmett says. "But I just thought that you two were a little closer than that."

Why on earth would he think that? Where does he get that logic? I'm not even close with him, let alone our sister who's over five years older than me and never cared to even look in my direction growing up. I roll my eyes, even though he can't see me. "Sorry to disappoint." I glance down at her contact, where only her phone number stares back at me. I don't even have a contact photo for her. It's sad, really. I wish Corinne and I were close. I wish I was close with every member of my family. Every *living* member.

"And you already tried calling Mac?"

"Yes," my brother replies, huffing a laugh. "You would think that her husband would respond to my dozens of texts and calls, but even he is unreachable."

"Maybe they did go on a vacation then, Emmett. Maybe they needed it. We might not need to worry."

"I would *know*, Holland. Unlike you, I talk to our sister regularly."

Ouch. It's not like me not talking to Corinne is a choice I make willingly–that's just the nature of our relationship. At the funeral, after Emmett yelled at me, I didn't even think to confide in her of my frustrations or sadness because we have never been like that. We just *don't* talk. But that doesn't give me a reason not to try to find where she is.

"Clearly not, given you can't find or contact her." I sound like I don't care, but I do. I love Corinne, always, even if we have never once told one another that. "Look, I can try to call her, and I'll let you know if I hear from her," I say, my voice reassuring.

"Please do. I'm getting worried."

chapter fifteen

Today, Sunday, the air has shifted at the festival with the same crew I spent the past couple days with, and not just because of the clouds covering the sky and late spring sun like a blanket. The festival doesn't have as many people here walking the boardwalk or riding the rides as the past two days, but I would still consider the festival a major success–if Kurt Gemini wasn't standing near the Ferris wheel with his two sons, or sidekicks, at his sides.

I have done my research on Kurt, so I know that it's him with his arms folded against his chest as he waits in line for the ride. I also know it's him because everyone next to me freezes in their tracks, clearly put off by the man standing before us with a condescending smirk plastered on his face. Kurt's attire and demeanor screams impertinent businessman, given that he and his posse are wearing black suits and ties at a festival in the brink of summer. Kurt's short brown hair is slicked to the side and his dark eyebrows are raised to his forehead, creating crease lines. His dark brown eyes narrow in on each of us as we approach him.

My own eyes shoot from Kurt to Roman, who is looking at me like he knows something I don't. The words he shouted at Atlas the other night float in my mind, and I immediately feel sick to my stomach.

"What do you think you're doing here?" Mabel asks, placing her hands on her hips.

Kurt's head tilts. "Excuse me?" he asks, his tone slicked with a faux politeness, but his eyebrows frown.

Mabel shakes her head. "You heard me. The three of you have a lot of nerve coming to an event like this."

"Is this event not for everyone?" Kurt asks, taking a step closer to Mabel, but Ed and Gill straighten next to her. Kurt notices, and he chuckles, then glances back to Mabel. "The fliers and other advertisements you all have put out didn't say that this festival was a private event."

"It's not a private event, but it's an event for those who actually care about the wellbeing of this community. People like you don't understand what any of that means."

Kurt places his hands over his heart, and his facial expression softens. "I understand community, Ms. Martin. It's people like you that don't."

Brady scoffs next to me. "What the hell does that mean? Of course she understands what community means. We all do."

"I don't know about that," the other male, who I'm assuming is Warren, says. He waves an arm through the air. "It would be my best guess to think that the entirety of this town believes in the same principles as those who settled here first. Historical, outdated ones. Tell me, Mr. Reyes." Warren zeroes in on Brady. "Are those same principles going to keep up with the future generations?"

"Oh, stop pretending you care about the residents here," Gill quips, rolling his eyes. "If you did, you wouldn't have ruined the hard work those owners put into those businesses on Main that you bought out." Warren shifts his attention to Gill. "There is an economic decline in Saltmere. The properties are so old that they are declining property value because they have been neglected for so long. This town has been struggling to support those small businesses because, news flash, no one comes to Saltmere. The schools here are underfunded. The younger generation is moving away. This town is so outdated and old school that you all resist innovation to make actual progress that will help the community."

Kurt nods at Warren, like they are speaking a silent language the two of them only know, then he looks back at the group. "This town is failing its residents. Gemini Development isn't the enemy of Saltmere. You all are."

While Warren's points weren't completely unreasonable, Kurt still deems untrustworthy with the way he tricked all of the store owners on Main Street. His solution, what he has done so far for the town, isn't the answer. The *correct* answer. The correct answer would've been to build trust, the foundation of all long-lasting relationships–not to communicate a creation of webbed lies with the motive to participate in the well-known backstabbing scheme and ruin the image for the residents here of the man who prides himself in his own version of *saving the town.*

It hits me like a bucket of ice cascading over the top of my head that Kurt and his sons do believe they are making a difference for this town, a difference for the better. They believe they are truly saving the future fate for a town as broken and rundown as this one by completely tearing down buildings that have been here for decades and erasing the history that brought Saltmere to life in the first place. That thought isn't as boggling as the idea that Kurt and I have similar grounds of motivation, but our tactics are completely different. I'm not a contractor, but I do have the purpose to build something as reliable as hope for these people here. Hope that this town won't inch closer to its downfall and wash away in a landslide straight to the ocean.

I *won't* be like Kurt. I actually want the trust of the residents of Saltmere, and I want to keep it.

I glance over at Mabel, who looks like she is seconds away from exploding. I think steam is blowing out of her ears.

She takes a step closer to Kurt and shoves a pointer finger right at his chest. "You have a lot of nerve saying all of that, you lying piece of sh–"

Ed pulls her back. "Okay! Let's all go, yeah?" He forces a smile at Kurt and his sons after gesturing with his head at all of us to start walking away.

Grace interlaces her elbow around Mabel and begins walking her away from Kurt, but, of course, Mabel resists her actions. She continues yelling at Kurt as she gets dragged away from the rest of us towards the ring toss booth filled with large stuffed animals. We all follow pursuit, leaving the three men behind us, but as I turn to catch up with Mabel and Grace, I feel a hand on my wrist. When I turn back around, Roman is smiling at me.

"You're the girl I saw the other night, right?"

I nod, cautiously. His gaze lingers, but instead of letting it make me shrink, I steel myself. He scratches the back of his neck, almost sheepish. "I wasn't in a great state of mind then. Sorry about that. Aren't you the writer visiting? How long are you here for?"

"Uh." I glance back to where the group is many feet away. Mabel is now fully occupied with plastic circlets in her hands, one arm cocked and ready to toss. Charlotte's gaze connects with mine, narrowing at the sight of Roman. I give her a slight nod before answering him. "Just a month."

"And you're writing about the town, right? Trying to highlight Saltmere's hidden treasures, bringing in more visitors?"

The way he says it makes my work sound almost whimsical, like a storybook project rather than serious journalism. His tone is lighter than the other night–still teasing, but not cruel. There's laughter threaded in his voice, like he's always on the edge of telling a joke he's not sure I'll get.

"Yes," I reply, tipping my chin higher into the cloudy sky.

He nods, and his vibrant blue eyes catch mine. He leans in slightly, just enough to lower his voice. "You're going to be the town's hero if you pull it off. The festival seems like a huge hit."

"I don't know about being a hero," I whisper.

"Well," he says, smile tugging, "if you ever need help, I'm around." His gaze flicks toward the booths, then back to me. "Do you know how much the festival earned this weekend? Whatever it is, I'll double it. Triple it."

I blink, taken aback. "And why would you do that?"

"Because." He looks down, nudging a pebble with his dress shoe. "Believe it or not, I want this town to do well."

"And I'm assuming your version of 'well' matches your dad and brother's?" My arms fold across my chest.

"No, actually." He glances behind him, and I notice Warren and Kurt are many feet away, watching us. Roman turns back to me. "I mean, maybe parts of it. But Saltmere isn't as perfect as everyone likes to pretend. Some things are failing. We're just trying to make the economy sustainable, give people reasons to move here long-term, not just swing by for a festival."

His words make me roll my eyes, but he finishes softly: "We are trying to help."

"By lying to the business owners? By tearing apart what they've built?" My voice sharpens. "That isn't helping."

His eyebrows lift. "You seem awfully protective of a town you just moved to."

I don't tell him about my mom's connection to Saltmere. He doesn't deserve that piece of me. "Because that's the reason I'm here. Tourists are what keep those shops alive. What I'm doing for Saltmere is actually beneficial."

"Sure, Holland." He chuckles again, and it takes everything in me not to grab him by the shoulders and shake him until he understands. Until he stops belittling my career like everyone else in my life.

But then his smile falters, his laughter fading. "I'm assuming Atlas knows you'll be leaving in a month."

I swallow. "Why do you care?"

Everyone knows my role here for the town. I am here for a month to write, then I'm going back to New York until I get my next assignment. My job description doesn't include long-term commitment, and it can't.

"I don't," he says quickly, then softens. "I'm just…curious about his life."

"Are the two of you friends or something?"

His laughter slices through the air once again, and his head falls back. "Is that what he told you?"

"No, he hasn't told me much, actually."

Roman hums, almost to himself. "Interesting. I'd have thought he'd mention the past by now." Before I can ask what he means, he shrugs and steps back. "Anyway. I'll see you around, Holland. It was nice to actually talk. Sober this time."

He grins, not a smirk, but something closer to genuine, and then saunters off toward the parking lot.

chapter sixteen

I'm settling down onto my couch with a romance book from the library in my hands on Sunday night when I see a flicker of movement outside the window of the living room. The sun has already set, and the remnants of it consists of bright pink and purple and orange streaks swiping over the clouds, but when I look at the water behind the house, I can see Atlas's figure on the dock, next to his boat.

My heartbeat flutters unexpectedly, and I freeze. I shouldn't get this worked up over a man I barely know, but I can't stop my hand from sliding over my lips, where his own lips have touched only once before. The kissing booth was two days ago, but our kiss has replayed over and over again in my head, especially before my mind drifts off to sleep at night.

I am freshly showered and wearing my favorite Taylor Swift concert t-shirt with blue sweatpants, but I trudge through the back door and onto the grass. He doesn't hear me until my slippers step onto the creaking dock, and he whips his head to me and plucks out an earbud. The string of it swings back and forth at his waist, but he smiles faintly.

"Hi," he says, his voice rough, like this is the first time he's spoken all day.

"Hi," I reply, smiling brightly. "What are you doing out here?"

He glances back at the boat that sways gently in the water. "I was just looking for something."

"In your boat?"

"In the compartment, yes."

I'm nosy. "What were you looking for?"

"A picture. But it's not in here." He shrugs. "But I did find these old earbuds. The left one is a little quieter than the right one, but they still work."

I huff a laugh and take a step closer to grab the earbud that swings at his side. But my slipper swipes out from underneath me, and I fall forward, right into his chest. I feel his arms hold me still, right at my waist, and my own hands are holding his upper arms, curled around his flexed biceps. I halt all movements except for my racing heart and panting breaths. My cheeks heat up in embarrassment, but that slowly turns into longing when Atlas's finger swipes at the bare skin of my stomach, where my shirt has ridden up from my trip. I push myself away from him and straighten, then chuckle nervously.

"Sorry about that," I say without making eye contact with him.

"It's okay, Holland," he utters, his voice lighter. "Here."

He hands me the other earbud, and I take it with shaky fingers and a small, wincing smile. Instantly, music blares into my right eardrum. ABBA's "Chiquitita" strums through the small hole, and I gasp. "I love this song!" I exclaim, turning to him.

"I know. It's one of the usual songs you play at night. I think the entire neighborhood knows this is your favorite song."

I can't even bring myself to apologize. My smile widens. "I bet you sing along, don't you?"

Atlas shakes his head, but he rolls his lips together to hide his smile. He gestures to me to follow him down the rest of the dock, and we sit down at the edge. I take my slippers off and roll my sweats up, then dangle my toes in the freezing water. Atlas does the same, and the two of us sit with the music thumping in our ears, and I sing along while Atlas listens and laughs when I sway from side to side.

We watch the sky and the water until the sunset colors disappear and the sky darkens in shade, listening to all of ABBA's most popular hits. It's peaceful and enchanting, sitting here with our feet dipped and swaying to the rhythm in the cold water. We stay until the wind quickens and the humid night air becomes too unbearable, and I begin to tell Atlas goodbye and walk back to my house, but he stops me with a simple look.

His long lashes batter up and down, his lips turn upwards, and he gestures with his head towards his own house. "Have you eaten?" he asks.

"No," I admit. "I'm just going to order something to-go from the diner, like I have been all the other nights I've been here."

"You do that every night?"

I huff a laugh. "I'm technically a tourist, so it makes me feel good to support them. Plus, me in a kitchen? That's a nightmare waiting to happen."

He snorts. "Well, the diner sounds great then. Come on, we'll go together."

He begins walking towards his back door, latching our hands together in a blur that I can't help but follow him or pull my hand out from his. My slippers slide and slither against the grass of his yard, and I take in the unfamiliar sight before me. Our yards don't share a fence, but now that we are facing the back of Atlas's house, I can see the army of gnomes scattering around the backdoor and along the edge of the grass and in front of the bushes to the right. They are in ranges of skin tones, poses, heights, and beard and hat lengths– all with different expressions plastered on their faces. Most are smiling with a circle of red swiped over their distinct cheekbones and holding a bundle of different colored flowers in their plump arms. Some are sitting on the tops of red, polka-dotted mushrooms, while others are busy with a task, either reading, sleeping, shoveling, or pail carrying. Some have their hats covering their eyes, and some have their hand up while they flip off the bypassers.

"Wow," I mutter.

"Yeah, I know," Atlas says, still walking. "My mom had a sick obsession with these things. It doesn't feel right to throw them away. But I keep them back here where I don't have to see them as much because they scare the hell out of me."

My laugh cuts into the air, and I toss my head back, before I really process his words. *Why wouldn't it feel right to throw them away?* But I don't ask him that. The fractional figment of Atlas's past feels like its own piece of treasure. I tuck it away into the files of my brain about him and step through his sliding glass door into the house.

The smell of his cologne and vanilla swarms in the air and hits me first, but my eyes wander around the layout of the space. It is the exact same format at the house I'm staying at, but flipped. The kitchen is to the right, the cabinets a dark brown color, while the countertops and island are white marble. There isn't any decor besides the single gold picture frame in the corner next to the sink, but from where I am standing, I can't make out what the image is.

The living room consists of a dark brown sofa on top of a brown, green, and white patterned rug, with minimal large plants on either side of the fireplace against the opposite wall. A full bookshelf with an arrangement of colored book spines stands as tall as the ceiling, with a few more picture frames scattered on top of the books that lay on their sides. The coffee table is made of dark wood that matches the cabinets of the kitchen. In front of the large window of the room are sage green curtains that drape onto the hardwood floor.

But because of what I see on the coffee table, I freeze in my tracks.

I walk over to it, then pick up the magazine that is making my heartbeat faster.

I turn to Atlas. "You read Wanderlight Journeys' magazine?"

It's an issue from over two years ago, when I went to Porto Venere, Italy and spent a month there creating a travel guide to one of Italy's less-touristy villages. The cover of the publication is me with my camera strapped around my neck as I stand in front of a row of multi-colored houses along the streets of the town. I'm glancing up towards a window three stories high to my left, where a local woman named Adelina, whom I had met on my first day in the town and have been close with ever since, is leaning out of the windowsill with a smile on her lips. A bundle of bright purple Fiordaliso flowers is dangling from her fingers towards me, the flower that is mostly seen in Italy. I'm not usually on the cover of the magazine–Jenny and our creative director, Lillian, usually choose a photo from one of any of the trips the travel journalists go on–but Jenny thought that this photo, especially with Adelina, captured the message and purpose of the magazine perfectly.

It's the only issue I'm on the cover on, and the butterflies in my stomach swarm rapidly at the idea of Atlas only having *this* one sitting on his coffee table, a place where anyone could see and pick it up.

The color of his cheeks pinken. "Maybe."

I put one hand on my hip and wave the magazine around with my other. "Why?"

He walks around the couch and snatches it out of my hands, then rolls it into a tube and tucks it underneath his arm without saying a word. He saunters towards the fridge in the kitchen, his tennis shoes crunching against the hardwood with each step. I follow him, because I want to keep questioning why he has only this issue of the company's magazine, but I stop when my eyes catch on the picture in the frame on the counter.

Now that I'm closer, I see that the photo is of a much younger, child-form Atlas wrapping his arms around a woman with matching brown hair and eyes. The woman's smile is so wide that it looks like the picture was taken as she was laughing, and Atlas is looking at her with adoration and awe dancing in his dark irises. He isn't paying any attention to the camera–all of his focus and attention is on the woman next to him.

"Is that your mom?" I ask, my voice soft. I point to the frame, but Atlas isn't looking. Through the thin material of his t-shirt, I can see his back muscles tense, and his shoulders creep up to his neck. He freezes in that position for a moment, and I begin to question if his mother is a sensitive topic for him, like mine is for me. *What happened to her?* The light of the open fridge casts a cone of white light on his features as he reaches in and retrieves a plastic water bottle, then hands it over to me. But he doesn't meet my gaze; he only glances at the picture.

I watch his throat bobble. "Yeah, it is."

"She's beautiful."

"Yeah." His fingers whiten against the handle of the refrigerator for a second before he shuts the door with a light amount of force. "She was."

Was. The word hovers in the air and sinks deep into my bones. I switch my attention from Atlas to the frame and then back again, memorizing the way the corners of his eyes soften and alleviate when he looks at the woman in the photo. I study the way his lips twitch as they rise slightly to the side, and the tip of his nose wiggles when he breathes in a sum of thick air. He's reminiscing about that specific moment the picture entails, probably listening to the sound of her laugh, to the sound of her voice. I do it all the time when I look back at photos of my mom. The habit is deadly– it freezes you to your core and can stop all progress of moving on, of advancing in this messed up life without them there with you, but the feeling of remembering how their laughter sounds like your favorite song or the sound of the ocean water hitting the sandy shore is spectacular, inescapable.

I restrain myself from touching him, from comforting him, because moments like these, when happy memories float through your brain and replay like a drive-in movie, can be rare. Those jovial moments of the past are so scarce before you blink and suddenly tears are streaming down your face and you can't stop them from dripping onto the ground, and you are reminded of the fact that you will never be able to see them again besides in your dreams; you will never be able to hear their laugh or be the one they are showing their smile to or be able to hold them in your arms and be in the proximity of their warmth.

Pity is often replaced for sympathy when one loses someone dear to them. Death is inevitable, but the concept is sinister. It's terrifying. But what are the rules for when consoling someone after death? One solution would be to pity the other, to feel the sorrow for their loss but put a distance between them that can feel condescending or patronizing. But that act can feel like someone is looking down on you when you are at your lowest state of mind, perhaps the lowest you'll ever be in your life. Or one can offer an understanding and an emotional connection that comes from a place of compassion. People get the two emotions mixed up and sometimes intertwine them together or spread them to pieces, which only harms the person grappling for strength against the war of grief.

I know how it feels to feel such a loss, so I don't pity Atlas, and I won't ruin this moment for him. I just let him feel out the memory while praying to whatever being above that he can know that he isn't alone.

Eventually, Atlas turns back to me, his eyes misted over, but he's smiling with his lips closed.

I match his expression, feeling my own eyes water. "Come on," I say quietly. "Let's go eat." I reach my hand out, and he takes it without any hesitation, and I lead him on unfamiliar grounds towards his front door, but I halt my movements when I take a glimpse at myself through the mirror on the wall of his entryway. I gasp.

"Wait," I utter, "I can't go dressed like this. I'm in my pajamas."

"You look great."

"Thanks," I reply, pinching at some upper corners of my t-shirt and looking down at it. "I'd like to think that Taylor would approve, too. But really, I have to change before we go."

Atlas laughs as he rolls his eyes. "Fine. I'll pick you up out front of your house."

chapter seventeen

The Heart and Honey diner is basically empty, and I'd like to assume that is because everyone else in the town is spending the evening at the last few hours of the festival. There's only one other customer in here, but the woman is facing the back of the diner in her booth, keeping to herself.

I order a plate of chicken alfredo with a side Caesar salad, while Atlas orders a veggie burger and fries. The waitress, Maya, brings out our food almost instantly, and as Atlas and I dig in, I can't help but let my question from earlier fall out of my very much full mouth.

Because I'm a nosy person, and because I don't know how to calm the butterflies in my stomach down.

They should try out for the Olympics with how many perfect flips and cartwheels they are performing at just the mere thought of Atlas reading an article I wrote. And keeping it on his coffee table.

"So, are you going to tell me why you had that magazine on your coffee table?"

The burger in Atlas's hands freezes midair, and his mouth hangs open before he clamps it shut and places his food back on his plate. He picks up a napkin from the dispenser at the end of the table, next to the salt and pepper shakers, and wipes the grease off his fingers.

"No."

I groan and roll my eyes like a toddler. "Why?"

"Because."

"What are you, a stalker?" He shoves a hand in the air and opens his mouth to answer me, but I quickly cut him off with a shrug. "My grumpy next-door neighbor, who oddly is all of a sudden interested in taking me out when we've known one another for a week, just *happens* to have a copy of the only magazine I'm on the cover of. Based on my wickedly good observation skills, I can only assume that you are, indeed, a stalker. Or a creep, if you will."

"I'm not a stalker."

"Where's your proof, then? Why do you have a copy of the magazine?"

The way Atlas's cheeks darken to a rosy pink shade, like they did when I first called him out for the magazine, makes me laugh. I pull out my camera from my bag next to me and hurry and click on the capture button before Atlas can protest, or even blink.

"Hey," he says, reaching over the table to grab the device. But there's a hint of a smile on his lips. "Delete that."

My squeal echoes off of each surface of the almost empty restaurant, and I pull the camera out of his reach, but it rams into the back of the booth seat with a loud *thump*. I gasp and flip the device around in both of my hands, investigating whether or not I scratched my second favorite item I own. The first is my notebook, since that spiraled bundle of paper is basically attached to me at my hip at all times.

The back of the seat I'm sitting on is a soft cushion material, but I still give Atlas a teasing glare. "This is my baby, Mr. Google Maps. You almost just hurt her."

"You gave your camera a gender?"

"Of course I did." I rub the camera as if it, *she*, is a dog. "She has been with me on every single trip I've been on with Wanderlight. If she quits on me, I don't think I'll be able to go on another trip." I glance down and smile, coddling the camera and rocking back and forth as if the device is now a newborn baby. "I'm pretty sure my mom would come back from her grave and yell at me if I ruined or broke this thing."

I freeze as soon as the words release from my tongue. Those words, my tone…I just made my first attempt at humor about the entire situation with my mom. And I, surprisingly, don't feel guilty.

Thankfully, Atlas chuckles. "Fine. I am so sorry that I *almost* broke your prized camera. I will never do it again."

I give him a pointed look. "Swear?"

"You have my word, Holland." He crosses an *x* over his heart and gives me a determined grin.

I nod. "Good." I give my camera one last pat and tuck her back in my bag. I take a bite of my pasta and groan when the sauce hits my taste buds. We continue eating in silence, the two of us too hungry to make any other conversation.

When my plate is scraped clean and Atlas only has a few fries left straggling, I sit back more in my seat. "Man, I really hope this diner doesn't ever go out of business. I would move here permanently if it meant that I could eat here everyday."

"I hope it doesn't either. This diner is definitely one of the selling factors of the town." He rests his chin on his propped up hand. "Won't you miss New York though?"

I shrug. "Maybe."

"What do you mean?"

"It's just, ever since I've gone back to New York in February, it hasn't felt the same." My gaze switches from him to the small window to my right, where I can see the lifeless road of Main Street and the line of the ocean water in the distance between buildings. "Too lonely. Too *big*. I don't know. I just think that I haven't really connected with the city. I'm always on the road or spending months at a time in a completely different continent, and I'm never in New York for longer than a few weeks before I'm sent somewhere else. But when I'm away, I'm not thinking about returning back to my apartment or office, or even missing the city at all.

"When I leave for each assignment, I feel thrilled. I love being able to go to all the places I can go to. It's like an escape for me and only me. I've never been in a new place for longer than three months, but those months are like I become a new version of myself. It's like I'm experiencing my own type of self-discovery with each town I visit. Because when I'm far from my usual routines and comforts, I'm forced to confront my true self. And I get to do it all in the most beautiful places on Earth."

When I meet Atlas's gaze again, his irises appear a lighter, softer shade of brown in this lighting. His eyes are narrowed slightly and he's nodding, as if he is really trying to understand my words.

"What about Chicago?"

I frown. "What about it?"

"Do you think that being there for those few months made you learn something else about yourself?"

I tilt my head and glance back at the window because I don't know how to respond. I did learn more about other people while I was back at home. The elderly couple that lived next door all our lives still treats my family like the children they could never have by the way they cooked and brought over dinner for the first two weeks. My own boyfriend had put work before flying to my hometown to be there with me for at least the funeral. Emmett mustered just enough strength to be the only one that could communicate to the lawyer about my mom's will without shedding a single tear. Corinne rested her head on her husband, Mac's, shoulder and cried tears I have never seen her release before, exhibiting a version of her that is so vastly different than the stone-cold exterior she shows to the rest of the world.

And my dad…I learned the most about him. I learned that he *loves* my mom. Not past tense, even though she's gone. Even months after the funeral, my dad still couldn't physically live a day without either breaking down in choked, slobbery sobs or dismissing everyone around him by staying completely silent and frozen for hours on end. There was no in-between. I had assumed that he loved her while she was alive, but their relationship had been so split up between us kids and the success of their careers. They hardly spent any alone time together, and they weren't the type of couple that displayed physical affection. My parents never fought, never talked to one another longer than what was shared at the dinner table or when they were getting ready for bed.

It was shocking to see the man that never showed much emotion besides numbness or disappointment show a vast amount of vulnerability about my mom, especially in front of me. But I didn't take it for granted. Not once. Not even after I left. I still text my dad daily just to live out the fantasy of having a stable relationship between us. He doesn't respond as often as I would like, but that's fine. I can deal with that.

I guess I did learn something about myself: I have the ability to become the human shield that casted protection and warmth over my dad when he was throwing up every single night and when he was refusing to take care of himself. I would never judge him or hold how much weight acting like I didn't just lose the only woman that truly understood me felt over his head because those three months were the first time my sheer presence didn't make my dad angry.

"Holland?"

I snap out of my thoughts and look back at Atlas. I blink and blink rapidly because, of course, my vision is blurred with a fresh layer of tears on the edge of falling down my cheeks. Atlas reaches across the table, slides over our discarded plates to the end of the table, and latches his hand with mine. His fingers are rough and callused, but he squeezes three times.

"Sorry," I mutter, swallowing down the emotion that stings my throat and is making me hot all over my body.

"You don't have to apologize–"

We are interrupted by our waitress, Maya, who brings over our check. Before I can even move an inch, Atlas slides his card out of his wallet and hands it to her, and she disappears again.

"You didn't have to pay for my meal," I protest.

"I know. I wanted to. It's the least I can do for making you upset."

I huff a laugh. "You weren't the one to make me upset, but thank you."

He shrugs, then his face gets serious again. "You don't have to apologize for showing emotion. Not to me."

It's my turn to shrug. "I know. But I've spent my entire life being the only one in my family to show emotion regularly. You would think that my family's coldness would've made me learn my lesson by now or something."

"Holland." Atlas sighs.

"What?"

He only shakes his head and takes a drink out of his watered-down Coke. Maya returns with Atlas's card and a small sized cup filled to the top with what looks to be a strawberry milkshake. She also drops a napkin that clearly has digits written in blue colored pen right next to the cup. Then Maya gives Atlas a wink and disappears back towards the kitchen.

Atlas looks at me with wide eyes, his cheeks darkening in color. I snicker under my hands. "Looks like you caught the eye of our waitress, Mr. GPS." I lean forward on my elbows. "I have to give it to her for shooting her shot while you are at dinner with another woman."

Atlas rolls his eyes as he slides the milkshake towards me. "Have it. I don't want it."

I eye the napkin, and my smile grows. "You better keep that, though."

"Absolutely not."

I take a spoonful of the shake and stuff it into my mouth. "Why not?"

He only shakes his head again, but instead of maintaining eye contact, his gaze droops down to my mouth as I swallow the scoop of ice cream, but I can feel a single drop of the shake dripping out of the corner of my lips. My tongue pokes out to swipe the excess away, and heat crowds every inch of my body as Atlas's eyes trace every movement. His jaw works, and his Adam's apple jumps up and down as he swallows hard.

The heat of the diner immediately increases, and I feel hot all over.

He clears his throat and begins to stand out of the booth. "Come on, it's getting late."

I take one last bite of the milkshake before he follows me closely behind as we walk out of the restaurant. Once we get to the glass door, he reaches ahead of me and pushes it open, but places his hand on the small of my back once again. His hand feels warm and calming against the material of my Taylor Swift shirt–which I decided to keep on and pair it with some faded blue jeans and my white Converse.

We step out into the dark, humid air and walk to the parking lot, and Atlas still doesn't remove his hand, but I don't mind. In fact, if I were brave enough, I think I would hold his hand right now. But that would be a senseless act to follow through given that we have only known of one another for a week. Yet my fingers itch to be laced with his again.

I must really be lacking sleep.

Atlas opens the passenger door of his truck, and once we have our seatbelts clicked and locked in place, we head back towards our houses. The short drive only allows one song to stream through the truck speakers, so I ask Atlas if I can play a song for him. He shuffles out his phone from his front pocket, unlocks it with a quick glance down, and hands it over to me.

My eyebrows shoot to the top of my forehead at the way he handed over his device so easily, but I waste no time finding his music app and searching for the song I'm looking for.

Music helps me find the right words to say and gain inspiration while I'm writing, but I'm always looking forward to car rides where I can hum or sing along or learn the words of any song that is playing. My brain might work differently than others when I'm reading or writing, but listening to music helps train my memory. Dyslexia can challenge auditory temporal processing, which often makes it difficult to detect the timing and order of sounds. I like to imagine the lyrics of whatever song is playing floating and highlighting in my mind as the song plays, and I like to associate each song I love with the moment that is happening right now.

The Temper Trap's "Sweet Disposition" seeps out of the stereo and fills the silence, and I rest my head back on the headrest and watch the minimal lights of the town pass by through the window, until I roll down the glass and let the wind take complete control over my hair. It blows all over my face, but I don't move a single muscle to stop it. I hear Atlas roll down his window, and when I look over at him, he's giving me a bright smile.

He continues going towards the houses, but he doesn't turn down the street towards them. I squint my eyes in silent question to him, but he looks back at the dark road, and as we enter into the outskirts of town, the only light is the crescent moon shining above and the cones of the truck's headlights.

I keep my head all but out the window, focusing on the line of the ocean water and watching the gentle waves curl in over itself less than a mile away as we drive. My hair swirls in its own personal tornado on the top of my head, and the blaring wind is making salty liquid streak down the corners of my eyelids, but I sing along to the words of the song that amplifies the giddiness I feel in this moment. The feeling swarming in my mind and chest and entire body feels ethereal, reckless, even though I'm not doing anything but driving with a man I'm slowly getting to know and oddly trust enough.

My smile widens like I'm a child, or a dog with their head hanging out the window, like I don't have a worry in the world and all is right. I know I need to call Corinne and I know I need to deal with the Geminis, but not right now. Not tonight. I haven't felt like this in well over a year, even long before my mom passed–careless and free. It shouldn't make sense, but in my head, it does. It feels like peace.

chapter eighteen

"Where are you taking me this time?" I ask Atlas once the song ends and another I had queued begins. I roll up the window so I can hear him, and he smirks over at me.

"Somewhere that you can write about."

A bundle of excited nerves swirl in my stomach. I haven't written any new material since before the festival began, but I'm required to submit a new article to Ariana before every Thursday until the end of the month, meaning that I will write four articles, and I haven't gotten the chance to explore any new areas of the town besides what I have already been to. My notebook is filled with what material I want to focus on each week that I'm in Saltmere, with this week's about the entire history of the town. Technically, that should've been the first article I published, but I couldn't pass up on writing about the festival, Saltmere's greatest tradition.

Next week's article will highlight the businesses that are still running–Heart and Honey, Velvet Bean, the art gallery, and the cozy bed and breakfast I have yet to visit that is run by Mabel's *mortal enemy*, Patty Corrington.

Now that I have a very attractive sidekick, who can't quite pull off his grumpy act, taking me to every new place that I can experience firsthand, I feel excited, and most importantly, *motivated.* There's a reason why Jenny waited so long to send me on another assignment since I returned back to New York from Chicago, and it doesn't have anything to do with my mom's death or Gordon's betrayal– although those events played a major role, obviously. But the true reason is that I lost my spark, my inspiration to write something I cared about that didn't just give me fast money to pay the bills. Jenny knew that, and I think that's why she wanted to send me here, when the timing was right, to explore the places she knew would help me bring back my ambition to create something memorable.

Time passes by quickly the entire rest of the drive, but the music keeps us company until Atlas turns the volume knob to the left and rolls down the windows as he turns off the highway and down onto a rough, dirt road. His tires crunch on the loose rocks, but I can hear birds chirping and singing in the close distance, up in the trees that dart down both sides of the road.

"Those sounds are Northern Mockingbird calls, even though they are mimicking the sounds of other birds. But I've been down here so much that I can tell the difference."

"Interesting," I respond, keeping my head out the window to listen to the sounds better. "Do you come over here often?"

The road ahead curves suddenly, so I clutch my hand around the handlebar next to the window and hold on as the truck shakes violently. But I'm too slow, and I smack my head on the top of the window frame of the vehicle. I groan as I slowly retreat inside the interior and glare at the man driving.

"Sorry," Atlas says, half wincing and half laughing. "I didn't mean to do that, I swear."

"You really did bring me out in the middle of nowhere to murder me, didn't you?"

He gives me a smile that makes the slight pound on the side of my head withers away. "It's not the middle of nowhere. It's my grandfather's backyard."

I gasp. "Really?" I glance back out the now rolled up window. "All of this?"

"Most of it. His old cabin is just a few more miles up this road, but we won't go there tonight. It's abandoned and a mess since there's no one left to take care of it besides me, but I'm planning on renovating it here soon and renting it out."

"You don't want to live in it someday?"

"It's too far from the warehouse and the ocean."

I nod. "That makes sense." I tilt my head. "So if we aren't going to the cabin, where are you taking me?"

"He has a treehouse that lots of locals know about but don't come to because they don't know where the turnoff is on this road. There are a few artifacts that my grandfather kept inside that give a glimpse of some of the history of this town, and I thought you would like to see them."

He drives for another ten minutes before turning off onto another dirt road that's worse than the first. I bounce up and down in my seat, and the seatbelt against my body rubs against my neck every time my body swings from side to side. Atlas appears unphased, as if he really has been on this road dozens of times, as the vehicle moves towards a more open area of the woods, where the trees have cleared out and a small pond takes over their place.

The water doesn't seem to be very deep since large logs and sticks poke out from the surface in various places, but on the limited trees surrounding the pond, a small treehouse made out of weathered planks sits about ten feet above the water. Moss and lichen cling to the lower edges of the support beams holding up the house where the large oak tree can't. A wide front deck wraps around the exterior that overlooks the pond and surrounding areas, where a rocking chair, a pair of muddy boots, and a fishing rod resting against the railing made out of logs and wooden panels. The roof is made out of sloped metal, its soft patina a blend of rust and silver-blue in the lighting of the moonlight, and the couple windows are framed with reclaimed wood, propped open with branches.

Atlas puts the truck into park in the middle of the road, at the side of the water's edge. "Wait in here for a second," he says to me before opening his door and hopping onto the dirt. He rounds the front of the truck, and I watch him trek through the neighboring tall weeds until he bends down and sticks a hand straight into the water. He wiggles the water around, the motion sending ripples in the surface down towards the opposite end of the pond. Then Atlas straightens and turns and jogs back up to my side of the truck.

"I'm just letting you know that the water's really cold," he says after he opens the door for me.

I gape at him. "Are we getting in?" I didn't bring anything besides the clothes I'm in, and even they aren't very warm.

"Before he cared for visitors, mostly the high schoolers that he thought would come to the treehouse at any time, my grandfather built the ladder for the treehouse in the middle of the pond. So we have to walk into the water to get up there," Atlas says, matter-of-factly. He then reaches a hand to me. "The water's not very deep, so it'll just be your feet that will get wet. I promise I won't let you slip and fall."

I narrow my eyes at him, flicking my gaze from his hand then back up to his face. "I don't know if I trust you,"

I joke, a teasing expression plastered on my face. We might have only known one another for seven days, but I think I do trust Atlas. He hasn't given me a reason not to, at least not yet.

He rolls his eyes, but a smirk rolls onto his lips. "I swear that I'm not going to pull you into the water as soon as you hold my hand. If I do, then you can pull me down with you."

"Don't tempt me."

I latch onto his hand and step down onto the dirt. We walk through the weeds until we get to the edge of the water, where Atlas tells me to hand him my shoes for him to carry. After rolling up my jeans so they won't get wet, I don't let go of his hand as my bare toes brush against the water in a trial run to prepare myself for how cold the pond really is, and I suck in a breath at the temperature. It's *freezing.* The skin of my toe already feels numb. The liquid swishes to the sides as Atlas takes a big step into the pond, as effortlessly as possible. Chills shoot down my skin and I exhale deeply and follow him in.

"Are you okay? Do you want me to carry you?" Atlas asks, not taking another step.

I shake my head. "Let's just walk fast," I respond, my teeth chattering against one another. I gesture towards the rest of the pond in front of us.

Atlas nods and chuckles softly, and he squeezes my hand once before we continue stomping on the bumpy, rocky ground, our footsteps loud and swishing the water as we walk. Dragonflies and other insects buzz lazily in the warm, humid air around us, but I can't pay attention to them right now. Now that I'm in the water, I can see that the ladder is behind the long branches full of leaves of the tree the house is built on. It's a swinging ladder made of rope and skinny wooden logs that doesn't look even remotely sturdy or safe, but I don't think Atlas would lead me somewhere where he doesn't think we will be okay, so I let those thoughts drift away.

He lets me walk up the ladder first, and my hands grip tightly around the log steps as I climb my way up. My once rolled up jeans slide down my legs with each step, but I ignore them and keep my eyes glued to the open trapdoor at the base of the treehouse.

I use all my strength to pull myself inside the small house, with Atlas not far on my tail. The ache in my arms simmers to a slight burn once I slide on my bottom towards the opposite end of the treehouse to create more room for Atlas to come all the way up. My eyes wander over the limited space, adjusting slowly and peering straight through a window below the slant of the roof that shows a perfect view to the sparkling night sky.

I hear Atlas stand, and seconds later, his footsteps creep towards a corner of the interior as he flickers on two battery-operated lamps that immediately illuminate the entire area. My jaw falls slightly as I take everything all in, from the tiny desk in the corner to the bulletin board on the wall with dozens of papers and pictures hanging slanted by thumbtacks. To the wooden floor that creaks with each step Atlas takes, the boards faded to a silvery gray. To the old, comfy chair that sits in the corner, its arm worn smooth where a hand has rested for years, beside a small, makeshift shelf lined with dog-eared paperbacks and a cracked pair of reading glasses. To the cobwebs that cling to every corner, to the red and blue patchwork rug laid across the floor, to the thermos with chipped enamel beside a tobacco tin repurposed for storing nails and screws. To the pair of old binoculars hanging on a hook near the window, its strap brittle with age.

There's a scent of cedar, dust, and pipe smoke swirling in the thick, dusty air. The space is quiet, but it hums with memory; not abandoned, but preserved. It feels like a place where one can come to work and to escape, to enjoy and listen to the sounds of nature in a place no one can disturb.

"I love it here," I say, my voice coated with awe. Atlas doesn't respond. Instead, he walks over to the desk and opens the first drawer, ruffling his hand through the array of items inside. He pulls out four smaller rectangle sheets of metal before turning towards me and sitting down on the rug.

He hands over the sheets, and I gasp. They are tintype photographs of all different portraits of people. My eye first catches on the photograph of a beautiful woman with dark skin, her lips curled up into a smile. Her eyes are squinted, as if when the actual photograph was taken, it was sunny outside. She's wearing a straw sun hat that has a colored ribbon tied into a bow around it, and she's wearing a collared shirt. Her wrinkled hands are propped up under her chin, and she's looking at me with a sparkle in her eyes. She's beautiful, and I feel drawn to her, as if every feature of hers is telling a story I am dying to understand.

I switch to another photograph, where this one is of a man with a long, streaked beard hanging from his chin. I can't tell what he is wearing, but his eyebrows are raised high towards his hairline, creating lined divots against the skin of his forehead. His long nose is curved and crooked at the tip, and his dark eyes are peering off to the distance. His darker-colored hair is disheveled in some areas, and his bushy eyebrows are burrowing together above his sunken eyes.

The next photograph is of a little boy, tilting his head to the side. His eyes are narrowed into slits, as if he was studying the camera as his picture was being taken. His irises are lighter and focused on something behind the camera. I can tell that his hair is blond, even in the black-and white photograph. His small lips are making an *O* shape, as if he was in the middle of speaking as the camera flashed. The soft, holed jacket around him appears to be too big for his small body because it bundles around his neck.

The last photograph is of a younger woman, probably in her late teens. Her long hair is in two braids that hang past her chest. She's wearing a light-colored t-shirt that hangs off of one exposed shoulder. She's not smiling. There's a shadow casting under her high cheekbones, and I can see a large scar that slashes straight from above her left eyebrow down to her jawline, the mark creased and crinkly as if her skin was in the process of healing over itself when this picture was taken. Her expression is sad and drained, and I can't help but wonder what her story is.

The corners of each plate of metal are smudged and have an exhibition of chemical marks coating them in various places, but each photograph appears to be unique to its own nature, telling a tale so deep within each person on them. I can't stop touching the plates or running my fingers over each face.

"Why are these here?" I ask Atlas, looking over at him.

"My grandfather was into tintype photography before he married my grandmother. He knew all these people."

My eyes snag back to the first woman in the sunhat. "What was her name?"

Atlas smiles, and he gently grabs the sheet out of my hands to look at it more closely, but he slides over closer to me. "This is Valeria Ramírez. She was my grandfather's nanny growing up. My grandfather used to tell me all about her, how she used to smell like cinnamon and flowers, and she wore her hair in one long braid that swung like a rope behind her. She called him *mi niño* sometimes, even though his mother said not to speak Spanish in the house. My grandfather didn't know why that mattered, only that Valeria's voice sounded prettier when she said it that way."

I watch Atlas as he continues to tell the story. "My great grandmother hired her when my grandfather was three, but it wasn't until he was five that he got to know Valeria. She used to sing while she cleaned. Not like church songs or his mother's records, but songs that drifted up into the rafters, kind of sad, kind of warm. One was about someone called *La Llorona*, and even though it was about crying, it didn't make my grandfather sad. He said it made him feel like he was part of something older. Like a bedtime story the world forgot to tell him."

Then Atlas's smile falters. "My grandfather's mother came home early one night, as Valeria was singing to my grandfather with the radio low, spinning around with him in the living room and pretending to dance like they were a part of a cast in those black-and-white movies. I'll never forget the way my grandfather described my great grandmother's face, how it was tight like the lid on the pickle jar in the refrigerator, and she turned off the music with a snap. My great grandmother screamed and yelled and accused Valeria of exposing my grandfather to her culture and lifestyle with the food she cooked and the stories of her ancestors she would tell, and how wrong that was for the Richens family. The next day, my grandfather had a new nanny, and he never saw Valeria again, until years and years later in a photograph he found in his mother's old nightstand drawer, when he was an adult. He kept it, and created this photograph of her so he would never forget about her."

Atlas hands over the metal sheet back to me, and I smile to myself as my gaze traces over all of Valeria's features. Her expression is warm and inviting, and I would've loved to know her in another lifetime. "She seems amazing."

"Yeah, I agree. I wish my grandfather knew what happened to her."

I nod, then switch over to the child's photograph. "Who's this?"

"That's my grandfather's youngest and only brother, Henry. He passed away from polio at age four, when my grandfather was seven. This was the only photograph his parents kept that he could find. His parents loved Henry, and when he passed, his parents weren't around much, hence why my grandfather always had a nanny taking care of him."

"What about this guy?" I switch over to the man's photo.

"That guy is Boot. He was my grandfather's best friend for over a decade before he realized who Boot really was." Atlas grabs onto the photo of the woman with the scar running down her face, his expression strained. "This is Anna. She was my grandfather's first love." Atlas sighs. "But Anna loved Boot, even when he hurt her more than he loved her in return. When my grandfather found out what Boot was doing, he never talked to his best friend again. He tried to help Anna escape Boot's wrath, but he was too late. Boot had killed her."

"Oh my god, Atlas," I breathe out. "That's *horrible*."

Atlas nods. "I don't think my grandfather ever got over Anna, even after he married my grandmother. He named my mom after her, Candace Anna Richens."

Wow. "She's beautiful," I say, a small, sad smile growing on my mouth. "She deserved better."

"Yeah, she did. I don't know why my grandfather kept this photo of Boot because he was a horrible person, but I do remember him always wishing he had a better, happier picture of Anna. An image where she wasn't hurting in multiple ways."

"She was strong. That's what this image represents."

Atlas looks over at me, his face morphing into a dozen of emotions as he registers my words. Then he gives me a gentle smile and another nod.

I mentally wince as I remember my bag and my camera is still in Atlas's truck, but I ask him, "Do you…do you mind if I take a picture of these for my articles? I would love to share these stories of these people, to give our readers more insight of those who lived in this town once before."

"That's why I brought you here. I'd like to think that my grandfather would like the world to know about the people in his life."

chapter nineteen

Atlas and I leave after another hour of him explaining every artifact inside the treehouse. The papers hanging in the wall are artwork his grandfather drew randomly that his mom loved and wanted to keep. The binoculars hanging on the hook were used to find the mockingbirds hiding in the trees and flying in the clouds. The chair in the corner was where his grandfather sat after his wife passed and read the books written and bound by her, which I asked Atlas if I could read after he told me how she never got any story of hers published.

I didn't take any pictures of the treehouse, but Atlas promised to take me again during the daytime another day to capture every detail more thoroughly in the natural light.

He walks through the freezing pond water and helps me inside the passenger seat of his truck. Before hopping inside the driver's seat, he reaches inside the back of the vehicle and retrieves a blanket underneath the backseat and hands it over to me.

"Thank you," I mumble, my entire body shivering against my seatbelt.

Atlas shifts the truck into drive and cranks up the heat so it blows out the bottom vents and straight onto my bare feet. I exhale and slouch more in my seat, my head resting back on the headrest as my eyes slam shut. "Wow. I didn't think I would need the heater on while living in a humid, North Carolina summer."

Atlas chuckles. "Me neither."

I glance over at him. "Thank you for taking me to the treehouse. I really appreciate it."

His eyes travel over to me, and he grins, and a dimple appears on his cheek. "Of course, Holland. I did promise you that I would take you places that you can write about."

"True, but I didn't think you would take me to a place as personal as the treehouse. Really, I think our readers are going to love reading about everything you told and showed to me. And the town folks, too." I wink at him. "It might help the rest of the people here want to get to know you better once the article is published. The elderly residents most likely knew your grandfather, and once they make the connection, they won't be as scared to be within two feet from you."

I watch him roll his eyes, and he scoffs. "No one is scared to be next to me. It's that I don't want them to."

"And you still haven't told me why, Globetool."

"What if I told you that I like being alone?" He turns his head to look at me again. "Maybe I don't want to make friends here. The people here tend to be nosy."

"Aren't they all in a small town? It's a given when you live in one." I huff a laugh. "Besides, do you blame them? Warren was right about one thing today; most of the people here are of the older generation. They can't help but always be interested in the lives of anyone around them."

"Warren?" Atlas's voice pitches upward with tension. "Why were you talking to Warren?"

The moments from earlier today, which seem like a lifetime ago, replay in my head. I scoff. "Warren and Kurt decided to make an appearance at the festival this morning. They said some things just to make Mabel and us others angry, and, well, it worked." I turn my head, squinting my eyes a little as I say in a quieter tone, "Roman was there too."

Atlas's grip on the wheel tightens, but he doesn't have the chance to respond before a loud *pop* sound pierces the air outside of the truck, like the sound of a firecracker. The steering wheel jerks under Atlas's hands, and instantly, the truck pulls off towards the right side of the road. I gasp and clutch onto the handlebar above my head, but Atlas stays calm as he controls the vehicle as best as he can, until he shifts the truck into park and shuts off the engine.

My chest rises and falls rapidly. I look over at him. "What just happened?"

"I think I just got a flat," Atlas mumbles before opening his door and hopping out of the truck. He opens the door behind his seat and retrieves a large box, presumably a toolbox, from the floorboard. His gaze flicks back up to me, and before shutting the door, he says, "Stay inside."

I watch his body and shadow cross through the cones of the headlights as he walks over and kneels down at the tire under my passenger door. I can't see what he's doing, but I hear metal tools ruffling together and Atlas sigh outside.

Yeah, I'm not going to stay inside.

I step out of the truck, my shoes landing on and crunching the rocky ground underneath. I don't say a word to him as he works, kneeling down next to his toolbox, facing the tire. I slide my phone out of my back pocket and swipe through the message thread with Corinne, only to find that the last message I sent her hasn't gone through. She doesn't have her read receipts on, but the other messages I spammed her with last night went through, so I know she had to have gotten them. *Did she shut off her phone? Or block me?* I had tried to call her four times last night, and, just like Emmett said, the calls went unanswered and straight to her voicemail. I type another message for good measure before sliding my phone back in my pocket.

A pair of headlights pierces the darkness as a police cruiser rolls down the curve of the highway only a few feet away, its red and blue lights flashing silently. The cruiser slows down as it nears us, tires crunching on the loose gravel at the road's edge as it comes to a halt behind Atlas's taillights. The engine hums and lingers beneath the rhythmic flicker of the flashing overhead lights, painting the trees and our bodies before a man steps out into the open and out of the car.

"Evening, strangers. You two break down or just stargazing in the middle of nowhere?"

I immediately feel relief coasting down my body at the sight of Sam. "Sam! Thank god. It's a flat. Atlas is fixing it, but I was two seconds away from Googling how to change a tire in the dark."

Sam chuckles, eyeing Atlas once. He props his hands against his hips, above his belt. "Well, lucky for you, he knows what he's doing. Probably. Right, Atlas?"

I glance down at Atlas, whose face is displaying a mixture of confusion and annoyance. His jaw is working, his lips are pursed, his eyebrows are frowning, and his nose twitches once. Atlas grunts, not bothering to look up from the tire. "Of course I do," he mumbles.

Sam returns his attention back to me. "You settling in okay? I haven't seen you since our meetup at the cafe. That article of yours sure did wonders for the festival. I don't think I've seen that many people visit this town in all of my years of being sheriff. And Patty was telling me that her bed and breakfast has never been full like it has been this weekend."

A blush creeps up to my cheeks, and I am grateful that it's dark outside and Sam can't see. I shrug and smile. "I'm just trying to do Saltmere justice."

His smile widens. "So, where were the two of you coming from?"

Atlas's gaze meets mine again, but this time, it's less angry and more encouraging. He gives me a slight nod, and I face Sam. "Atlas was just taking me home from showing me a place for my articles."

"What kind of place?" Sam asks, keeping a small smile on his lips as he turns fully to me. "There's nothing but marsh and woods over here."

I take another glance down at Atlas, reading his face as best as I can in the darkness that surrounds us to make sure I can share this information. He gives me a small smile before washing it away from existence and returning his focus on the tire.

"There's a pond and a treehouse up in these woods, actually. They belong to Atlas's family."

Sam blanches before looking down again at Atlas. "Which side?"

"My mom's." Atlas's voice hardens in tone.

The two men lock gazes, holding them so intensely that questions act like alarm bells in my head and threaten to fall off my tongue. But I seal my lips shut and let the odd, uncomfortable moment pass between them.

Sam is the first to look away, refocusing his attention on me with his smile returning. His tone is light, but slightly too pointed when he says, "So, you two are spending a lot of time together, huh? I heard about what happened at the kissing booth between you two."

Atlas visibly stiffens, and the back of my neck warms. There's something unspoken here, like something I am within reach but unable to fully understand, and I suddenly feel like I'm under a microscope.

I huff a laugh, my nerves in my stomach growing rapidly with each passing second. "What, like it's a scandal?"

Sam raises his eyebrows. "Small towns run on gossip, Holland. People notice things. You happen to live next door and somehow encouraged the town's most mysterious, reserved guy out of his shell to participate in a kissing booth. You are riding around town with him, letting him take you to different places…let's just say that a few folks are curious."

A beat of silence streams through the air, and neither Atlas or I speak. Sam's eyes flick over to him again, and Atlas stops moving his tool around in front of the tire. The pressure to say something boils over in my chest and throat, and before I can stop myself, I blurt out, "We're dating."

Even the crickets that have been singing to us this entire night stop chirping as soon as those words fall off my tongue.

Sam blinks once, then a couple million more times before he laughs awkwardly. "Well, now. That…wasn't on the community bulletin board."

My voice grows higher and higher. My heart might as well beat straight out of my chest and fly away into the clouds, because it's going too fast. "Yeah. Uh. Surprise?"

Atlas stands slowly, brushing his hands off on his jeans. He looks at me like I've grown a second head, and I might as well have with how deranged I have come to be from saying something as insane as *we're dating*. But Atlas turns his head and registers Sam's surprised expression, and something shifts in his posture.

"Yeah," he says, calmly. "It's new. Kind of wanted to keep it quiet."

Sam grins and raises his hands up in surrender. "Well, I won't blow your cover." Sam clicks his tongue. "But just so you both know, the people of this town are going to lose their minds when they find out." Sam tips his head to me, his face still locked in its amused expression. "Hope your articles' got room for romance now. Saltmere sure loves a good love story."

He nods to Atlas, then heads back to his cruiser. In a matter of seconds, the blue and red lights shut off, and darkness surrounds us once again. But the air hangs thick, overwhelming, after Sam drives off and only Atlas and I stand facing one another.

My shoulders crouch to my neck as I wince. "I panicked."

"Yeah, I noticed," Atlas responds, dryly, rolling his eyes. "Naturally, the best way to handle a little social pressure is to throw us both into a town-wide performance. Solid instinct."

"I didn't know what else to say. He was looking at you like…like you were hiding something."

Atlas swallows. I stare at him, but he doesn't respond, only kneels back down to finish changing the tire.

"I didn't mean to mess anything up," I utter, quietly.

Atlas only shrugs. "Too late now. Guess we're dating."

I release a loud sigh, my mind spiraling in endless directions. *What was I thinking?* Sam's right; I haven't been in the town long and I still know that the people of Saltmere are going to lose their minds at the news of me and Atlas. Not because of who I am and my mission here, but because

Atlas *has* been a mystery for every resident here. He doesn't interact with anyone. He doesn't *like to* interact with anyone.

I opt for humor to make light of the situation because I'm embarrassed by my actions. "I mean, I guess we can go on that date you were wanting to go on."

He doesn't respond, doesn't even laugh or do anything. *God, this is miserable.* I think I'd rather sit and listen to Mabel's rants about Patty Corrington and their issues than stand here awkwardly, towering over Atlas as he finishes securing in his spare tire onto his truck.

Eventually, he finally stands, grabbing onto his toolbox and dusting his hands off on his pants. He saunters towards the backseat of the truck, opens the door, and sets his toolbox back on the floorboard, then finally turns to me.

His brows are furrowed together. "I'd rather not go on a date where the woman I'm interested in feels forced to go out with me just to prove a point to the rest of the town."

His voice is firm, unbreaking. It makes my heart beat faster in my chest. "It doesn't have to be forced," I quickly say, then I shake my head. My body feels like I've stepped into a billion degree sauna from how sweaty I have become from this conversation. "I just mean, it would be like dinner earlier today. I wasn't forced to be with you then. You could say that was a date, too."

"It wasn't."

"Why not?" *What the hell am I saying? I didn't want it to be a date. It* wasn't *a date.*

"Because I wouldn't take a woman out for the first time to the town's old diner."

I huff. "Fine, even though there's nothing wrong with that diner. It's cozy and the food is delicious." He opens his mouth to speak, but I cut him off by shooting my hand straight up in the air. "You also took me to the art gallery. That could've been a date, too. I wasn't forced then, either."

He raises an eyebrow, but there's a shadow of a smile ghosting his lips, like he wants to laugh. It brings relief down every inch of my body, and I deflate by exhaling loudly. He takes a step closer to me, folding his arms against his chest. "What's your point, Holland?"

My name rolls off his tongue smoothly and deeply. I swallow. "That you don't force me to be around you."

"Even to go out with me?" He leans down, his lips just inches above my ear.

Chills spiral down my arms and legs. I release a shaky breath. "Y-yes."

When he straightens, he's smirking. He rubs a hand over the stubble on his chin. "If we're doing this, we're doing it *my* way."

"There's a "your way" to fake dating?"

"Yeah. Rules. Boundaries. Groundwork. Otherwise, we are waiting for a disaster to happen, and I can't afford that."

"Okay, Mr. Logistics. Lay it on me." I give him a determined nod.

"Rule one: We act like a *normal* couple in public. Handholding, sure. Maybe a kiss on the cheek." He pauses, looking back at his truck before back at me, and he clicks his tongue. "But nothing…*real*."

"Okay."

"Rule two: We don't tell anyone the truth about us. Not Charlotte, not Grace, and certainly not Mabel. Or anyone else on the festival board."

"Oh, I don't plan on it. I think we already get plenty of attention by just being out together as friends."

"Rule three: This ends cleanly. No one gets hurt. When the time comes, we break up quietly. No drama, no tears."

"Pssh. Easy." I swipe a hand through the air. "I don't cry in public. And I'm leaving in a month anyway."

"Rule four," Atlas says, his voice quieter. His gaze pierces through mine. "Rule four: I don't fall for you, and you don't let me."

My breathing hitches. "Atlas–"

"You said you weren't ready. I respect that. I won't and never will push you to do something you don't want to do. I will still take you around Saltmere, but don't ask me to fake something that feels real, not unless you're damn sure it's just an act."

I feel time stop in its tracks for a single moment, and I can't say anything. My body freezes, and I can only blink in response to Atlas's words and look away from him. The wind picks up, drafting warm air that ruffles through my hair and my clothes. The leaves of the trees surrounding us on either side of the road tousle against one another. A few tools that Atlas left out roll along the gravel, away from us until they lay against a bundle of green weeds.

I glance back at him. "Okay. You've got a deal."

chapter twenty

The drive back to our houses is silent. My left knee won't stop bobbing up and down in my seat, and I can't seem to stop fidgeting my hands together in my lap. It's so dark outside my window that I can't make out anything as we drive back to town, nothing for my eyes to hyperfixate and focus on to distract my mind from reeling over what Atlas and I just agreed to.

I mean, we've already kissed once. We've seen each other basically every day since I've moved to Saltmere, and it isn't very awkward between us. We are, I think, becoming *friends*. He must tolerate me enough since he asked me out just a few days ago. Nothing has to change. Everything's going to be fine.

I just wish my heart could be convinced so it will stop racing in my chest. The organ might as well be performing in a marathon, with my ribs individual hurdles for my heart to try and jump over.

I haven't felt this nervous in front of anyone since I first went out with Gordon, even though we had been good friends before ever becoming official. It had been my first date since my three-month relationship with my high school boyfriend, Michael. The first date jitters with Gordon made me so sick to my stomach that night that we ended up taking take-out back to his apartment instead of going to Neil Simon Theater to see *MJ*. I haven't seen or been with anyone since him, and there's clearly a reason.

He pulls into his driveway, and I unbuckle and murmur a quiet *thank you* without looking at him, afraid that if I meet his eyes, I'll say something too honest and too soon. Shutting the door behind me, I walk around the front of the engine and trudge through the grass towards my front door, keeping my arms folded against my chest and tucked tightly against my body. But I hear another door shut, and when I turn my head back to Atlas's truck, he's stepping on the curb of my yard.

"Did I forget something?" I ask quietly.

He stops, his shoulders sagging downward. "I…" His mouth hangs open, his dark irises searching for answers within mine, but I don't have any.

I frown, tilting my head to the side, my heart again knocking against my ribcage sporadically. "What's wrong?" My feet inch back towards him.

He hesitates like his words are stuck in between his chest and his throat, bringing one hand up to drag down his face. His eyes flick back up behind me, to my house, then back down at me. The porch light hums its own melody in the background, casting a glowing spotlight directly on the two of us. "I just…" He cuts himself off again, inhaling a sharp breath. "I just didn't want to leave things weird between us. About us…dating now."

A sliver of nerves evaporates out of my body and into the thick, humid air at his vulnerable words. "They already are weird."

He nods, slowly. "Right. Yeah." He swallows. "I know."

The silence stretches thin between us. It's not angry or cold, but rather heavy with how quickly things have changed for the two of us in such a short amount of time of knowing one another; our kiss at the festival, our newfound fake relationship, the way I just left his truck awkwardly like I was running away from him.

"You just seemed quiet," he finally says, "after. On the way here."

"I was just tired," I lie, shifting on my weight and keeping my eyes glued onto the individual strands of grass at my feet. "Right." He shoves his hands in his front pockets.

Another long beat of silence passes by us, but I make myself glance up at him. His jaw is tense, and his eyebrows are furrowed together on his forehead. There's a hint of restlessness pulsing inside of him, like he's forcing himself to stand still but itching to move. Or to speak.

"You don't have to check up on me," I utter. "We don't owe each other that."

He nods, exhaling. "I know."

The breeze picks up around us, causing ripples in both of our clothing and rustles in the trees surrounding the houses.

"I just didn't want to go without," he begins, shrugging and not meeting my gaze once again. "I don't know."

I take a half-step closer, and we are only less than a foot from one another. Our eyes lock. We're so close now that one wrong breath could change *everything* in a heartbeat. He doesn't move, and neither do I, until his hand raises slowly, cupping the side of my face. His pointer finger swipes gently, slowly, against the edge of my jaw, and I hold my breath and withhold a shiver because I don't want him to stop. I don't want him to pull away.

I rise to the tips of my toes and lean in, angling my head so our lips are only centimeters from touching. *Kiss me,* I want to say to him, *please.*

"Holland," he whispers, his voice strained and foreign. His breath flutters on my cheeks, and I so badly wish he would let himself lean all the way. "We can't." He swallows just as I lower onto my heels. "We shouldn't."

Suddenly, my mind clears from the imaginary, desperate fog that my mind was lost in. *We can't.* Not when he was the one to make the rules for how we have to navigate this new…dynamic between us. The one that *I* put on us. Not when I know that if we kiss again, I don't think I can fake it. *But nothing real*, he had said just over an hour ago. He's right, we can't. Kissing each other would change everything between us.

He blinks once, and it is like his entire mood has shifted. He straightens and takes a step back, dropping his hands to his sides and I so desperately miss the warmth of his touch and proximity. I stand, frozen, watching him from a distance as he takes another step closer to his house.

"I'll see you tomorrow?" he asks.

I nod, swallowing up my embarrassment and praying to whatever above that he can't see how red my entire face is right now. "Yeah, tomorrow."

"Goodnight, Holland."

He gives me a small smile, but I can't return it. "Goodnight, Atlas."

I turn and walk to my house, shutting the door behind me without another glance.

chapter twenty-one

I wake up on Monday morning with dark circles around my eyes and a raging headache. The rays of the sun stare back at me through the rows of the blinds I was too tired to close last night before crashing into my bed, and I squint and groan into the air.

Sunday was one of the longest days of my life. Between trying and failing to contact my sister and worrying about what the hell is going on with her, to spending the morning with the festival crew and running into Kurt Gemini and his evil minions, to learning even more about Atlas and his family and then ruining the evening by telling the town's sheriff that we are *dating*, I feel mentally drained. And equally embarrassed on the last one.

I don't know how many more times I can listen to Corinne's voice on her voicemail without the fear of where she might be ringing through my head like the blaring sounds of a tornado warning. I don't know whether or not to contact my dad, because if he doesn't know about Corinne's sudden disappearance, I don't know how he would handle it. I texted Emmett last night to see if he's talked to our dad, but, of course, he doesn't answer me either.

I'm trapped in a limbo full of unease and doubt, so I snatch my phone from the nightstand and press on my dad's contact. Even if I make this worse for him and he doesn't know about Corinne, the least I can do is talk to him, since

I'm stuck in a town across the country and can't physically be there to find information of my sister's whereabouts.

He answers on the last ring. "Hello?"

"Hi, Dad. How are you doing?"

"Oh, uh, I'm doing alright. How are you?"

I physically restrain myself from shuddering at the awkward tension coming through the line. "I'm doing great. Listen, I know you're probably busy at work, so I won't take too much of your time. I was just wondering if you have talked to Corinne recently."

"Corinne? Uh, yeah. She called me last Thursday, I think."

Relief soars through my bones, and I release the breath I had been holding. "Oh, good," I mutter. "Did she say anything about what she was doing at the time? Or maybe if she was going anywhere?"

"What's going on?" My dad's voice raises in concern. "Did something happen to my daughter? Is she okay?"

I swallow down the sting of how he referred to Corinne, as if she is his only daughter, because that doesn't matter right now. "She just hasn't been at work, and Emmett couldn't get a hold of her. But if she's talked to you recently, she's probably fine. What did she say on the phone?"

My dad's quiet for a few seconds, before he sniffs and shuffles through something on his end of the line. "It was a little odd, the conversation we had. She seemed upset. She kept asking about your mom's unfinished painting in her old studio. But, you know, I don't go in there. That room is locked and will stay locked until I leave this planet and see my wife again."

The hair on the back of my neck stands. "Oh, okay." *I have the painting.* No one knows that, though. *Why would Corinne be interested in that painting?* My eyes travel towards the closet in the corner of the room, where I know the canvas is leaning against the wall. "Did she say anything else?"

"No, just that she would come and see me in a couple weeks. Then she hung up before I could even respond."

Shit. This conversation has only left me with more questions. "Alright, thanks. I'll keep trying to get in touch with her."

"Holland, you're making me nervous right now. Is Corinne okay? Did something happen to her? Should I catch a flight to California? What about Mac?"

"I don't know, Dad. I'm sure she's fine. Stay in Chicago. I'll keep trying to talk to her. Don't worry, okay? I'll let you know when I hear from her."

"Alright," he responds. I'm about to end the call when I hear him sigh and ask, "Are you still in New York?"

He hasn't been reading my texts. I informed him that I am spending the summer in Saltmere when I first arrived here. "No, I'm in Saltmere, North Carolina for the next couple months. Have you seen any of my messages? I told you that I was here for my next assignment, Dad."

"Saltmere?"

"Yes."

My patience is running thin, and it won't be very long before emotion stings in my throat at the reminder that he doesn't care about my career or life, or care to even respond to my desperate texts.

"Your mom loved Saltmere," he utters, his tone light and reminiscent, like he's replaying a memory in his head. "Did you know that, Holland? Did you know that she loved that town? Man, I wish I could've visited it with her." He's quiet for a moment. "I wish I could've done a lot of things with her. I wish I was better for her. I wish she was still here."

I can't help but let the fresh tear fall down my cheek. "I know, Dad. I know she loved this town, and that's why I came here. For her."

He sniffles down the line. "I miss her."

It doesn't matter that he's showing me his rare side of vulnerability right now, because when he gets in this phase, it doesn't matter who's listening. He just wants to express to anyone with ears that he misses his wife. He's not showing this ounce of rawness because he wants to relate and reflect with his daughter, but sometimes, when he gets like this, I pretend that he is confiding in *me* with *his* feelings because he *wants* to.

But that will never happen, so I shove down the hopes of that fantasy, swipe at the tear about to fall off the edge of my chin, and clear my throat. "I can send you pictures of the town, and you can read my article, if you want. I'll be writing a bunch while I'm here. But I have to go, Dad. I'll talk to you soon."

I hang up before I can hear the disappointment in his voice.

My head crashes back down on my pillow, and I stare at the ceiling.

Talking with my dad shouldn't hurt as much as it still does. Hearing his voice leaves me in a state of discomfort because of where our relationship stands–where it has always stood, all of my life. I *should* be used to his lack of presence and attention, but because I grab on with sweaty, shaking hands to the sliver of hope whenever he shows me an ounce of care, I rope myself into disappointment. It's exhausting, but I can't dwell on that right now. I have a portfolio to accomplish in Saltmere, and I have to try and find my sister.

And manage, somehow, not to have anyone find out that Atlas and I are now fake dating.

A loud rumbling sound outside jolts my shoulders up into my neck, and I shoot up in my bed and step towards the window. I peel the blinds apart and peek through them, only to find Atlas rummaging through his boat against the dock.

Part of me wants to go out there, like I have before, and talk to him, hang out with him with our feet dangling off the dock and listen to the music he knows I love, but the rest of me wants to glue myself to my bed and never leave it because of what I said to Sam about us last night. The embarrassing moment replays in my head, and redness coats my cheeks and the back of my neck in humiliation and shame. *We're dating.* Do people know now? Did Sam tell anyone? And why on earth do Sam and Atlas not like each other?

I can't go out there. Atlas is probably upset over the entire ordeal. I'd rather not bother him anymore. I have done enough damage to his desire of not wanting anyone to be involved in his life.

I start to walk away from the window when Atlas straightens his legs and stands, his body still facing his boat, but his head is turning in the direction of my house. He doesn't look at my window, but rather the back door in the living room, his facial expression covered with concern and…*want*? His eyebrows are frowning, and his eyes are squinted, like he's focused intently, but one corner of his lips is curled up, his chin is slightly raised to the sky, his shoulders are still and stiff, and his hands are fidgeting at his sides before he folds his arms against his chest.

His gaze stays on my back door for what feels like multiple minutes before his eyes move back down at his feet, and I step away from the blinds and out of the room, in case he looks back up and sees me watching him. With confusion lingering in my mind, I step into the kitchen and make myself a cup of coffee. I sip slowly, forcing my eyes to not wander off and out of the window, where I know Atlas is still outside on the dock. My stomach soars up and down with nerves, my arms cover themselves with chills, and the hair on the back of my neck rises, as if he is looking back at the house and can see me.

I hurry and place my mug back in the sink and head straight to the bathroom to get ready for the day. My agenda for today is to visit the library and Charlotte so I can check out local history books and chronicles of Saltmere. My article is due in two days, but if I spend the majority of the day browsing the library and writing down all the information I can find, I can finish it by tomorrow. I still have the tale of the beginning of Saltmere written down that Sam told me a few days ago, and I plan to find more details and preferably *factual* evidence that those events actually happened. I'm hoping that Charlotte is there today to help me.

I leave the house thirty minutes later, wearing my black denim overalls and a white tank top, paired with my red Converse. I have my hair tied back in a low bun, thankfully tucked away from sticking to the thin layer of sweat on my neck already forming as I walk to my car. But as I'm walking around the front of the exterior and I glance up towards the street, I frown.

A baby blue beach cruiser is leaning against the black mailbox. I freeze in my tracks and swivel my head from side to side, but no one else is around. There's nothing but a quiet street and morning haze. I take a step closer to it, and when I peer down the basket tied to the front of the bike, I see a note with my name written on it.

Cautiously, I pluck the folded piece of paper out, where a legible, typed out font reads:

So you don't have to rent one.

-A

My heart thuds against my ribcage. My jaw drops, my eyes tracing and making sense of each letter over and over. I turn and glance behind me to Atlas's house, where all of his blinds are closed shut, but I know that he is probably still in the backyard, at the dock. *When did he have time to get this?* My eyes flick back to the bike. It's *perfect*, the type of bike that has a separate purpose just for pedaling along the seaside, or up the path to a cozy cottage, or coasting up the boardwalk. I *love* it.

This isn't fair. He isn't playing fair. *He shouldn't be getting me gifts, not after I embarrassed both of us in front of Sam last night.*

"Do you like it?"

His voice comes from behind me, low and just amused enough to make my pulse jump.

I turn slowly. Atlas stands at the edge of my yard, a few feet away from me, holding out a to-go cup I recognize from the cafe and trying very hard to appear casual, like he hadn't just left a wildly thoughtful gift in front of my house.

"Why did you get me this?" I ask, my voice rough and unfamiliar.

"You've rented a bike every single day from Megan's shop. That has to be getting expensive. Thought you might want one to have while you're here."

It *was* getting expensive. And there's only so much I can expense. "I can't accept it."

"Sure you can."

"After last night?" I scoff. "After the *humiliation*? God." I wince. "I can't even relive my own stupidity."

"It's not that bad, Holland."

"I told Sam we are *dating*, Atlas."

"I know."

"Sam might keep his word and not tell anyone about us, but we live in a small town. People talk. People are going to notice us and put two and two together. Besides, we already kissed in front of everyone."

"Yeah," Atlas says, a slow smile tugging at the corner of his mouth, "we did."

The air stretches between us like a pulled thread. I glance at the bike again, at the tan stitching on the seat, at the bell with the tiny star etched into it, and I exhale. "I don't want you thinking I'm asking you for anything," I mutter, fidgeting my hands together in front of me and refusing to look up to meet his gaze. "I've already done enough to…*interrupt* your desire to be left alone."

Atlas takes a small step forward. "Holland." His voice is low again. "You don't control me. You don't dictate my actions or tell me what to do. I do things because I want to. And I wanted you to be able to have your own bike." He nods at the cruiser. "Ride it or don't. But either way, it's yours."

Atlas smiles then. Not a big one, but better than the one he gives other people. Just a quiet curve of his mouth, like maybe he is giving me the option to speak or stay silent, and he'd be fine either way.

I stare at the bike once again, then the note that's back in the basket. "Thank you."

He nods once, then hands over the to-go cup. "It's a vanilla latte with oat milk."

God. *How does he know my order?* He really needs to stop being so *nice*. I take it, and not at all gracefully. My fingers brush against his, and for a fraction of a moment, the light breeze stops. The birds circling the sky quiet their chirping. The sounds of the ocean halts. Everything freezes.

But Atlas blinks once and turns, walking off back to his house, leaving me alone in my driveway and in a state of mind resembling standing in the eye of a storm I can't see coming.

chapter twenty-two

I push open the heavy door of the library and step into the quiet hush of dust. The building is almost completely silent as I walk on the toes of my shoes towards the front desk, mentally rehearsing what I'm going to say to Charlotte–something casual, like "Do you happen to know where I can find the oldest books about Saltmere?" and *not* "I need a distraction from the man who just bought me a bike so let me hyperfixate on obscure town history."

But Charlotte isn't behind her desk.

Instead, a small girl sat in the big rolling chair, swinging her little legs side to side and peeling strands off a string cheese with the precision of a surgeon. She's wearing a pink t-shirt with a purple unicorn on the front and denim shorts, paired with pink and white striped tennis shoes. Her curly black hair is thrown up in a high ponytail, and her round glasses are sliding down her nose as she keeps her head down.

When she finally looks up, little brown eyes narrow in on me. "You can't check out any DVDs for the day because my mom said the player is broken and she doesn't know how to fix it."

I blink. "Uh, okay. Good to know. Is Charlotte around?"

"She's shelving. I'm in charge."

The girl takes a victorious, slightly vicious bite of her string cheese, eyes locked on me like she's a miniature librarian judge.

"In charge?" I echo, trying not to smile. "Aren't you a little young?"

"Yes, in charge. And I'm eight and three-quarters, but I have *credentials*." She points to a folded piece of paper on the counter that reads "LIBRARY BOSS" in pink glitter pen.

I nod, then try again. "Well, *Library Boss*, I just wanted to ask Charlotte something. Do you know where exactly she's at?"

The little girl sits up in her chair. "You can tell me. I'm very mature. I read chapter books *without* pictures in them."

I glance around. No Charlotte in sight. "Okay, fine," I say, lowering my voice like I'm about to discuss an international secret with her. "Do you know anything about the old history books about the town?"

The girl squints her eyes, then slides her glasses up on her nose once more. "Define 'old'."

I hum. "Well, they don't have to be old. Just anything that will tell me the origin of this town."

"You like to read history?" She frowns, and her eyebrows curl down in disgust. "Solomon Hobert likes to read history books, and he's not very nice to anyone."

"Who's Solomon Hobert?"

"This kid in my class. He doesn't have very many friends."

I snort. "And that's because he reads history books?"

She shakes her head. "No, it's because he used to have a crush on my best friend, Tabitha, but Tabitha likes Aaron, and Aaron and Solomon used to be good friends before Solomon pushed Aaron off of the swingset at recess last week."

My eyebrows shoot up. Second grade drama is way more intense than I remember. "Wow, that's horrible."

"Yeah. Tabitha also likes Wesley, but Wesley is my cousin. And he has a crush on Amanda, but Amanda doesn't like anyone. She thinks that boys still have cooties."

"So you know all the drama about everyone, huh?" I ask, my smiling widening.

The little girl scoots off the chair. "I know *everything*," she says, matter-of-factly, then leans in towards me. "For example, I know that you're the girl who is dating the mystery guy that doesn't like to talk that much. Atlas."

My breathing hitches, and every bone in my body stills. "Excuse me?" I blink and blink. "Who told you that?"

"Patty Corrington was just in here not that long ago, and she told me all the tea, like she usually does. How you guys kissed at the festival, how she can see the way you two look at each other. She said that Atlas has the 'smolder'. That means he's hot *but in a tragic way*."

I press a hand to my forehead. "Oh my god."

"I saw Atlas at the grocery store awhile ago. It was a Monday, and my mom was off somewhere looking for her favorite yogurt that she says helps her "digest emotions" or whatever, and I was in the cheese aisle. I like the cheese aisle." She pauses to hold up her string cheese, giving me a wide smile. "It smells like feet, but, like, in a good way."

I cringe and huff a laugh, but she continues, swiping a hand in the air. "Anyway, I'm standing there, just admiring the beautiful selection, when I see Atlas turn down the aisle. He stops in front of the shredded mozzarella like some kind of lost wizard who got dropped off at the wrong section of the store. But I knew exactly who he was. Because everyone's been talking about *the new guy in Saltmere* like he's Bigfoot or something. Patty told me a couple days before that he has a "mysterious past" and Gill Colthorpe said that he saw him petting a raccoon while he was walking home from the boat dock by the boardwalk. So obviously, I had been on high alert to meet this guy."

"Obviously," I say, blinking, hiding my smile.

"But guess what? He's real. And tall. And wearing a big coat in the grocery store, even though it's, like, eighty-four degrees outside. Also–and I swear on my cat Burty's life–he had a coffee mug *in his* coat pocket. Not like a travel one, like…ceramic. With a chip in the handle. Just in there, like he forgot to put it in the sink on his way out of his house like a normal person."

She rolls her eyes, and I decide that I could listen to this adorable stranger tell stories for the rest of my life.

"So I'm staring at him," she continues, "and he stares back. It gets really awkward for a moment before he says, "*Do you like Gouda?*" Which is a weird first question, but because I am *me*, I answer, "*Only on Tuesdays.*"

"And then this man…he laughs. Really, really loudly. Like I just told him the world's funniest joke. He says, "*That's what I told the Queen of Denmark.*" *The Queen of Denmark.* I mean, who even says that? I don't know what it means, but I respect it. Then he pulls a coupon out of his *sock* and gives it to me. I didn't even ask for it! He just says, "*Only the brave get dairy discounts.*" And hands me thirty cents off some cheese I can't even pronounce. But then he walks away, just disappears down the cereal aisle next to the cheese one, like a weird, nice ghost."

Her eyes flick away, and she shrugs. "I told my mom all of this afterwards and she said he probably just moved here and needs some time to adjust, whatever that means.

But I think he's definitely from somewhere cool. Like a secret island where cheese is how you pay for things and everyone bows down to the Queen of Ricotta and wearing long coats with mugs in the pockets is normal. Anyway, I still have the coupon. It expires Thursday. And if I run into him again, I'm asking him if he knows the Queen of Denmark personally. Because now, I need answers."

The girl–*finally*–inhales a deep breath, but her break in speaking isn't long before she bursts with a new shade of excitement and says, "Oh my god! You can ask him! Since you guys kiss and stuff!"

Before I can even respond, or defend myself or simply explode, Charlotte appears, her arms full of books and her eyebrows already raised on her forehead. "Piper, what did I say about interrogating the patrons?"

"I'm building my social skills, Mom," Piper says primly, then offers her mom the rest of her string cheese like a peace offering.

Charlotte sighs, then turns to me. "I leave for five minutes and she starts digging into people's relationship status and Gouda trauma."

I raise both of my hands in the air. "In her defense, she's extremely efficient." Then I sigh as well. "So, I'm assuming you know, too?"

"About you and Atlas?" Charlotte asks, her shoulders crunching into her neck as she smiles excitedly. "*Oh yeah.* The two of you dating is the town's favorite gossip right now. But I have to say, I thought that I would hear about your sudden new relationship from you, or maybe Grace, or maybe even Mabel. Not Patty Corrington."

"I haven't even met Patty in person yet." I run a hand down my face.

Charlotte slaps a hand on the counter and snickers. "Well, she sure knows a lot about you." She glances down at her daughter, who is busy swinging around two tiny slices of cheese in the air. Charlotte covers Piper's little ears with her hands. "So, did you and Atlas decide to get together right after the kissing booth? I need to know the details."

I exhale. "Not exactly," I mutter. I want to tell her the truth, that it's all a facade, but that would go against Atlas's rules. "We are taking things slow right now. He's taking me around the town to places I can write about in my articles." Yeah, that's not a total lie. "I just can't believe Sam would spread the word about me and Atlas that fast. I mean, he did say that he would keep quiet about it last night."

Charlotte's eyebrows frown. "Sam? The sheriff?" When I nod, she tilts her head to the side, her black curls falling down her shoulder. "Wait, you two were with Sam last night?"

"He saw Atlas and I stuck on the side of the road. Flat tire," I say, shrugging. "Sam was looking at Atlas like Atlas was hiding something, and there was so much tension between them, so I blurted out that we were dating–just to change the conversation. But Sam has been so kind to me since I've been here, and I just thought that he wouldn't spread the word. At least, not that fast." I scoff.

Charlotte hums, glancing down at her daughter, then muttering under her breath, "So that's why Sam was late." Then she looks back up. "Well, it wasn't Sam that told us. Patty said she saw you guys on a date at the diner last night."

The only other customer in the diner. Shit. "It looks like I have to meet her, then."

"I love Patty, though she *does* thrive on drama, whether that is being a part of it or hearing about it. She has at least three different enemies that I can think of in this town at the moment."

"And Mabel is one of them, correct?"

Charlotte tosses her head back in a laugh, the sound loud and foreign and real. The action makes her hands fall from Piper's ears. "The two of them have hated each other for years. When you go meet Patty, you'll have to hear how she tells that story. It's priceless."

But her earlier words stick out to me. "Wait, what do you mean *that's why Sam was late*? Are you two…?"

Charlotte gasps and presses her hands back on her daughter's ears, then scowls at me. "Shh!" she chants. Then whispers, "I can't have my drama running around this town, too."

I huff a laugh, my jaw falling. "I've been here for a week and my relationship status is already the talk of the town, and you can secretly run around with the town's sheriff and *not* have anyone know?" I keep my voice quiet, even though no one else is inside the library and Piper is busy reading through a graphic novel from the pile of books Charlotte dropped off, not caring that her mom is covering her ears. "That's not fair!"

Charlotte only shrugs, but there's a smile ghosting her lips as she picks up the rest of the books she was holding previously and whirls away, heading towards the stairs. "Follow me, little lovebird," she says, glancing back at me with a subtle grin, "let's go somewhere where little ears can't hear."

chapter twenty-three

"I didn't know you were a mom," I say, following Charlotte up the stairs of the library.

"Yep. Though, I don't know how you couldn't tell, given that my purple eyebags are now permanent and there are strands of white forming around in my scalp as we speak. Piper sure keeps me on my toes." Charlotte takes two steps up at a time, her pink and purple tie-dyed skirt swishing with each step she takes. "And, yes–I know you're interested but too nice enough to ask–Piper's dad and I have a good relationship. Rob doesn't live here; his dental office is two towns down in Waverly. Piper sees him every other weekend and three weeks throughout the summer. She was with him all last week."

"I bet she fills him in on *all* the drama in Saltmere," I say.

Charlotte laughs. "Oh yeah. Rob hates it, but he loves his daughter, so he deals with it."

"That's so great. I think I could listen to her all day long if I could."

Charlotte halts her movements on the final step of the stairs. "Did you just nonchalantly volunteer to babysit her anytime?"

One eyebrow of mine shoots up, and I put my hand on my hip. I take a glance down the steps, back to where Piper is sitting at the desk, still reading her book. I lower my voice anyway and whisper, "If it means that you will go out with Sam, then yes. I can even babysit for free." Charlotte's face lights up, and I stick a finger in the air. "*But* you have to tell me all the details with you two, since you basically know all of mine with Atlas."

"I hardly know anything, but you got yourself a deal." Her hand extends for me to shake, so I do, snickering. She resumes walking towards the non-fiction section, as if she is leading me right where I need to browse. "So, tell me. What's it like being with the town's mystery man?"

"Is that how everyone refers to him?"

"Basically, yeah. If you haven't grown up in this town, or you don't have family that live here and haven't visited at least once every summer, people that are newcomers automatically get nicknames. And they usually stick with you forever." She stops in the aisle with the last names *A* to *M*, tilting her head up to scan the higher shelves. "Take Legal Beagle Pierce, who had to move to Saltmere five years ago to defend Alabama Jones, the town's infamous bakery owner who found herself in a legal affair with a bride that didn't pay for any of her wedding's desserts. This bride decided to come into the bakery and steal them while Alabama had her back turned to help other customers. Anyway, enter Pierce Vanderbuilt, a fancy-pantsy attorney from Charleston who once, on a day where he wasn't working on the case, walked his pet Beagle down Main, and Brady saw him. We have him to thank for Pierce's nickname, which is still in effect, since Pierce decided to move here after the case was resolved."

I can see where Piper gets her pleasure to share all the details of one's life. But my stomach swirls. "What's my nickname?"

"The journalist. Which, in my opinion, isn't creative or original at all. It's actually horrible. Saltmere could've done better with that one."

I laugh, relieved. "I'd rather have that than anything else, to be honest."

Her eyebrows wiggle. "Even the mystery guy's new girlfriend?"

"Ugh. Don't remind me." I groan, tossing my head back towards the ceiling.

But she freezes in her tracks, the book she is attempting to put away stuck in mid-air. Her lips curl down into a frown. "What do you mean? Do you not like him?"

"Oh, uh," I stutter, "yes, I do. It's just that, again, we didn't want everyone to know about us."

"But why? What's the harm in everyone knowing?" She tilts her head and swipes a hand through the air in front of her. "I mean, besides the town not going to be able to leave you two alone. And I'm warning you, they *will not* be able to leave you two alone."

Because the truth of us fake dating is more likely to slip out. Because now Atlas and I have to act like we really are together, which I know that I'm not ready for. I don't know if I'm ready for a relationship, let alone a fake one. Pretending can be fine, to an extent, but with the small gestures Atlas is doing for me? Our kiss at the festival and our *almost* kiss last night? I *really* want to tell Charlotte that it's not real. I want to tell *myself* that it's not real.

I sigh. "Let's not talk about my dating life anymore." I glance up at the shelves. "Can you help me find books about Saltmere's history?"

Thankfully, Charlotte drops the subject with a simple nod, and after I help her put away the books in her hands, she leads me towards the section of the library that I need.

The section is limited, but she hands me three books that could be useful for my next article. I check them out and thank her, but before I can exit the library in peace, Piper's head pokes up from behind the counter again. She has purple headphones on top of her hair, and she plucks them off as she gives me a wicked smile. "Ask Atlas for another cheese coupon for me, Holland!"

chapter twenty-four

I ride my new bike all over town today, heading from the library first to the cafe for my second cup of coffee this morning. I convince myself that I *definitely* need it after the past two days, and since I carry around my laptop everywhere with me, I figure I can sit down and flip through the pages of the new books I checked out and write down more notes for the next article. I still have the notes of the legend of the town that Sam told me when I first arrived at Saltmere, and I plan on factchecking those details before I write them.

I order another vanilla latte and take a seat in the corner booth, emptying out my back full of books, my laptop, and my camera. The morning sun seeps through the open blinds of the window against the wall, warming me as I wait. My thumb taps against my lap as my eyes roam around the building. The cafe isn't busy, with only a few elderly couples chatting with the baristas at the bar, and a few teenagers sitting in another booth on the opposite side of the room. Everyone is minding their business, not paying me any mind or attention about my recent relationship status, and for that, I feel my shoulders relax and my posture slacken against the booth cushion. *The town* can *leave me alone about me and Atlas*, I think to myself, mentally arguing with Charlotte's logic that she left me with before I shut down the conversation. *I'm fine. Everything's fine.*

After I receive my drink, I take a sip and open my laptop and slide over the first book on the table. The book title is *Saltmere: The Town Time Remembered.* The book cracks as I flip to the table of contents page, scanning through the list. I then flip to each chapter, where I gather that the entire book is full of carefully compiled, local historical records of the town. It is complete with archival materials, oral histories, letters, newspaper clippings, and photographs, both black-and-white and colored. The book explores the town's rise, its mysteries, its cultural quirks, and the lives of its people across generations.

I stare back in awe at the pages as I read over some excerpts that have been collected from multiple centuries, including both written articles, letters, notes, and journal entries. In chapter two, titled *Saltmere Claims Itself*, the journal entry written by Mayor Joanna Linwright, in her address on the Town Green, called ""Founders Festival Speech – Excerpt," The Saltmere Sentinel, June 10, 1872" reads:

"*...and so, as we gather here to mark eighty years of this town's proud history, let us remember our founding, not by decree, but by presence. There are those who say Saltmere was never officially founded, that we are a misprint in the county ledgers, an accident of maps. But I say this: Was the wind ever granted permission to blow? Did the river file its course with a magistrate? We built here, we named here, we stayed here. That is enough. Saltmere did not wait for the world to recognize it. It simply began.*"

The old wood of the booth chair creaks under me like it, too, remembers something. The books crowding the table are full of ghost voices; images printed onto the pages of scraps of letters, brittle journal pages, ink faded to the color of old bruises.

Another journal entry, from one of the original shipwreck survivors named, Captain Elias North, wrote on August 11, 1792:

"We buried the last of the sailors this morning, Jonas, who took a splinter to the leg three days before we hit shore. I'd never seen a man rot from the inside while still whispering prayers. The dunes here shift like smoke. But there's water, and fish, and wood enough if you don't ask where it came from. I built my shelter from the ribs of the ship. I think she'd have liked that. Our old vessel, giving us one more favor. We're calling it Saltmere now. It's what the marsh water tastes like when it dries on your lips: bitter, but not unwelcome."

This excerpt, the captain burying his men and naming the town with salt on his lips, hits harder than I expect. It isn't the grief that strikes me, exactly. It's the resignation. The quiet, resigned note of *bitter, but not unwelcome.* It echoes something in me, not homesickness, but something deeper. A kind of genetic sorrow.

Another survivor, Annabeth Cole, wrote a letter to her sister in Norfolk during October of 1793, a little over a year since the shipwreck:

"Dearest Ruth,

I cannot say if this place is good, only that it holds us. We are not meant to be here, but here we are. The men have built a wharf–barely more than a row of teeth against the waves–and the cottages lean like old thoughts. But there is fish, and we've begun trading smoked cod with the coast walkers who come down from the north. I found a piece of blue glass on the shore yesterday, smooth as a worn coin. The children say they're messages from the sea, like the ones we never got when the ship went down. If you can forgive me for staying, then I can forgive myself."

The letter makes me pause. It feels almost too intimate. Like a thought I haven't realized I had until someone else wrote it down two centuries ago. I can't help but place myself in Annabeth's shoes, who just wanted to survive and search for an ounce of forgiveness that only her sister could give her, who I can imagine as the person who was Annabeth's greatest and closest friend. I *long* for that type of relationship. I don't know where Corinne is, but I would do anything to talk to her, to inform her what my life is like now, to ask for forgiveness of not trying enough to connect with one another if it means I can have her within arm's reach for the rest of our time together on this planet. I glance up towards the window, where the afternoon sun filters through the glass in dull, watery light, and for a second, the room seems to be suspended. Still. Like the town is listening.

My skin prickles as I continue flipping page after page of each of the other books as well, losing track of time as I immerse myself into these excerpts, these stories of the people who made this town. My skin prickles–not in fear, but in recognition. I want to explore through the marsh at night, to step into the mire and walk through the same lands that these people did long ago, to be able to feel *them*, to hear their stories in the waves of the sea and listen to their echoes.

Sam was, in fact, not lying about the beginning of this town, but reading these excerpts brings a bittersweet feeling inside of me. The excitement to use these *real* elements for my articles whizzes in my blood because I want everyone who reads my work to feel for these people. To understand their feelings and their drudgery. But these same slices of evidence make my stomach whirl in unease. These are real feelings, real issues, real *fights* that this town's residents' ancestors went through, and I suddenly feel that I won't be the right person to accomplish delivering their life stories to the public. I didn't grow up here. This is my first time visiting Saltmere, and I'm leaving in a matter of weeks. *Will it all be forgotten once I leave?*

I close the last book, slowly. Not because I'm done reading, but because it feels as if these books will start reading *me* back. I continue making notes in my notebook, determined to write down every single detail because these small fractions of real-life pieces of history will serve as a portable element of time travel for the magazine's readers. I have never wanted anything more than our readers to learn more about the past of this town. I just want to be the right person to accomplish the task.

"Hi there, dear," I hear one of the baristas say after the door of the cafe jingles. I look at the customer walking in, and my heart *drops*.

It's…my sister.

It's Corinne.

chapter twenty-five

"Corinne?"

My voice feels foreign and quiet over the clamorous sounds of the cafe, but I know she hears me.

My sister looks over, her dark brown hair waving and falling down her back. Her skin is slightly darker than the last time I saw her, like she's spent hours on end underneath the rays of the summer sun. She's wearing a navy blue buttoned t-shirt and white capris, matched with silver sandals. I don't think I've ever seen her in such casual attire. She's always striding around in colored pantsuits that scream business and respect that I used to laugh at the idea that she probably wears them to bed–but now, in the natural light that pours into the cafe, she looks as if she belongs somewhere near the beach, somewhere warm and inviting and currently embracing the summer season.

Like Saltmere.

Her dark brown eyes beat into mine, the corners near her eyelids crunching together as she gives me a bright, warm grin.

"Holland," she breathes out, disregarding her spot in line at the counter and strolling over towards my booth. My legs immediately shoot up and straighten, and in less than a second, her arms are extended out to her sides and she's wrapping them around me. My chin lands on her shoulder, my face lost in her wispy hair. I close my eyes as I breathe in her scent, strawberries and vanilla.

I don't even remember the last time we hugged like this–not during any holiday, not at the funeral, not when she got into Harvard, not at any of our graduations, not when her and my mom were visiting New York over three years ago for an event regarding Corinne and Emmett's firm. But *this* embrace feels long overdue, like a sense of much needed reassurance. It feels like a beginning.

"What are you doing here?" I ask, ending the hug but keeping my hands wrapped around her elbows. A boulder's worth of relief casts down my entire body at the fact that Emmett and I can stop worrying about where Corinne is currently.

But, then again, we still need to worry about *why* she's here, and *why* she suddenly fell off the planet for a while and is now standing before me.

Her glossy lips crack a smile, displaying her white teeth. "I came to visit you."

I frown. "Me?"

She nods, taking a step back and then sitting down in my booth.

I blink at her, frozen in place, because this has *never* happened without our mom present. We don't just visit one another *casually*. We don't talk to one another unless we have a specific need or a task that has to be accomplished. Hell, we don't even interact without any member of our family around us–not because we don't have anything to say to one another, but because it's so damn *awkward*. It's like our bodies gravitate in opposite directions because we don't know how to act like normal sisters, or even normal humans.

Slowly, I sit back down, narrowing my eyes as I search for any type of indication that she is hiding something. I trace over every feature of hers, over her long lashes that shower air down her cheeks with every blink, over the slant of her freckle-clad nose, over the dimples indenting on her cheeks near the corners of her smiling mouth.

This woman sitting here in front of me is *not* the same woman I call my sister.

My sister is cold, serious. Never smiling on her own will, unless it's showing a rare amount of affection towards her husband, Mac. Mac, who buckled down over a decade ago and did everything he could to win over his icy queen, who yells at more people than she gives a curt nod to as a *hello.*

I've never *not* gotten along with Corinne, necessarily, but I don't know what to say to her, or how to act. I don't know what she needs, or if I can even help her, given the state of our relationship right now. *Wait.*

"Is this about the painting?" I ask her.

Corinne takes a sip from *my* drink, like that is the most normal thing to do right now. If my dad's words about how Corinne had asked him where our mom's last painting was weren't currently ringing in my head, I would stare at her in shock. And in awe. "What do you mean?"

I shake my head. "Dad told me that you asked him about Mom's unfinished painting recently. Is that why you're here? Because you know how much she loved Saltmere?"

She takes a deep breath, now fidgeting with her red-painted fingernails. *She used to hate fingernail polish.* Once, when I was five and she was almost eleven, I spilt my glittery pink nail polish on her favorite cardigan, and I thought that I was going to be locked up in her mental ice castle and be casted out of her life forever because of how mad she was at me. She didn't talk to me for *three months.* I knew, even back then, that I would never be close with her, because we were, and are, so different.

She glances up at me again and gives me a closed-lip smile. "I missed you, baby sister."

Yeah, she's definitely going through something. Maybe a mid-life crisis.

Boldly, I reach forward and place my hand over top of hers. "Are you doing okay, Corinne? Dad, Emmett, and I are really worried about you."

"What do you mean?"

"Well, Emmett called me and told me that you haven't been at work. And he *never* calls me, so I know that he is worried that you aren't okay. Dad said that he's talked to you not that long ago, but you didn't sound like yourself, and you were suddenly interested in Mom's painting. You haven't answered any calls. You haven't gone to work. You fell off the face of the earth, and your own husband won't answer us, either. What's going on, Corinne?"

"Mac's not my husband anymore."

My jaw hangs, and I suck in a breath. "What?"

"We are separated and filing for divorce."

I shake my head again, my cherry earrings smacking into the sides of my neck. "Hold on." My hand raises, and I stick a pointed finger into the air. "What do you mean you two are filing for divorce? You two were good at the funeral. I saw you guys."

She laughs–*laughs*–like I just told her a joke. "Oh, baby sister. How naive you are."

I flinch. "Naive?"

"Mac and I were separated during the funeral. Everyone knew that, I thought."

"I can guarantee that none of us know that detail about your life. Emmett would've said so on his phone call. Same with Dad."

"Oh." Her eyebrows curl down into a frown on her forehead. "Hmm. Well, I thought it was obvious. We haven't been happy together in years. And after…" She pauses, takes another drink of my mug, and sighs. "We just weren't working out. I don't even know if I actually loved him."

My heart cracks for her, and confusion consumes me. "You were married for almost eight years, though. You didn't love him the entire time?"

She shrugs. "There was a point where I was content. But I think I always knew I wasn't satisfied, you know?"

She's asking me the question, as if she is looking for justification for her decisions, but the truth is, I don't know the specifics of her life to truly know anything. We have never been close enough to share these types of details with one another. But I give her a small smile and change the subject. If she wants me to know about the details of her life, I think she will tell me, since she says that she's here for me. "So, where are you staying? And for how long?"

She seems grateful for the topic change, given that her shoulders and chest visibly deflate and she sinks more into her seat. "I researched hotels here–which don't exist, by the way–and found a bed and breakfast at the end of town. I tried calling to reserve a room, but the line was busy each time, so I'm hoping they have something for me."

That will definitely need to be changed, if this town wants tourists to visit. I really need to meet with Patty.

Corinne smiles at me again. "I plan on staying for a while."

"Were…were you going to call me?"

She tilts her head, then glances down at the table. "I know we haven't been close, Holland. And that's my fault. After Mom's funeral–" she stops herself when her voice breaks off slightly, "I realized just how bad our relationship has been all of our lives. Losing Mom made me realize that I don't want our relationship to be so strained anymore." She glances up, tossing me a watery look. "I'm sorry for not being supportive of your career. You are clearly talented, and you are doing so great. I've read your work. *All* of it. Every single article. You're amazing, Hol."

A stinging sensation burns and crawls up my throat. She couldn't possibly know how much I have craved those words from her. "Thank you, Corinne. That means a lot."

She nods. "I hope you don't hate me for coming here. I don't want to get in your way while I'm here, but I hope you don't mind me wanting to get to know my baby sister better in this beautiful town that our mom loved."

I latch our hands together across the table. "I would love that." I suck my teeth as a thought crosses my mind. "Why don't you stay in the extra bedroom of the house I'm renting? It's on the outskirts of town, close to the ocean." The words are flowing out of my mouth rapidly, and I don't want to stop them. I *want* my sister around. "The area is to die for, and I think seeing one another every day would help us get to know each other quicker."

Her entire face lights up. "Are you sure? I promise, I didn't just come here to use you, by any means–"

"I don't think that." I squeeze her hand. "I just want to become closer with you."

Her smile warms me. She resembles our mom so, *so* much–umber eyes, long lashes, golden undertones painting every inch of her skin–that tears spring to my eyelids and threaten to fall, but I blink them away, finally exhaling the breath I hadn't realized I'm holding. Because a sense of belonging rings through my blood and calms every doubt of my displacement in my family with just her words and her presence before me.

chapter twenty-six

Corinne just happened to rent a car with a bike rack on the back, so once we load up my bike, we drive towards my house. The car ride isn't filled with awkward silence like I was worried about, but rather filled with remembering old memories of us as kids and some funny stories from the places I have visited for the magazine. My heart feels light giggling together like this, her hand swatting my forearm affectionately when I tell her something she can't stop laughing at that she accidentally snorts, which only makes us both laugh even more.

It's relieving to act like this together because *this* is how it should have always been between us. But I can't change the past, and if it wasn't for the distance I have felt from my family members, I probably wouldn't be the person I am today. I have Corinne now, and that's all that matters.

She doesn't go into any more detail about her marriage or any acknowledgement about my mom's painting, but I don't press her on those issues. We pull up to the side of the road, and I can't help but flick my gaze over to next door. Atlas's truck isn't in the driveway, and all of his blinds are still shut. An ounce of disappointment falls through me, when it shouldn't. I shouldn't want to see him, especially since my heart is all over the place and we are now, as the town already knows, dating.

I think to tell Corinne about that slight detail of my life, because I'm sure she will find out eventually, but when I open my mouth to tell her on our way up towards the front door, she turns to me, wrapping her hand gently around my upper arm.

"How on earth did you find this place?" she asks, her eyes squinted up towards the house. "This is probably the cutest little thing I've ever seen."

I chuckle. "Yeah, I agree. My boss, Jenny, found it for me, but I'm good friends with the owner, Mabel. You'll probably meet her soon. She's always around."

"I can't wait. I have never been more excited for this mini vacation."

I help her unpack her suitcases–plural–and it doesn't fail to occur to me that she packed *a lot* for this *mini vacation.* I haven't been to her apartment in Los Angeles, so I don't know what her closet looks like there, but I would like to assume that her wardrobe must be much larger than mine. The guest bedroom of the house is smaller than the main, tucked away past the kitchen, and the closet doesn't have enough room for all of her fifteen pairs of jeans, eighteen blouses, twenty-four plain colored t-shirts, twelve tank tops, seven pairs of denim shorts, four baggy hoodies from her years at university, two pairs of flowy overalls, and nine different pairs of sandals.

Yes, I count each and every item, because I'm in shock. *If we continue getting closer, maybe she'll let me borrow some of these clothes. Sisters do that, right?*

I have taken clothes of hers before, back when she left for college and I was still in middle school. She had left years' worth of concert and graphic tees hanging in her closet–not deemed worthy enough for her years at Harvard–and I snagged them and still wear them around when I'm lounging around at home. I don't think Corinne even realized they were gone, but I always hoped she didn't, because I loved that I got to wear something she once loved before.

I pluck out the last shirt from the last suitcase that I missed, one that is rolled tightly underneath one of her sandals. I unfold it and shake it out, but a taste of nostalgia and resentment licks at me when I register the design and paint smudges on the front of the shirt.

"This is Mom's painting shirt," I blurt out.

Corinne leaves the closet and is kneeling next to me immediately, snatching the shirt out of my hands and standing up once again. "I know," she says quietly before grabbing onto another hanger and hanging the shirt up on the rack, next to her other tees.

"Why do you have it?"

Her head pokes out from behind the closet door. "Why do you have Mom's painting?"

My jaw slams shut. The silence fills the limited space of the bedroom, bouncing off the walls, as we stare at one another, unrelenting. I pretend to act like I have no idea what she's talking about, forcing my lips to curl down into a frown and my eyebrows to burrow together. I shake my head. "I don't."

Corinne exhales before returning back on the floor with me, interlacing our hands together. She doesn't meet my gaze when she quietly says, "I know you have it, Hol. You don't have to lie. No one's going to be mad at you."

"Is that why you came here?" I ask, matching her soft tone. I don't want to fight with her already, not when this has been going so well. "To get the painting?"

"Of course not," she defends, her head snapping up to look at me. "I came to see you. To see this town that

Mom loved once upon a time." Her shoulders fall, and her eyes fall back down to our hands. "To get closer to her."

My thumb swipes over hers. "You were close with her, Corinne."

Her lips roll together, and she sucks her teeth. "No, no I wasn't. I didn't have the relationship the two of you had."

"That doesn't mean you weren't close with her." I give her a small smile. "We all had different relationships with her."

"But it does. I tried so, *so* hard to be just like her, but because of that, I resented her for it. All my life. And the shitty part is, she never once put pressure on me to get the most perfect grades or go to Harvard for law or become the best attorney. She didn't care what I did with my life; she never once gave me the praise I always wanted for being as successful as her. Or trying to, anyway." Her sigh is loud, and one tear falls down her cheek. "Mom's heart was as big as the sky, with love, warmth, and kindness for everyone around her. She was the perfect embodiment of a loving person that you could laugh with or to go get advice from. Or even a hug, because she was just *that* amazing. But I never saw her like that, not until the last few *months* of her life. I blocked out the wondrous parts of her. I put an imaginary pressure on myself because I thought that becoming another version of her would make her love me *more*. Would make her finally proud of me.

"She never gave me any indication that what I did or didn't do in school mattered. Dad did, but Mom just wanted me to be happy. But her doing that made me feel like what I was doing wasn't enough to earn her applause and praise, so I kept pushing myself. Every single day. And then I hated her for it."

"I had no idea," I whisper, my own tears already threatening to fall. "I had no idea that you resented her. It always seemed like you two were so close."

"I didn't want to make it my entire personality to hate her to her face–only behind her back. I was the one tearing our relationship apart, and I couldn't stop myself, not even when we found out that she had cancer. I was so sick in the head, so fed up with my own problems in my marriage and my resentment for her." She wipes her nose with the back of her free hand, her crying getting louder and more out of control with every second that passes. "I will never forgive myself for treating her so horribly those last few months. I wish I could turn back time, Holland. I wish that I didn't–"

Corinne stops herself, covering a trembling hand over her trembling lips. Her eyes lock shut, making more tears cascade down her face and trickle down onto the carpet at our laps. I squeeze her hand three times, but I let her cry this clearly pent up emotion out, let myself be a safe space for her to release everything she needs to.

Eventually, once her tears have stopped crowding her eyelids and her sniffles have replaced her sobs, she looks back up to me. "I used to resent you, too. For the relationship you had with her. I was so jealous that the two of you spent so much time together growing up. She was always helping you with your homework every single night, always taking you out shopping or even let you watch her paint in that room of hers. That's why I never tried to get close to you. Because I was so damn jealous."

She huffs a laugh, shaking her head. "I'm so, so sorry, Holland. For being such a bitch to you about your career choice, about just wanting to do what you loved. I'm so–"

"I have dyslexia," I cut her off, meeting her gaze. "That's why Mom would sit up at the table with me every night. I couldn't read any of my homework." My tone isn't harsh, but a weight on my chest feels both heavier and lighter with every word that comes out of my mouth. Heavier because I don't know what her reaction will be; lighter because I'm not ashamed of my disability like I once was. "I worked with Mom and multiple therapists throughout school to perfect my reading, writing, and comprehending skills so I wouldn't keep falling behind the rest of my class. And it worked." I smile. "It worked so well that I grew a love for writing. *That's* why I chose my career. Not to just be the outlier of the family or to go against what everyone else was doing. I found something I loved that I worked really hard to become great at, and I wanted to do something with it."

Corinne's crying again. "God, I really am a horrible sister." I open my mouth to argue with her, but her hand slips out of mine and shoots up in the air, stopping me. "No, I really am. I had *no* idea. I didn't even question you on why you even wanted to become a journalist. I just assumed my own reasons and tried to convince you to not go through with your dreams."

"Well, to be fair, no one knew about my challenges. I didn't want anyone to pity me or look at me differently." I shrug. "I already was giving Dad trouble for being his most difficult child; I didn't want him to change his perspective of me just because I had an actual reason for my struggles in school. I wanted to prove to him that I can be just as successful as my siblings." I lace our hands back together, lowering my voice. "And as for you, I don't hold anything against you. Or Emmett, or even Dad. Sure, I was hurt when I felt that the entire family was against me for wanting to become a journalist, but I also know that I didn't tell you all the full truth of why I wanted to become a journalist. I kept everything to myself."

"But that doesn't excuse our behavior, Hol." She sighs, then adjusts herself so we are sitting side-by-side, our legs touching and her head leaving on my shoulder. "I should've been supportive no matter what. *We* all should've. I'm sorry."

I rest my cheek on the top of her hair. "It's okay, Corinne. I promise. I'm doing good."

"Hell yes, you are," she replies. "You are an amazing writer. And from now on, I will support you no matter what, even if you want to write about boycotting to-do lists or how to fall in love with your alarm clock." I laugh, but she continues, tapping her hand on my knee. "I will read whatever you write and love it." She sits up again. "How are your articles coming along here? Your one about Saltmere's festival made me wish I got on a plane here sooner."

I smile. "That one turned out really great, actually. I haven't talked to Mabel, who is on the festival board, since yesterday morning, but I think the event turned out really well."

"That's amazing, Hol. I'm so proud."

"Thanks," I say, a coat of red swiping over my cheeks at her praise. It feels unreal and ridiculously good to hear her say that. "My next article is due on Thursday. I was actually reading a couple books about the town's history at the cafe for my next one."

I tell her what else I have planned to write while I'm here, and after unpacking the rest of what's left in her suitcases, we return to the living room. It's only a little after three in the afternoon, but Corinne hasn't eaten since she left the airport in Raleigh, so we order dinner from the diner to pick up. When our food's finished and discarded on the coffee table, we slouch down against the couch cushion and sigh towards the ceiling, and Corinne flips on an episode of *Friends*, both of us lounge in sweats and some of her graphic t-shirts.

The grin on my face never leaves as we watch the show, but I'm not just smiling at the jokes and the characters on the screen. I'm happy because I am sitting here with Corinne, doing something together as trivial yet monumental as laying down on the couch and watching reruns of her favorite show. Because occasionally, she turns her head to me, her cheek dimples indenting more and more with every laugh she makes. Because when she's hunched over, heaving in laughter, she tosses a hand over that lands on my forearm, like she's including me in this comical moment so neither of us is alone. I should be writing my article right now, but there is nothing that could stop me from spending the rest of the night like this.

Corinne doesn't want to talk to Emmett or our dad quite yet, but I don't question her reasons. She promises me that she will tell them the news about her and Mac tomorrow, since they don't know about their problems either. Episode after episode streams on the screen, and we only get up from the couch to pick up the box of donuts we Doordashed from Alabama Jones's bakery that I haven't even visited in person yet off the front porch.

We are interrupted by the ring of the doorbell around six. Corinne sits up, and the blanket wrapped around her legs falls to the ground as she stands. "I'll get it. Stay here, baby sis."

"It's probably Mabel, the owner of the house. It'll be good for you to meet her," I say as she walks towards the front door. I shift my gaze back to the television screen, grabbing onto the remote to turn the volume down.

"Well, hello there," I hear Corinne say. The door is wide open, and she's leaning her hip against the door handle, but my breath sucks in when I see Atlas's full head and shoulders poke above Corinne's five-foot eight frame.

I'm walking to the door before I even realize it.

"What are you doing here?" I ask him, my eyes trailing up and down his body. He's wearing a cream colored collared long-sleeved, denim jeans, and nice shoes–a completely different attire from what I have been seeing him in the entire time I've been in Saltmere.

But what surprises me the most is the bouquet of tulips in his hand.

It must show on my face because Atlas smiles and tilts his head to the side. "I'm here to take you to the tulip fields."

"What?" I ask, dumbfounded, my head rearing back and a frown tugging on my lips.

He glances down at the flowers, then hands them to me. His sleeves are rolled up, and the veins of his forearms run like river paths across the surface of his skin, and I can't help but stare at them. I stay stuck and speechless in shock, and Corinne saves me by snatching the flowers out of Atlas's hands. I look over at her, blinking a million times a second, and she gives me a knowing look. "You didn't tell me you had a boyfriend, baby sis." She turns back to Atlas, stretching her hand out in front of her. "Hi, I'm Corinne. Holland's sister."

"Oh," he replies, nodding. He shakes her hand. "Good to meet you. I'm Atlas." His gaze flicks over to me, and he narrows his eyes in a silent question.

"My sister surprised me by coming to Saltmere," I say.

My voice doesn't even feel like mine because it's so strained. I'm still trying to register Atlas's actions and the way he looks standing on my doorstep, his hair falling just past his ears in slightly tousled waves, clean and pushed back with a lazy flick of his fingers. It's not wild, not scruffy like it usually is, and he doesn't have his usual ball cap on or his cowboy boots. He's still a country boy from the way he stands, relaxed but alert, and the look in his eyes that says he's seen storms and silence alike. But tonight, he's dressed to impress. And it suits him.

"That's awesome," he finally says, turning to my sister. He gives her a wide smile, a gesture that shows his dimples, a gesture I wish he gave me on the first day we met because it's so immaculate. "Saltmere's great. Lots of good people, lots of things to do."

"Like visiting the tulip fields?"

Atlas huffs a laugh. "Yeah, if your sister will answer me about going together."

Both of them turn to me, their stares nothing but burning a hole right through me as they wait for my answer. *Of course* I want to go. Jenny said I should visit the fields and write about them anyway. I just hate that I have to lie to Corinne about being in a relationship with Atlas.

"Will you be okay alone here?" I ask Corinne, and she only rolls her eyes.

"I'm in the cutest town on the East coast. Of course I'll be okay." But her face softens. "Go have fun, baby sis. I'll see you when you get home." She takes another glance at me up and down, then grabs onto my elbow and pulls me back inside. "Actually, Mr. Atlas, give us a second to get Holland changed. She will be right out in less than ten!"

chapter twenty-seven

In exactly ten minutes, I'm sitting in the front seat of Atlas's truck, wearing my white, flowy skirt that hits my ankles and Corinne's denim, buttoned tank top, my hair thrown up into a high bun. Corinne also let me borrow her gold hoops, some gold bangles, lip gloss, brown sandals, and her shimmery highlight that she spread against my cheekbones.

Corinne was putting the bouquet of flowers in a vase as I waved her goodbye, and now I stare straight ahead, my seatbelt rubbing too tight against my chest. Nerves dance like shadows flickering against a wall under candlelight in my stomach, and my knee won't stop bouncing in its place. My body is swaying back and forth like I'm a child on a rocking horse. I keep rubbing my hands together on my lap, taking deep breaths to calm myself down, but nothing is working.

I don't know why I'm freaking out. I've been to many places in the town with him. He listens to me and is kind, he's funny and protective. But, to the entire rest of the town, we are *dating*, and I can't keep track of my feelings growing for him, or of our kisses–almost or not–or his kind gestures that leave me speechless.

"Do you like your bike?"

I whip my head to him. He is already glancing over at me, a shadow of a smile present. He doesn't look nervous at all. I swallow and nod, then look forward again. "Yup!"

"Are you okay?"

"Yup!"

"Holland." Atlas frowns. "What's going on?"

"Nothing, silly." I swat at the air and laugh awkwardly. "Everything's awesome."

"Are you acting like this because of Corinne?"

"What? No, it's not her. She's super great."

Atlas hums in disbelief. I lean forward and adjust the air conditioning to blast it on my face. "Really, it's not her. She's actually really cool. I've never been close with her before, and it's like I'm learning so much about her. It should be weird, getting to know your only sister at age twenty-three, and it was at first, but I had so much fun with her today."

I'm rambling, but I can't seem to stop. "She surprised me. She's going through a lot in her marriage, and I don't really know all those details yet, but I just want to be there for her. I want to become strangers to best friends, like those twin sisters on the *Parent Trap* or Anna and Elsa in *Frozen*. You know what I mean?" I don't let him even have the chance to actually answer that question. "She's so great. I could listen to her stories and her laughter over episodes of *Friends* forever I think. Does that make me weird? Probably. But I'm worried about her. I don't–"

I gasp softly when Atlas reaches over the middle console to grab my hand, the one that has been rubbing back and forth nervously against my thigh like a total weirdo. His hand flexes and his fingers interlace with mine. "Holland," he says, "take a breath."

"Right. Sorry." I can't look at him. *What the hell is wrong with me?* I turn my head to look out the window, where the shops on Main whiz by. I stare at the wonky reflections of Atlas's truck as we drive by the windows of the buildings.

There's a beat of silence. "Are you being like this because of me?"

"What? No, of course not." I laugh again, but it sounds more like a hyena. I even snort. Loudly. *God. This is so embarrassing.* "Don't flatter yourself, Map Boy. I'm perfectly fine."

"Listen, if you didn't want to come toni–"

I, *finally*, take a deep breath. "I did. *Do.* I want to be here." I glance over at him. "With you."

The corners of his lips rise. "What did you do while you were getting dressed? You're acting like you pre-gamed this outing with me with a shot of espresso."

I slap his arm with my free hand, reaching across the console because I don't want to release his hand. "I'm not acting *that* bad."

"You snorted." His smirk widens.

"It was a *dignified* snort." I straighten my posture like that helps my case.

He chuckles under his breath, eyes scanning my face like he's trying to memorize it. I feel a blush crawl over my cheeks. "Okay, well. Dignified or not, it was cute."

I groan and cover my face. "I think I'm dying. This is how I will die."

"You die on a date with me?" he says, mock-offended, one eyebrow raised. "That's a bit harsh, don't you think?"

"No, I die because I can't stop saying weird stuff around you and my body is malfunctioning under this imaginary pressure. My brain wants to tell myself to shut up while my mouth wants to tell you that you look like one of those men on the cover of a romance novel. Seriously, why do you look like you can sand mahogany down by hand and still somehow smell like cedar and good decisions?"

He blinks, his other hand on the wheel sliding down it. He wants to smile. "Did you just say that out loud?"

"No," I say, shaking my head. Then I wince and sigh. "Yes, I guess I did."

Atlas laughs, actually *laughs*, and I want to bottle up the sound and use it to erase all my future embarrassing moments in front of him.

"Well," he says, "if it makes you feel better, I think you're charming when you're spiraling."

I narrow my eyes at him. "Charming in a *wow-she-needs-help-and-needs-to-learn-how-to-act-on-a-date* kind of way?"

He shrugs. "Maybe." He looks over again, swallowing. Suddenly, all of the light, joking air is sucked out of the vents of the vehicle. "You called this a date."

I make a face at him. "You called it one too. Is it not?"

"I was thinking it was, but I wasn't sure if you thought so."

"We *are* fake dating, Mr. Directions, which means that we have to go on dates in front of others." My voice gets quieter as I remember earlier today at the library. "The town already knows about us."

"Yeah," he says, glancing once at our hands still latched together, then back at the windshield. "I know."

There's another moment of silence, the only sound being the air conditioning and a small buzz of the static noise coming from the stereo. "I ran into Gill at the warehouse and he asked me why we haven't told anyone ourselves." He huffs. "I can't believe I thought we could trust Sam."

I have to break the news to him. "To be fair, it wasn't Sam. It was Patty Corrington. She saw us at the diner."

Atlas hums. "Still. I don't trust Sam."

I tilt my head. "Why?"

I watch Atlas chew on the side of his cheek, losing himself to his thoughts as each second passes. "It doesn't matter."

If we don't talk about it now, we're never going to. "But it does. You two looked at each other like you either wanted to kill the other or you were seconds away from confessing some sort of mind boggling, life ending secret."

His grip on the steering wheel tightens, displaying his white knuckles. I wait for him to answer, to give me *something* regarding more of his past and the weirdness he has with the town's sheriff, but he doesn't respond. I lean my head against the headrest behind me and glance back out the window to my side. Atlas might not respond, but he does swipe his thumb gently against the back of my hand. My heart stutters. *Yep. I'm still spiraling.*

My phone vibrates in my bag. I pull it out with my free hand, but my stomach plummets when I read the contact and message.

`Just skimmed over the latest piece about Saltmere's festival,` Gordon writes. `Still overwriting like you're trying to impress a professor instead of gaining an audience, I see. Thought we worked on that?`

My mouth goes dry. I clench my teeth together and withhold a groan.

`Good to see that you're still at it. Don't forget: a clean narrative doesn't need theatrics. Hope to talk to you soon!`

I stare at the messages, my thumb hovering over the keyboard, blinking down the anger rising inside of me. Then I lock and shut off the screen without replying.

But his words still sit heavy in my chest, like I swallowed them whole. Typical Gordon, always more teacher than partner, always measuring my work against an invisible scale, the prize dangling at the far end and never within my reach. I *hate* how much his judgement gets to me. He might care about the success of my career only because how well my articles do affect how good his reputation can withstand, but he doesn't care about anything in my personal life. Hell, he probably didn't even know I was in Saltmere until my article was published. Maybe he didn't deserve my silence, but he definitely doesn't deserve a response to those messages.

"Are you okay, Holland?"

I startle in my seat. Atlas is looking at me with confusion plastered on his face.

"Yeah, why?" I force myself to say.

His eyebrows knit together. "You're holding onto your phone like it has offended you somehow."

I glance down. My knuckles are white around my phone case, my grip so tight that my fingers begin to throb. Slowly, I loosen my hold and slide my phone back in my bag on the ground, wincing. "It's nothing," I reply.

"Who texted you?" He searches my gaze before returning his eyes back on the road, lowering his tone. "Was it anyone from your family? Gordon?"

My head rears back, and I blink rapidly in surprise. "What makes you think that it was Gordon?"

He shrugs one shoulder, clicking his tongue against teeth. "Just the way you look really angry right now."

"Yeah, I am." I exhale a deep breath. "He read my article about the festival. Gave me his…notes."

"Let me guess," Atlas begins, flicking a look over at me, "helpful, constructive, and laced with superiority?"

A laugh escapes out of my throat, sharp and humorless. "Right on brand."

"I don't think you should listen to what he has to say." He gives me a small smile, a sight that makes a sliver of my anger flutter away. "You shouldn't believe any of his words or opinions about you."

"I know," I murmur. "It's just hard. He used to edit all of my work. It's hard to unhear that voice in my head, you know? He likes to torment me with his *criticism*."

I watch Atlas's shoulders slouch against his seat, nodding his head. He stays quiet until he says, in a quiet tone, "People like that don't know how to let go unless they believe they still have some sort of power over you."

"He doesn't," I quickly say. "Have power over me, I mean. At least, not anymore."

He looks over at me again, his eyes slightly narrowed, like he's searching for the lie in my words. Then his gaze softens, and there's no judgment. Only patience. Steady, unwavering patience. "I believe you," he says. "But I think that maybe a small part of you still thinks that."

His truthful words sting as they shoot straight for the beating organ in my chest, the piece of me that gives more than it should to people that only misuse it. I glance away, biting the inside of my cheek.

"I don't want him in my head anymore," I whisper. There's a nip in my throat at my vulnerability. "He's ruined my confidence in being a writer, almost cost me my career because of how harsh he was to me about my work right after my mom's funeral." I sigh. "I hate that he still takes up space in my mind."

"Don't give it to him." Atlas's voice is gentle, soft. "You've already outgrown whatever version of you he thinks he knows."

There's a slice of hope glimmering in my chest, sparkling with light. I don't know if it's the words he just said or the way he said them, but the glint in his eyes makes me believe everything that comes out of his mouth about me. Like what he is saying is factual and true. Like he sees something in me that I have forgotten is there.

"You're good at that," I say, getting more comfortable in my seat. "Saying the exact thing I need to hear."

"I mean everything I say, Holland. Especially to you."

Maybe that's what makes me continue to want to spend time with him. I might not have known him for long, but Atlas isn't the type of person that says something he doesn't truly believe. Everything that comes out of his mouth is valuable. He means everything he says, not to win, not to wound. *Especially to you.* Just to remind me who I am. And for the first time in what feels like a lifetime, I think I'm starting to believe it, too.

I don't respond, but I don't feel as awkward as before. Instead, I keep a ghost of a smile on my face at this re-found purpose in myself.

He lets go of my hand for a second, and I watch him slide his own phone out from his front pocket and click on his Spotify app. Taylor Swift's *folklore* album begins to play. I gasp, placing my hand over my chest. "Oh my god, is Atlas Richens secretly a Swiftie?"

"A man who isn't a Swiftie is lying. Her music is good," he replies, nonchalantly, like this isn't a valuable piece of information. "I saw you wearing a concert shirt of hers the other day and thought you liked her."

"Oh, I don't just *like* her. Taylor Swift is my moral compass."

Atlas huffs a laugh. "I'll pretend to understand what that means."

I sing along to the music as Atlas drives out of town, where green, open fields take over the landscape out the windows. We drive further and further away from the ocean, and after another ten minutes, Atlas turns off onto a rougher gravel road. I'm transfixed by the view; my forehead presses against the glass of my window as my eyes catch onto the sight. Rows upon rows of tulips lay in every imaginable hue: deep crimson, buttery yellow, creamy white, coral pink, and even dramatic purples that look almost black in the sunlight. The way their waxy petals catch the sunlight looks like a stained-glass piece of art, and when the slight breeze rolls through, the entire field ripples like a painted sea. Dozens of people are roaming through the narrow paths, some bending down to smell and run their hands through the earthly beauty, some posing for pictures with their loved ones, some children darting and laughing through the field like there isn't any other place they would rather be.

"Oh my god," I say, in awe. We pass vehicle after vehicle on the road, and we bounce in our seats until we reach the end of the road and pull into a parking space. My feet hit the ground and I shut the truck door behind me, and Atlas appears at my side, stretching his hand out for me to hold.

I don't know if it's to continue on with a show to the people around us or if it's because he wants to hold my hand again, but I grab onto it anyway. He pulls me closer into his side, thumb swiping mindlessly against my hand as we walk and completely ignoring the way I visibly shudder because my heart is racing wildly in my chest at the gesture. He leads me towards the field entrance at the end of the lot, where a wooden beam arch wrapped in greenery and faux, colorful flowers stands tall like a mountain. There's a woman wearing a purple t-shirt, khaki shorts, and a tan bucket hat sitting behind a plastic foldable table taking cash to enter into the field, and Atlas hands her a twenty-dollar bill and tells her to keep the change.

She winks at me as we pass her, and I give her a smile and focus on what lies ahead, trying to keep my breathing normal and my falling jaw in place. The color of the tulips is so much brighter up close, and I pull Atlas around groups of people and families towards a less crowded section of the field, where a large windmill stands tall in the distance. The only other person nearby is a mother pushing a stroller on the paths, humming along to the music streaming through her headphones, minding her own business as she walks farther away from the entrance.

I whip my head up to Atlas. "I think this is one of the most beautiful places I've ever been."

"I think so too."

I have my bag hanging from my shoulder, so I pull out my camera and snap an absurd amount of pictures from all angles. Some of the guests smiling and enjoying their company, some of the foot trails that appear to lead to the end of the world, some of the weathered bronze statue of an elderly woman holding a watering can in one hand and a bundle of tulips in the other, some of the windmill that moves slowly around in a circle. It's cinematic, the way the Earth can create such beauty and the way my camera can capture it all.

I can't wait to write about this place.

Atlas is quiet the entire time I take the photos, but he rests his hand on the small of my back and keeps it there until I finish. I slide my camera back into my bag and adjust the strap onto my shoulder, but he takes the bag from me and holds it so I don't have to.

I cock my head to the side and smirk at him. My bag is bright pink and has cartoon ladybugs on it. "My bag really compliments your outfit, Atlas."

He shrugs, the corner of his lips tugging at the side. "Then I guess your bag's into me. Should I be worried?"

We walk for another hour, but it's my knees that begin to ache because of how many times I bend down to smell each color of tulip in every row. We run into Frank Adamson, a farmer and owner of the field, and he tells us that he planted about fifty thousand bulbs this season in the span of his eight acres. He explains that he plants them, some by hand, some by his machine, late November, before snowfall, so they can bloom the entire month of May and into June. He says that most of them begin to blossom at once, explaining that different varieties bloom at slightly different times so he staggers planting them a bit to help stretch out the season and the colorfulness of the field. I take notes in my notebook of all of the information with his permission, and he gladly lets me when I promise to send him a physical copy of the article so he can frame it.

When more people begin to clear out of the paths, we follow them towards where four different shop stands are, close to the entrance. The first shop's sign reads: *Annie's Cookies*, and I pull Atlas that way.

"God, these cookies smell *so* good," I say, pointing my nose high in the air to smell the rich, buttery sweetness looming around the stand. There's a woman behind the wooden counter, her bright red hair thrown up into a high bun with some pieces curly and hanging near her cheekbones. She has freckles coating her nose and forehead, with ruby red lipstick spread on her lips. She's wearing a black tee that says *Annie's Cookies*, but her name tag says *Wren.*

"Hello there," Wren says when it's our turn to order. "What can I get you?"

The small glass display shows six different cookie options: classic chocolate chip, snickerdoodle, oatmeal raisin, lemon sugar cookie, peanut butter with chocolate drizzle, and double chocolate fudge. "We'll take a box of each," Atlas says behind me, his hand again placed on the small of my back. I lean more into him when his fingers lightly trace small circles, grounding me in the moment. The scent of fresh cookies and blooming tulips mingles around us, warm and calming. I glance up, catching his gaze already on me just as he offers a small, closed-lip smile.

"Good choice," I say, my voice quiet. "I don't think I would've been able to pick."

He nods twice, the smile widening on his features. Then he straightens his head up towards Wren and hands her his card. His hand squeezes my back gently, and for a moment, everything feels lighter, easier. Like maybe, just maybe, I want this moment to last a while. This peaceful, this cozy, serene atmosphere is intoxicating, and I don't want to leave, especially when Atlas continues to either keep his hand interlaced with mine or his hand on my back to keep me close to him. Both are simple gestures that make my stomach flutter endlessly like a storm of nerves that continue to swirl and tumble over one another. No one has come up to us to ask about our sudden relationship, or even gives us the time of day or has given us a judging, concerned glance in our direction, but Atlas's touch doesn't feel like a show. It doesn't feel fake. It feels *real*, just like the friendship that is unfolding between us, just like the kind heart that is buried deep within Atlas's chest that he doesn't often let the rest of the world see.

There are multiple tables in front of the stands, and the area is lit by string lights that cast a golden glow over the open space. The soft flicker of the bulbs twinkle like stars in the daylight caught above the gathering crowd. Laughter and quiet conversation drift through the air around us. It's a perfect little oasis, welcoming, inviting, and timeless, with everyone lost in their own small moments.

"I love it here," I say when I take a seat on the bench of a table next to Atlas, who places the box of cookies down on the surface before us. I watch him flip open the lid of the box and reach for the lemon cookie, breaking off a large piece and swiveling it in my direction.

My eyebrows shoot up in surprise, but I open my mouth anyway for him to feed the piece of cookie to me. Our gazes remain locked, while goosebumps spread down every inch of my body. He watches me chew like it's the most fascinating thing he's ever seen, and a slow grin pulls on both sides of his.

"Good?" he asks, his tone too low for me.

I nod and swallow, words gathering on the tip of my tongue but failing to come out. My heart continues to beat rapidly in my chest, pounding against my ribs. He still hasn't looked away. Neither have I.

"You've got," he begins, his thumb now reaching up towards the corner of my mouth, "a little bit of icing. Right here." His thumb brushes over my lip, so slow and deliberate that I want to squirm in my seat, but I don't. I hold my breath even after he places his thumb into his own mouth and sucks off the icing I supposedly had on me, and my eyes widen. He smiles wider this time, registering my shock with a small chuckle.

He breaks off another piece of the same cookie and feeds it to himself this time before facing me again. "I love it here too," he says, glancing around us. "I've been to Saltmere a couple times growing up and I've never been here before."

I swallow. "Too bad this place can't be open all year long." I grab the chocolate chip cookie and take a bite. "What do you think Frank does in the wintertime?"

"Probably wishing he owned a Christmas tree farm or something," Atlas says. "Or maybe his wife wishes that. I once saw Frank around with Emily at the grocery store in the holiday decorations aisle, and Frank looked like he wanted to be anywhere else in the world besides there listening to his wife sing along to the Christmas carols streaming through the speakers the entire time."

I gasp, some chunks of the cookie in my hand falling down on the ground at our feet. "Oh my god, I *completely* forgot."

"Forgot what? How to chew properly?"

I narrow my eyes at him, then roll them. "No, what Piper told me about her meeting you for the first time."

"Piper?"

"Yeah, Charlotte's daughter? I met her at the library this morning and she told me the craziest story about you. I mean, I could assume that you had some weirdness to you, but carrying a mug in your coat pocket? Giving an eight-year-old a cheese coupon?" I lean forward, resting my chin on my propped up palms. "You really are committed to being the town's cryptid, aren't you?"

Atlas chuckles, huffing air through his nose. "First of all, that cheese coupon wasn't real, it was given to me as a prank. But it's a really good pretend gift to give a very inquisitive individual. And second of all, mugs are much more practical. Why is everyone still pretending that paper cups are better?"

"But why not leave it in your truck like a normal person?"

"Normal is overrated."

"That's probably something Piper would say."

"The kid's smart," Atlas replies.

I grin. "She made it seem like you pulled out your mug like magicians pull doves out of their hats. She thinks you are a wizard."

He shrugs, as if this piece of information isn't news to him. "I didn't feel like correcting her."

"Of course you didn't," I say, rolling my eyes again. But my smile grows.

"You know, you could start carrying around a mug with your camera and notebook in your purse. We could be wizards together." His eyebrows wiggle up and down on his forehead like a crazy person, but the playfulness in his tone makes me laugh.

"Tempting," I huff, twirling a strand of my hair near my face in my fingers. "But I think you've got the whole mysterious, mugman-obsessed-with-cheese bit handled. I'll just stick to being the town's journalist."

"Fine," he says, sighing like he's truly disappointed. "But when Sargento or Kraft offer me an unlimited supply of any kind of cheese for being so generous for my community outreach efforts, don't say I didn't try to include you or come running back to me about wanting a discount."

"Oh," I say, swiping a hand through the air, "you won't need to worry. I'll just be here jealous and mug-less."

He smiles. "Your loss."

I shake my head and chuckle, grabbing onto another piece of a cookie and putting it into my mouth, chewing slowly as I glance around again. But both Atlas and I jump in our seats as someone sits across from us. *Three* people sit across from us.

Mabel, Gill, and Ed–each of them an array of different expressions.

Shit. *Here we go.*

chapter twenty-eight

The top of Mabel's black curly hair is wrapped with a red bandana, and she's wearing black sunglasses to cover her eyes, but I can *feel* her concerned or angry or confused gaze on me. Her lips are turned down into a frown, and she has folded her fingers and is resting them on top of the table's surface.

Gill and Ed, however, look pleased with matching smiles plastered on their faces, probably either from the company sitting in front of them or the show that Mabel is seconds away from making. Or maybe both.

"So," Mabel begins, "when were you going to tell us that the two of you are dating?" She whips off her glasses. They tumble on the table across from her. Her dark brown eyes find me. "And why did I have to find out from Patty Corrington? You know how much I can't stand her. I thought you and I were becoming friends."

She's clearly upset, and it makes the disturbed part of me want to laugh at the reasoning behind why. "I'm sorry, Mabel. We are friends." I glance over at Atlas, who doesn't appear phased or upset that this interrogation is happening at all. I feel bad that I have to lie to her, but no one can know the truth. Not if this is going to work. "Atlas and I just wanted to keep things quiet for a while, but we didn't know that Patty saw us together at the diner last night until Charlotte told me this morning at the library."

"Excuse her, Holland," Gill chimes in, gently tapping Mabel's forearm. "She's bitter because she just found out that Patty's the neighbor of the month for June in the neighborhood."

"That's a thing?" Atlas asks, finally using his voice. "I thought that only happened in the movies."

"Oh, it's a thing," Ed says. "It could be compared to winning an Oscar around here. That is, if the Oscar came with a yard sign, a bouquet of petunias and leaves of dogwood trees, and passive aggressive letters from angry neighbors about recycling habits."

Mabel scoffs, folding her arms against her chest. "I didn't *forget* about recycling day. I was just testing to see if the raccoons were still around."

"Right," Ed says, deadpan.

Gill nods. "A noble scientific endeavor."

I look again at Atlas, who is trying very hard not to crack a smile and laugh. I feel a hint of unease floating away from my body at the sight because just a week ago, he wasn't friends with any of these people. His eyes meet mine, amused laced within them. We are probably thinking the same thing, that Mabel is probably seconds away from unleashing her hatred for Patty on all of us. "So," I say, "what does one do to earn this title?"

"Excellent neighborliness," Ed replies, his voice as monotone as if he is reading off an imaginary description on the back of a product. "Patty won because she hosted her infamous cul-de-sac chili night that we just happened to not be invited to, drove the elderly living in the retirement home to the eye doctor, and repotted the flowers in the pots along Main. And she did it all in a week."

"Wow." Atlas hums. "She sounds like an overachiever."

"She is," Mabel mutters, "but I don't trust her. How could she be neighbor of the month if she didn't even invite the three of us to her chili night? She's probably lying about everything that makes her qualify to run."

"She couldn't have possibly lied about any of the things Ed listed," Gill says, giving Mable a stern and confused look. "My neighbor, Danny, said that his dad can finally see the marigold and lantana flowers in the pots because he has a new set of glasses, thanks to Patty. Danny didn't even know his dad's vision was like that until he saw him get emotional over the flowers. Do you really think that Patty forced Danny to make something like that up, Mabel?"

"And whenever I go to the library, Piper won't let me forget that Patty's homemade brownies she made for the chili night are much better than the ones I made for Christmas three years ago," Ed says, his bottom lip curling down into a pout. "That girl doesn't tell a lie, even if it hurts my feelings."

Mable huffs some air out her nose, making her hair blow up in different directions around her face. She leans back in her seat and folds her arms against her chest. "Fine, I'll stop being upset about Patty, but none of you can come running back to me when you find out that Patty has been lying the entire time to gain some sympathy and give out free meals. Because I'll only tell you that I told you so." Her mood immediately changes when she looks back and forth between me and Atlas. Her head tilts, studying the two of us, and a sly smile coats her lips. "So, the three of us just interrupted your second date then, correct?"

"Well," I begin, "Atlas was just taking me here so I could–"

"Yes," Atlas interrupts. "The three of you have interrupted our second date."

Atlas glances over at me, a hint of a smirk tugging at his mouth, but his eyes are as firm and steady as ever, like he's daring me to correct him. My heart stutters in my chest, and I open my mouth, but nothing comes out. His eyes flick down to my lips, just for a moment, before they land on mine again, staying there.

From the corner of my eye, the others exchange confused glances with one another, but I can't focus on anything other than the way my cheeks brighten in color from the intensity of Atlas's stare.

I briefly hear Gill say, "Well, don't let us stop you from doing whatever second date thing you were doing. We'll…just be over there. By Olivia's soap-making shack. Or maybe even the parking lot. Quiet. Invisible."

Atlas chuckles, softly, a sound that courses down the surface of my skin and licks it with an arrangement of goosebumps. He still doesn't look away from me when he mutters, "Too late for that." He finds my hand under the table and latches our fingers together. "We're leaving."

"We are?" I ask, my eyelids blinking faster than the butterflies flying around the field.

"We are." He grabs onto the box of cookies and stands, and I follow.

I take one last glance over at the others, my gaze landing on Mabel, who is only giving me the largest smile I've ever seen her give to me. She gives me two thumbs up, and my shoulders crunch up to my collarbones when I give her an awkward grin and a shrug before I follow Atlas towards the parking lot.

chapter twenty-nine

Atlas takes us back onto the highway, leading back towards town. I want to ask him where he's taking us this time, or if we are just going back to our houses and our *second date* is complete, but the glint in Atlas's eyes back at the table tells me I shouldn't question what his plans for us are and to just trust him. It's empowering, the feeling beating in my insides, the feeling of longing for someone who lets me breathe, who makes the world feel wide again. Atlas doesn't ask me to be a specific person for him to make him like me more, not like Gordon, not like Emmett or my dad or used to be Corinne.

It's refreshing, because with Atlas, it's as if I've stepped outside my weight, as if I've stepped into some sort of dreamlike state and I don't have to hold everything that has been pulling down on me with imaginary ropes–my mom's passing, my recent break up, my need to prove myself that I can still be the writer I once was, the rocky tug-of-war relationships with my family–alone.

The wind slips through the small crack in Atlas's window, warm and noisy, and when I turn my head to look over at him, he's already looking at me. It's a silent act of reassurance, no question in his eyes or in his expression. He's looking at me like I'm something worth watching, worth holding onto, worth spending time with, even in the quietness surrounding the limited space of his truck and the chaos outside of it.

I could ask him where we're going, but his gentle smile says in the silence that it doesn't matter.

It's not about the place, even if I can write about where he takes me.

It's about the person. It's about *him.* It's about us, fake or not.

It doesn't matter to me anymore, not when this hasn't felt fake at all. This is only day two of our fake relationship, but I don't feel like pretending anything with him.

I can be myself, and that feels like the biggest breath of fresh air I've ever taken.

I lay my head against the headrest and watch the hills and the beginning of the sealine out my window. The sun is moments away from falling below the line of the sea, casting golden ripples on the surface. Eventually, Atlas turns off towards a neighborhood behind the grocery store I never would've known about. The road is full of potholes, but Atlas serves slowly around them. Except for when he slams on his breaks and my chest tightens behind the restraint of my seatbelt.

"Shit," he mutters under his breath, bringing the truck to a stop. I lean forward in my seat, glancing over the tall dashboard just to see a stray black and white striped cat prance in the middle of the road, only a few feet away from the front tires of Atlas's truck.

The tiny fur ball stops right on the white dotted lines of the street, sits down, and participates in a stare down with me and Atlas, daring us to try and drive around it.

"It's so cute!" I proclaim, my hand already pulling at the door handle of my door. It swings open, and I step out onto the pavement. Atlas mumbles something behind me, but I ignore him. Slowly, my feet tiptoe towards the adorable animal, who only blinks at me, unbothered, like it's the one who owns the road and I'm a guest passing through.

"Here, kitty," I coax gently, sauntering toward it before I lower to a crouch a few feet away. I stretch out my hand like I've done this before. "I'm not going to hurt you, I promise."

Behind me, I hear a faint *click* of Atlas shifting the truck into park and the sound of his door shutting. "Holland," he calls out, his voice laced with both annoyance and amusement. "You're going to get yourself mauled by a feral cat."

"You don't know that it's feral," I say, my eyes still zeroed in on the animal. It still doesn't move. "It's like a tiny zebra."

The cat flicks its tail and raises its neck into the air, sniffing. Atlas comes up beside me, towering, arms crossed over his chest. "You are going to try to pick it up, aren't you?"

"Obviously." I withhold an eye roll.

"What if it bites you? What if it has rabies?"

"It's worth it," I retort. "Just look how adorable it is."

The cat finally stands and stretches in slow motion, then with a dramatic swish of its tail, it struts over to me. I hold my breath and watch with wide eyes as it gets closer and closer, rubs against my leg once, then circles around Atlas's shoes for good measure. The cat flicks his ears a couple times before sitting peacefully at Atlas's feet, glancing up at him like it's waiting for him to pick it up.

"Oh my god," I say, a gasp escaping my lips. "I think it likes you!"

"That makes one of us," Atlas says under his breath. His eyes flick down to me, and I know he wants to smile but is forcing himself not to. "You sound jealous."

I stand, my knees protesting in the process. I fold my arms against my chest. "Of course I am." I look back down at the adorable bundle of fur, its black beady eyes beating into mine. Atlas then bends down and grabs the sweet thing, and it *purrs* in his hold. *He thought you had rabies, and you still let him touch you?* I pretend to be upset and stomp my foot. "How could something so cute choose you over me?"

Atlas narrows his eyes at me, and even though he has faux anger plastered on his features, he brings the cat closer to his chest. My smile widens, and he sighs. "Get in the truck before I lose what's left of my dignity," he says.

"Too late," I sing, shrugging and walking back to the passenger side. "But at least we gained a friend."

Atlas groans as he trails behind me, then he gets inside the truck. He sets the cat down on the middle console in between us, keeping one hand around it so it doesn't slip. I check for a collar, but it doesn't have one.

"I think we should give it a name," I say.

Atlas begins to drive again, and the cat saunters the two steps to me, resting in my lap. I pout affectionately and grin, gently swiping over its little ears and back.

"Pothole? Bandit? Piano? Domino? Zebra? Inkwell? Oreo?"

I gape at him. "God, you're terrible at coming up with names. *Pothole*? I'm still questioning why this cat went to you first." I glance down at the little thing. "I like Oreo, though."

Oreo is in fact a boy, and he stays still the entire drive to wherever Atlas is taking us. He even purrs in my lap, and I erase all my false hurt for Oreo liking Atlas first. I've never had a pet before, but I know for sure that I'm keeping this one. That is, if he doesn't already belong to someone else.

The sky turns into a dusky blue with a golden ring around it before Atlas finally turns off onto a road with small homes arranged in a colorful pattern. Couples walk hand in hand with their large dogs on a leash on the sidewalk, and kids are still playing out in their front yards, running in swimsuits around the sprinklers shooting straight up in the air. But Atlas continues driving until the end of the cul-de-sac, pulling up the only house probably on the entire block–or even the entire town of Saltmere–that looks as if it's been waiting centuries for someone foolish enough to come knock on its door. The siding of the house has faded to a dark gray, and the paint is chipped and peeling in long, curled strips, like an individual with claws has scratched at it. The home is at least two floors, and one of the upstairs windows has cracks that spread like a spiderweb crawling over the glass, and behind the window, darkness looms. The entire roof is sagging in various spots, boards warped and splintering under its weight, and the front door isn't visible behind the wooden slabs nailed down in front of it. The ivy slithering up the house looks like it wants to strangle it, and the grass and weeds in the yard are multiple feet tall, appearing like the home's personal jungle.

"Are you taking me here to murder me or something?" I keep my voice quiet and pull Oreo closer to my chest. Luckily for me, he doesn't protest.

Atlas huffs. "No, Holland. I think I've made it clear that I'm not a murderer."

"Then why the hell are we at a haunted house right now?"

"Just wait before you judge it," he says, shifting the truck into park once we are stopped right up next to the curb. He shuts off the engine, unbuckles his seatbelt, and hops out of the truck. Before shutting the door, he tilts his head, giving me a confused look. His eyes bounce from my face to my arms that hug Oreo tightly against me. "Are you coming?"

"Are you *insane*?" I scoff. "It would be nice if I knew what in the world we are doing, Captain Coordinates."

"We aren't going inside the house at all, I swear. We are just going around it. There's something cool in the backyard."

"What, a graveyard?" I shoot back, half joking, half completely serious.

Atlas just grins at me, then he shuts his door and saunters around the front of the vehicle. He opens my door and holds out a hand in front of him, and I hesitate. "Are you sure we will be okay?"

He steps a step closer to the entrance of the truck, his boots crunching on the loose gravel on the edge of the curb. Atlas reaches out his hand and swipes a short, loose piece of my hair that has fallen from my bun behind my ear, keeping a small smile on his face. I want to shudder at his touch, but I stay frozen, staring into his brown eyes. "I won't let anything happen to you, Holland," he tells me, his tone soft and quiet.

My body instantly leans into his hand that is now cupping my cheek. His fingers gently trace the edge of my jaw, and his irises flick down to my lips and linger there. I lick my lips, and he traces the movement before swallowing and meeting my gaze once again. "Can you trust me?"

I nod, and his hand falls out onto the open space between us again, waiting for me to grab it and step out of the truck. I finally do, but I keep Oreo in my free hand as Atlas interlaces our fingers together and leads me up the cracked and weed-filled driveway. Chills fall down every inch of my body when we step closer and closer to the house, and the sun continues to sink lower and lower under the horizon, making the sky darker and my fear strengthen by the minute. I squeeze Atlas's hand three times. He squeezes mine back, glancing down at me occasionally to check on either me or Oreo. But Oreo doesn't seem to mind us walking into the shadows of a clearly haunted house. He just seems content to be held.

Instead of heading towards the front door, Atlas leads me to the side of the house, where an overgrown greenery archway stands in the middle of a fence that divides the front and back yard. The gate creaked open with a sound of a sigh at Atlas's touch, revealing a path of uneven stones that shimmered faintly under the growing moss. *It's a flower garden.*

The air back here smells weakly of damp earth, metal, and lavender, and every plant seems slightly too vivid. Vines twist like veins around rusted iron trellises, clutching at broken and cracked statues that stand as tall as the house and choked flowerpots. Rose petals black as ink curl like fire and smoke have made them welt at the edges and bloom in places they probably shouldn't. Lilies with pale silver veins bobble up and down in a wave to us as we walk, even without any help of the nonexistent wind. A stone water fountain sits in the center of the garden, chipped and dry, but still drips water droplets every once in a while.

Oreo fidgets in my hold, his hind legs kicking at the side of my stomach. With a glance up at Atlas and his reassuring nod, I slowly let Oreo down onto the stone pathway. He scatters off instantly, winding through the cement pots of dead flowers and into the trees that surround the garden.

Atlas must read the concern stuck on my face. "The garden isn't very big, so Oreo can't get lost. I promise," he says.

His words don't help me feel at ease, but I nod anyway. "How did you know this was back here?" I whisper to him.

He talks in his normal tone, not seeming at all afraid. "My mom used to love coming here growing up. The owner actually took care of the house and the garden, once upon a time, and my mom said it was the most beautiful place she had ever been to. The flowers were always in full bloom during the summers. But the owner died the summer my mom turned eighteen. The new owner of the property tried to take care of this place, but it's not an easy task, so they gave up and moved out almost two years ago. This garden has looked like this ever since."

My heart warms at the glimpse into Atlas's personal life, and at how he brought me here to share this memory with him. "I would love to," he continues, "find someone that can revamp this place. I used to come here a lot as a child once I found out my mom loved it. I would love to find someone that can make it beautiful again like it used to be." He looks down at me. "Maybe you can write about it, and maybe one of your readers knows someone who is an expert in flowers. It would be amazing to turn this place into an attraction for tourists. Or, even if you don't write about it, I still want to find someone who wants to help make this place feel alive again. Not just cleaned up, but really cared for." His voice softens, and he scratches at the back of his head. "I don't know, maybe that sounds dumb. But I just hate seeing it like this. Like it's forgotten."

I squeeze his hand again. "It's not dumb at all. I would love to write about this place."

"Really?"

I bump into his shoulder with mine. "Of course." I glance around at the garden once again, and that fear from earlier disperses. Appreciation takes its place in my heart. With Atlas's words floating in my mind, I can envision the beauty that used to reside here, can imagine a young Atlas running through the aisles in between the pots of colorful petals and bees and butterflies dancing and fluttering and bouncing from flower to flower. I can see how lively this garden could become to the public once again, but the terror of a house in front might still be a problem. "We might have to do something about the house if we want people to come."

Atlas lets go of my hand and digs in his front pocket. He pulls out a single silver key and holds it up. "That shouldn't be a problem for long."

"You *bought* this place?"

"Yep." He glances back at the monstrosity. If I look closely enough, I can see the shadows that loom out of the cracks in the windows on the second floor. And if I squint, I think I see a white, ghostly figure with red eyes standing behind the back porch door. I withhold a shudder as I look back at Atlas, giving him a not-at-all scared smile. He immediately registers my expression and tilts his head to the side. "Don't worry, I don't plan on living here. Ever."

I nod and exhale in relief. "So what are you going to do with the house then?"

"Tear it down, extend the garden. Or rebuild, I'm not sure yet. But we will have to hire a priest or someone to deal with the ghosts." He runs a hand through his hair. "Can't have them scaring off the future visitors."

I snicker, the tension in my shoulders loosening. He makes it seem like performing exorcisms are a totally normal weekend activity, something to check off a to-do list. "I'm sure Saltmere has someone for that, maybe has a two-for-one deal for cleaning spirits and weeds."

He smiles, his eyes sparkling with the help of the light from the half-moon rising above us. "I'm not sure if the ghosts will even want to leave." His grin falls, though, when he looks back at the house, up towards the windows. I follow his line of sight. His voice gets quieter when he says, "Maybe they are just waiting for someone to notice that they're still there."

One corner of my lips rises, and I turn to look at him. "I guess we all want that," I murmur. "To be noticed."

His gaze meets mine again, and his eyes linger. "I think you already are," he whispers, and redness crawls onto my cheeks and warms them with the intensity of his stare and the earnestness in his voice.

I glance away, rocking on my heels. "Let me know if you need help with the ghosts. I'm not certified or anything, but I'm great at talking to things that don't talk back."

He chuckles, low and genuine, and it vibrates everywhere in my body. "I'll keep that in mind."

We are both facing the house again, and for the first time, it doesn't feel like it's watching. It feels like it's *listening*.

But the moment doesn't last because a loud yowl and hiss comes from somewhere behind us in the trees, and I don't have time to register anything else before Oreo dashes straight into the back of my legs. My entire front jolts forward, my face smashing against Atlas's chest. His arms tighten around me to hold me still, and he mutters a low "what the fuck" before I slowly straighten.

My own hands are clutching around Atlas's biceps, and when I glance up at him, he's already looking down at me. "Are you okay?" he asks, eyes scanning all over my face and body.

"Yeah," I say.

He turns his head around to look for Oreo, who is now sitting calmly on his hind legs on top of a flower pot several feet away.

I frown. "Did our new pet just try to be a wingman?"

Atlas keeps looking at the cat. "Yeah, I think he did."

Turning my head towards the trees, I squint my eyes and search for any other plausible reason why Oreo would freak out like that, but I don't hear any other scurrying in the bushes near the tree trunks.

I sigh. "The cat's a genius."

"I can't even be upset with him."

We both watch as Oreo jumps off the flower pot and saunters back towards the trees, disappearing from our sight just as quick as he entered it.

"Neither can I."

Atlas trails the tips of his fingers up the backs of my arms leisurely, and I fight the chills that want to spread down every inch of my skin. We keep our eyes locked on one another's, until his hands travel up to my bare shoulders, then to my collarbones. My hands fall down to his waist, and I clutch at his shirt at his sides.

"You're beautiful, Holland," he says.

His finger drags over the pendant of my necklace, then over the chains that keep it in place. My tongue parts my lips and darts over them, and he catches the movement with his gaze. "What are we doing?" I ask, my voice hoarse and unfamiliar.

"What we should've been doing this entire time."

I'm dizzy, out of breath. "What about our rules, Atlas?"

"Fuck the rules."

His hands are now behind my neck, and I'm rising on my toes. But my mind is wandering and stumping over the logistics we *just* talked about last night. "We can't," I whisper, and I want to slap myself for trying to push him away right now. Just a little under twenty-four hours ago, I was wanting his lips on mine. Hell, I do *right now*, but he's the one that made the rules, the one that stopped us from moving forward. I don't blame him, because I'm the one that was hesitant first, but I don't want him to regret this. I don't want him to regret *me* once he realizes what he's doing. "You didn't think that way last night."

"And I hate myself for that," he says, his warm, minty breath hitting my face in various spots. "I just didn't want to pressure you. I *never* want to pressure you." His words cause him to blink several times, like he's processing what he just said. He swallows and his hands begin to loosen and slide back down my body, but I pull him closer so both of the fronts of our bodies are pressed up together.

"No," I say, my tone demanding. "No, don't think you're pressuring me right now. You aren't."

One of his hands swipes another piece of my hair behind my ear. "I just can't help myself around you, Holland. It's consuming, the way I want you."

"I want you too, Atlas," I whisper, and it might be too soon, too sudden, but I don't care. I want him. Everything he's done for me in this short amount of time has been more than anyone else has ever done for me, and I'm tired of fighting my attraction and want for him.

As soon as the words fall off my tongue, Atlas's lips crash onto mine.

chapter thirty

He doesn't hold back, and neither do I. It's messy and beautiful and reckless, our lips swiping against each other's and our tongues colliding like this is our only source of air. Like we've been holding our breath this entire time and finally reached the surface, together. It's mesmerizing and electric, charged with an abundant amount of energy that both pierces through my heart and solidifies my desire for him.

His hands leave my neck and fall back down my waist, until they land on the backs of my thighs. Before I know it, he lifts me up, and I'm grateful that the skirt I'm wearing is flowy and loose enough that I can wrap my legs around his middle. We don't break our kiss as he walks me several steps and sets me back down gently on the cold surface of a cement flowerbed. My head tilts up when he cups my jaw in his palms. He presses his lips on mine for a moment longer before trailing kisses near my ear, then down my neck. I arch my back for him, internally begging him not to stop. My skin hums with need, with his touch, and my core begins to burn when his tongue licks over my collarbone.

My hands slip under his shirt, and he kisses the corner of my mouth. Against his lips, I pant, "I'm on the pill. I'm clean. Please, I just want to feel you."

He halts his movements. Our breaths mix together, our chests falling up and down. "Come home with me," he says.

I can't respond because words are stuck somewhere between my throat and the wild thrum of my heart, caught in the heat of his gaze and the pulsing ache of wanting more. I nod instead, pulling his head back down so he can kiss me one more time before I stand before him.

"Okay," I breathe out.

He doesn't hesitate. He grabs my hand, and I follow him to the line of the trees, where Oreo is laying behind a rose bush. Atlas grabs him with his free hand, and the three of us head back to the truck.

The drive back to our neighborhood is treacherous. It's quiet and thrumming with agitation, but my imagination runs wildly as I picture Atlas on top of me, imagining his fingers traveling down my stomach and curling around the strap of my thong and tugging it to the side. I have to clench my thighs together as I picture his finger drumming inside of me in a rhythm designed just for my own pleasure before I unzip his zipper and slide my own hand around his length–Oreo's *meow* interrupts my thoughts.

Atlas chuckles, like he knows exactly what I was just thinking about.

I adjust the air conditioning so it's blowing directly on my face, slowly easing the scarlet that has crawled all over my skin. I give myself a distraction to send a text to Corinne saying that I will be home late, but she only sends me a million winky face emojis that don't help.

When we finally pull into his driveway, Atlas guides me up the porch steps, holding Oreo in his other hand. Once he opens the front door, Oreo scurries out of his hold and straight towards the kitchen, like he's been here a million times already. But I don't have time to question Oreo's sense of direction because Atlas places his hands on my hips, backs me up against the door, and kisses me again, that same sense of urgency from the flower garden burning through my veins once again.

He trails kisses down my neck as he hoists me up, and my legs wrap around his middle when he walks us straight to his bedroom. He gently lays me down on his mattress, then takes a step away to peer out the door before shutting it.

"Will Oreo be okay?" I ask in a whisper.

"There's nothing harmful in this house that he can get to," he responds, "and he's currently chewing on one of the couch pillows." Atlas's body hovers above me, and I sit up on my elbows and bite my lip. He takes off his shirt with one hand, and my eyes trail up the indents of his abs and the line of his *v*.

"Are you sure you want to do this, Holland?"

I nod frantically, desperately.

"When you want me to stop, just tell me."

I nod again. "You promise you aren't faking this?"

"Does this feel fake to you?"

He tugs at my hand and drags it down to cover his bulging erection through his jeans, and I inhale sharply. There's a darkness wavering in his irises as he waits for my response. I shake my head. "No, it doesn't."

"Nothing has ever been fake for me, Holland, no matter what bullshit rules we made. It doesn't matter that we declared that we are fake dating just a day ago. I don't want this to be pretend. Not with you."

"Me neither," I whimper. And I mean it.

He kisses me again, gently this time, and he lowers himself onto the mattress next to me. Running a hand down my chest, his tongue swipes in circles around mine, and his fingers tug at the buttons of the denim tank I'm wearing, starting at the lowest one. Chills travel down my skin every time his finger brushes against my stomach. Slowly, he unbuttons them all until my breasts are fully exposed for him, and I hear him groan.

"Fuck, Hol," he says. His finger circles around my nipple, teasing it in between his pointer finger and thumb. I sigh, arching my back slightly and my eyes flutter shut. His hand continues to trail down to the waistline of my skirt, and I hold my breath. The pressure is already building in my core just from his gentle touches and from the fact that I haven't been touched like this in over eight months. In too long. I know that if he sinks his hand below the flowy material he will see just how badly my body wants him, just how wet I am for him.

He does just that, slipping his hand under my skirt and swiping a single finger over the material of my thong, and my back arches even more. Atlas continues kissing down my neck and chest as his finger dances over my pussy. He lifts the material and shoves it over to the side, and my lips tremble and my breathing rattles when he slides his finger over my center.

"Fuck," he says again. "You're so wet."

He sinks his finger in, and I jolt, opening my legs as wide as my skirt will let me. I moan into the crook of his neck as he pumps faster and faster, building a rhythm I know I will lose myself to. My hips grind in their own movement to increase the friction. "Yes, baby," I hear Atlas say above my ear.

The seconds that pass by are blurred together, my eyes opening and shutting when he adjusts the speed of his fingers driving inside of me. He grunts when my skirt continues to get in the way, and he slides the fabric down my legs before resuming. I can feel myself coming closer and closer to the edge, but just as I am about to fall, he pulls his fingers out.

My body shivers at the interruption, at the way my pussy immediately misses him being inside. He shifts his position so he's now on top of me with my legs bent at his sides. There's a smirk plastered on his face, but I don't have time to question his motives. He props himself on his knees, wraps his hands around my calves, and lowers his head to my exposed middle, his heavy, warm breath trickling on the wetness down there. My entire body explodes when his tongue flicks back and forth against my clit.

I moan louder and louder. "Fuck, Atlas. I'm close."

He slides his finger back inside, but keeps his tongue brushing against me. My hips continue riding him, jerking up and down. My hands tug at his hair, strands parting in between my knuckles. I switch between tightening my eyelids together and watching the stars behind them blink back to me and focusing on how the line in between his brows deepens with every stroke of his tongue against me. His gaze burns into mine, and I keep slipping between wanting to hold the intensity of it or needing to keep my eyes closed to not fall apart too quickly. Every nerve of my body, every inch of my skin, is alert and lit up with so much exigency, but Atlas continues tethering to my every need, every longing desire I haven't dared to acknowledge until now. Because before I met him, I was gliding through the days without any thought to take care of myself the way he is taking care of me right now.

It's like he is reading the ache between my breaths and answering each silent wish of mine with his hands, his mouth, the steadiness of his presence. The pressure builds and builds, and before I can even fully process it, I'm releasing onto his tongue.

It's euphoria that streams through every cell of mine, in every vein. It's bliss, exhilaration, to be cared for in the hands of a man I could see myself falling for, could spend the rest of my days on this spinning, floating planet. He pulls his hand out from me and gently kisses up my thighs, my stomach, my breasts.

And when I lean up to tug at his pants to convey to him that I'm ready for him, ready for this new step in our relationship, he listens without either of us speaking a single word. We are anchored, bound with one another, connected by the same invisible string, the same ache, the same unspoken pull. I watch with adoration dancing in my irises as he stands to take off his pants and briefs, and they both puddle at his feet before he's back on top of me, one hand gripping the base of his hard, strained cock.

There's already a bead of precum dripping down the head, and as he kneels in between my open legs, I watch it fall onto my pussy. I bite my lip and brace myself for this, for him, when he whispers, "Are you sure, baby?"

I nod. "Yes. Please, Atlas."

"I'm clean. I haven't been with anyone in a long, long time," he adds, and I nod, tugging him by his waist to pull him closer to me. I'm absorbing a sense of neediness, but only for him. I just want to feel him inside of me. I want to drown in the feeling of him filling me, mesmerize the way both of us will become undone for one another.

When he finally, slowly, sinks inside, my back arches again and I moan breathily. One inch at a time, he moves in a rhythm I'm comfortable with until he's fully inside and I can't take anymore. "Fuck," I whisper-shout, my eyes rolling to the back of my head.

"Eyes on me, baby," he says, his callused fingers grabbing at my chin so I can look at him with all of my attention. He pumps again, harder, the tops of his thighs slamming against the bottoms of mine. I whimper. I scream his name like he's my own personal prayer. It's when I feel my second orgasm on the verge of crashing down on me when he increases in speed, messily, and my body tenses just as his does, and we release together.

We stay that way until our breathing and pounding hearts calm. He finds me a rag from his towel closet and helps me clean myself, a smile stuck on his lips. I want to kiss him and repeat this over and over again. I just want him.

We disregard our clothes after I go to the bathroom and he lays back down beside me, wrapping his arms around my middle and pressing a kiss to my shoulder. In a whisper, several minutes into soaking up the melody of our breaths and the hum of the silence, he says, "I don't think I've ever felt this way about someone, Holland." He swallows, and my heart increases speed once again. "I've never wanted someone the way I want you."

chapter thirty-one

My hand twists on the doorknob of my front door, and I tiptoe inside the house. All of the lights are off, and I release the deep breath I had been holding and slouch my shoulders down as I shut the door behind me and walk down the foyer to the living room, when–

Corinne flicks on the lamp next to the couch.

"Well, well, well. Look who finally decided to come home."

"What are you doing up?" I ask her in an unnecessary whisper.

My sister crosses her arms against her chest. On one side of her head, her hair is tangled and wild, while the other is perfectly combed and slicked down. She's wearing a matching, baby pink silk pajama set and bunny slippers.

"Are you performing the walk of shame right now?"

I gape at her. "*What?*"

"You just got laid."

"I have no idea how you could possibly think that," I say, turning my head to look towards the kitchen. I focus on the steel of the refrigerator, the handle of the microwave, the designs on the coffee mugs on the shelves. Anything else that will make the blush creeping up my skin dissolve.

"We might not have been close before today–well, yesterday, technically– but I know the look of someone that just orgasmed at least twice."

I run a hand down my face. "I don't need you to remind me. My body will be feeling the aftermath for at least a week."

Corinne giggles, then stretches her hands out in front of her and tugs on mine, pulling me down next to her on the couch cushion. "Tell me *everything.*"

Her want, or need, to hear of the events of today makes me feel giddy because this is another normal activity sisters do together. Tell each other about their recent hookups. Except, I don't tell her *all* of the details of said hookup, only about the tulips and the garden. And about our new cat, who is currently sleeping on top of Atlas's laundry hamper in his bedroom. Oreo looked so cozy as I was leaving his house that I didn't want to wake him.

"He took you to see a tulip field? Then to a not-haunted house with a flower garden in the backyard?" Corinne gasps. "God, that man is in love with you. No man on the planet would willingly spend time surrounded by flowers if he wasn't completely and utterly obsessed with making you happy."

"Your standards are incredibly low, Cor," I say. "But no, Atlas is *not* in love with me. You can't fall in love with someone you met only over a week ago."

She shrugs. "My standards are so low that I started dating Mac because he held the door open for me once and didn't smell like Axe body spray."

I grimace. "That's your baseline?"

"Hol, that was my *green flag.*"

"That should be your *bare minimum.*"

"Exactly. And we see how well that worked out." She leans forward to retrieve a grape from a bowl resting on the coffee table. "Honestly, I've had more chemistry with hot baristas that remember my drink order and call me 'sweetheart'."

My eyebrows skyrocket at this new information about her. I tilt my head, narrowing my eyes at her. "Were you planning on flirting with the barista before I yelled your name?"

She shrugs again. "Honestly, yeah. I was thinking about it. She was handling those machines like a boss bitch and was rocking that hot pink apron like it was her sole purpose to. I have no further comment." I stifle a grin and toss a pillow at her. "You fall in love over caffeine. You don't get to judge me."

She catches the pillow and leans back. There's a smug smile coating her lips. "Oh, I'm not judging. I'm observing. And I'm observing your face going all soft when you talk about him. Or when he shows up on the doorstep with flowers in his hands and a giddy grin on his face."

"I do *not.*"

"You so do," she sings, then points straight ahead at the dark television screen a few feet in front of us. "Go ahead. Check your face out."

I throw another pillow at her, and she ducks. And I avoid looking at the screen because I know that she is one-hundred-percent correct.

chapter thirty-two

The next day, I bring Corinne and Atlas along to go to Patty's bed and breakfast. We take my car, since the small, yellow cottage-like building is about thirteen miles from the neighborhood. We stop by the library so Atlas and I can drop off our rentals, and Piper won't stop asking Atlas for another cheese coupon and Charlotte won't stop giving the two of us weird smirks and not at all sneaky winks. All I can do is roll my eyes and hold in a laugh.

We pull into the grovel parking lot of the bed and breakfast, but each slot is filled with vehicles and a few motorcycles with Louisiana plates. In fact, every license plate is from a different state other than the maroon minivan in the back corner that has a vinyl sticker that reads *Patty Mobile* in white lettering on the back window.

Atlas nudges his elbow against mine. "Looks like your articles worked." There's a proud, excited feeling brewing in my chest. I smile. "Looks like they have."

We enter through the lobby door, and we are instantly hit with the smells of fresh linen, coffee, and lemon. The lobby is small, with a brown leather sofa in front of an old but beautiful fireplace that has beachy decorations on top of it. The walls are cream colored, and there are multiple seaside paintings hanging on them.

"It's so cute in here," Corinne says next to me, then heads straight to the front desk window, where a woman with bright white, short curly hair and a pink blouse stands behind, smiling affectionately at us. The woman has dark blue eyes and dark pink lips, and her bright gold earrings dangle near her jaw.

If Betty White had a twin, it would be Patty.

Patty leans over the wooden counter, resting her elbows on the surface and beaming at us. "I can't believe who I'm seeing." She straightens, and her shoulders crouch upwards. Then she claps, and both Atlas and I jolt at the sudden sound. Patty glances straight at Atlas, pointing a red painted finger at him. "It's about time I have you and your lovely girlfriend stay here at my place. I was waiting for the time you finally came out of your shell and snagged a beauty like her. Took you long enough."

"Oh," I begin, cheeks heating red, "we–"

"Do you even have any rooms available?" Atlas interrupts. "Looks like you got a full house judging from the parking lot."

He turns his head and winks at me, and I mouth a quick *thank you* to him. The less attention on me and us from this woman, the better. Afterall, she is the reason the entire town knows about us.

"Oh, yes. It's been crazy. I don't think I've ever had this many guests all at once. I'm going a little insane, just a bit." She widens her smile, gesturing at me. "Seriously, thank you so much. You will never know how much this all means to me and my little business."

And Mabel hates this woman? She's kind, even if she's the town's biggest gossip.

"Of course," I say. "I'm just happy to help with what I can. I'm planning on highlighting businesses here in Saltmere for my next article, but it seems like the new tourists have already found some of the charm of this town on their own." I take a look around the lobby, at the paintings. Then at the few pictures in frames along the wall of what must be happy customers. "Do you mind answering some questions about the place?"

An hour later, we head to the diner, then to the cafe, then to the art gallery to ask the same questions to all of the owners of the businesses. All of them were ecstatic to contribute their stories of their startup journeys and their hopes for the future, and it sent a current of energy through my bones. My hand aches from writing so much, but I couldn't feel more elated to showcase all of the hard work the owners have put into each of their small businesses.

When the sun lowers to the horizon, Atlas takes Corinne and I to his grandfather's treehouse so I can take more pictures for my last week's article next Thursday. Corinne babbles the entire time, expressing just how much she loves this small, radiant town, and I agree right along with her. It's like the two of us, with the help of Atlas and the people of Saltmere, have found what home really feels like.

chapter thirty-three

The rest of the week passes by in a blink of an eye. I submit my next article on Tuesday to Ariana, and she has it edited by nightfall Wednesday so Wanderlight can post it on Thursday morning. Corinne and I spend every morning riding bikes to the cafe, where Corinne does, in fact, flirt with Cierra, and I let her while I sip my coffee and listen. She clearly wants the attention from Cierra, whether it's to gain a platonic relationship or to distract her from her downfall with Mac, but it doesn't matter the reason. I'm just happy my sister is smiling and laughing.

On Wednesday, Corinne and I adventure over to the library, and Charlotte and my sister hit it off immediately by giving me shit about my recent *relationship* with Atlas. I try to tell them that it's nothing serious and it doesn't need to be the town's *headline of the week*, but Charlotte just raises her eyebrows at me like she's reading straight through my lies. My sister makes a dramatic gasp loud enough that it echoes through the aisles of the empty library, and Piper hears it through her headphones. She tugs them off of her head and plasters on an annoyed look at us for interrupting whatever she was listening to on the tablet in her hands.

"You *so* like him, Holland. You need to stop fighting it," Charlotte says, leaning over the reception counter.

"I don't," I lie. It's as convincing as a child with chocolate on their face and trying to deny the fact that they did touch the cake.

Corinne snorts next to me. "You're blushing again."

I reach over the counter and grab the nearest book on the stack next to Charlotte's computer. The title reads *19th Century Plumbing Innovations*. I flip it open, ignoring their stares that feel like overwhelming bullets of fire on me. "I hate both of you."

"You both are worse than Bailey and Mary gossiping at recess," Piper pitches in on my behalf, giving her mom and my sister an irritated expression.

"Are those your friends?" Corinne asks her.

Piper scoffs. "They wish. But no." Then she turns to me. "Don't worry, Holland. I also think you're lying to yourself about your feelings for the mysterious cheese man, but I think he likes you back. I don't think you have to panic and swim away in the ocean to the nearest island or change your name or anything. Just, like, maybe tell him you like his face. Or give him a can of soda. That usually works in cartoons."

She shrugs before plucking her headphones back over her ears and goes back to doing whatever she was doing on her tablet.

"I love her," Corinne says.

"Me too." Charlotte focuses back on me.

The doors of the library open and close, and Grace saunters up to the counter, wearing a paint splattered apron and black jeans. Her hair is in a tangled messy bun on the top of her head, and paint streaks take over her face instead of makeup.

"Wow, girl. I'm loving this new look on you," Charlotte says to her, eyebrows raised up to the ceiling.

Grace only responds with a loud sigh. She walks around to the back of the counter, and drops down on the empty chair against the wall next to Piper with a dramatic thud. Grace leans forward, bracing her forearms on her thighs, and covers her face with her palms to muffle her groan that sounds like it's coming from deep within her soul.

"What happened?" I ask cautiously.

Charlotte puts a hand on her hip. "Yeah, why are you wearing more paint than what we bought together the other day?"

"That stupid fucker of a developer keeps bothering me at the gallery. He decided to stop by this morning while I was painting."

Charlotte and I share a look, and her teasing smile vanishes. "Again?" she asks.

Grace nods. "He wanted to talk numbers. *Again.* Which, to him, only means throwing money around that I don't want in my face while pretending he's doing me a favor."

I wince. The Geminis always make my skin crawl, with their slick smiles and louder-than-life presence, like they own every corner of Saltmere they step into. I want, *need*, to stop them, to push back before they take over what's left of this town, but the thought alone makes my stomach knot tighter.

"I have told him time and time again that the gallery isn't for sale. I'm not falling for his traps like the other businesses have. But Kurt just told me that I'm being unreasonable *and* emotional." Grace finally pulls her hands from her face, dragging down her skin dramatically. She flops her head against the wall behind her. "It took all of me to not throw my dirty paint water at his face and call Sam to get him off my property."

"Did you?" Piper pitches in, taking her headphones off again and tossing them and her tablet onto the counter. "Please tell me you did. I have to tell my friends something that doesn't include me finding my friend Josie kissing a boy behind the rec center."

"I thought about it," Grace responds. "Vividly."

Next to me, Corinne blinks up at Grace before quietly saying, "Honestly, you would've been completely justified." The four of us all look over at Corinne, who's been quiet the entire time, fidgeting with the silver and gold rings layering on her fingers. But now, she's only focused on Grace, the color of Corinne's cheeks turning into a soft pink color.

Grace tilts her head to the side. "Sorry, you are…?"

"Oh! Sorry." Corinne's body jolts, like she suddenly remembers she has a spine. "I'm Corinne, Holland's sister."

Grace offers a tired but amused smile. "Nice to meet you. I'm Grace, the owner of the art gallery, if you didn't already catch that."

"She's also known as the local art goblin." Piper adds.

Grace gasps. "I am not!" Then she flicks her gaze over to Charlotte. "Am I?"

"I can neither confirm nor deny." Charlotte throws her arms up in surrender, and Grace only groans again.

Corinne, however, lets out a breathy laugh that she tries to cover up with a cough. "I…I really like your apron."

My eyebrows skyrocket to my hairline, but all of us shift our attention back to Grace's apron. There's at least seven shades of dried paint, a smear of what might be clay, and one bottom corner that's half-singed and blackened like it's been burned recently.

"Thanks," Grace huffs, "it's a one-of-a-kind disaster."

"I like disasters," Corinne replies, but she blinks rapidly and shakes her head. "I mean, uh, not *actual* disasters. Just, um, messy. People. That kind of disaster. Not like hurricanes or tropical storms or anything like that."

Charlotte bites her lip across from me, failing to contain the smirk forming on her face, flicking her eyes back and forth between me and them.

Grace smiles at Corinne, softer this time. "Cool."

The color of Corinne's cheeks darken to scarlet. Charlotte's eyes connect with mine once again, and her shoulders crunch into her neck with excitement, wagging her eyebrows up and down on her forehead.

"What should I do about Kurt?" Grace swivels her head to Charlotte. "I need him to stop coming into the store and pretending to buy something just to get me to talk to him. If I wasn't such a people pleaser, I would tell him to fuck off the second I see his stupidly handsome face." She scoffs. "I mean, why does someone so evil have to be so hot?"

I quickly glance over at Corinne, and her shoulders slouch down at Grace's words. I'll have to ask her about her sudden *interest* in my new friend when we get back home.

"I think we had to have been punished in the astral plane or something, because having Kurt and his minion sons lurking around the town feels like cosmic sabotage." Grace exhales loudly.

"You should tell Sam anyway," Charlotte replies gently. "Maybe make him aware that Kurt needs to mind his business and get the hell out of town before he makes everything in Saltmere crumble to dust."

"I wish it was that easy," Grace says. "I've tried to talk to the other owners that lost their businesses, but they all just push me away because they don't like talking about it. I think they view themselves as failures and are ashamed they fell for all those lies, and it's all Kurt's fault."

"I could try to set up an interview with him," I point out. "I've been wanting to ever since I first moved here."

Ever since I talked to Sam the second day I moved here and I found out exactly what Kurt Gemini and his sons were doing to this town from Sam, I knew I would need to set up an interview with him. Maybe to trick him, maybe to catch him slipping, maybe just to look him in the eye and see if he flinches when I ask him how it feels to bulldoze the historical elements of the town. I know I have to get close enough to hear him lie straight to my face. I'll try to reach out to either him or maybe trick Roman into assembling a meeting with the man behind the fall of Saltmere. I could pretend that I need to talk to him about…Atlas? Given the only two times I've talked to Roman, Atlas seems to be his only topic of interest. Maybe even Sam can help me, help guide the conversation perfectly to where I can catch onto the plans Kurt has for the businesses he swept in and bought and warn the other business owners.

I'm typically not one to write articles that dive deep into tearing down businesses or careers, but since this town and the people have warmed their way into my heart, I can't just sit back and let someone like Kurt Gemini steamroll over it without trying to do something. It might not be my job to play the town's protector, but it feels personal now. This place is starting to feel like mine, too. And if I have a voice people listen to, I want to use it towards another thing that matters for the wellbeing of this town.

"Oh my god, that would be amazing!" Grace shoots off of her chair, instantly zooming the few steps towards the counter. "Could you actually do that?"

"Would he even agree?" Charlotte asks.

"I have no idea, but I want to try." I pull out my journal from my bag on my shoulder. "When I met with Sam, he gave me Kurt's contact information. I'll schedule a meeting with him even if it takes me the rest of my time here to find out what he's got planned."

Corinne seems to have regained her earlier awkwardness. "That kind of sounded badass, baby sis." She's giving me a wide grin.

I beam at her. "Thanks. I've been working on my investigative journalist voice."

"It's giving NPR but with a vengeance." Charlotte nods.

Grace leans on the edge of the counter, resting her chin on her propped up palms. "I don't know, I kind of like it. Holland's on a mission. It's heroic. *Very* courageous. Someone should paint her mid-speech with wind blowing through her hair."

"Oh my god," Corinne utters, "don't encourage her. She's already the most prosperous one in the family." She drags a hand down her face and groans, but my smile widens on my face at her words. A grateful, happy feeling coasts down my body.

"I'm not encouraging her," Grace says, turning her head to look at Corinne. "I'm just impressed. Clearly, it runs in the family."

Corinne's teasing expression falters, her face now stuck in shock. She gasps softly when Grace winks at her, but Grace doesn't look at my sister for long before she pops a hand on her hip and focuses on Charlotte. "Now that my rant about Kurt Gemini is off of my chest," Grace begins, "I think it's time for *someone* to come clean about something."

Charlotte's face reddens like she knows exactly what she's about to say. *Does Grace know about Sam too?* "Do you mean Holland? Because she and Atlas are the talk of the town right now. They went on two dates together and everything."

Grace flicks her gaze to me. "Oh, I'll get there." She glances back at Charlotte, smirking and pointing at her chest. "I'm talking about you, Miss *Single* and Hot Librarian."

Charlotte grabs onto Piper's headphones discarded on the counter and plops them back over her little ears. Piper, who was busy flipping through a graphic novel that was left near the computer, frowns at her with confusion, but doesn't say anything when the faint streamline of music flows into her ears.

Charlotte faces Grace with a stern look, eyes wide and lips pursed. She whispers, "You know better than anyone else that my daughter has the biggest mouth in town and will tell *everyone* what she hears."

Grace throws her head back in a laugh, her blond bun flopping over to the side. "That's because she learns it from her own mother. Remember what happened when you told half the farmers market that Timothy Chen was secretly in love with Whitney Gardner just because they were standing next to each other at the peaches stand?"

Charlotte scoffs. "That man was staring at her like *she* was the peaches. Do you blame me?"

"We're getting off topic," Corinne, to my surprise, pitches in. "I want to know the tea Grace was about to share."

Grace grins, glancing back at Piper for a brief second before facing all of us. "Little Miss Librarian isn't so single after all, isn't she?" She doesn't let Charlotte say anything. "I was just talking to Patty Corrington this morning at the cafe, and guess what she told me?"

"Hopefully something about Holland and Atlas?" Charlotte grimaces.

Grace shakes her head. "Nope. Well, yes, but not at first. She told me that you and the town's sheriff have been running around together when you two think no one's watching." Grace folds her arms. "When were you going to tell me about Sam?"

Charlotte shifts her gaze over to me and sighs. "Looks like you aren't the only one that people will gossip about in this town."

I huff a laugh. "I'm just glad I won't have to bear their stares and questionable opinions by myself."

Grace gives her a big smile. "Welcome to the fishbowl, Charlotte. Population: everyone with eyes and way too much free time."

Charlotte snorts, then slouches down onto her desk chair with a loud thud. "Great. This is just great."

"To small town fame, selective hearing, and someone probably watching us through the blinds right now," Grace says, leaning against the counter and picking up a cup full of pencils and pens near the computer. She raises it in the air. Corinne raises Piper's empty Capri Sun pouch, Charlotte raises her cold mug of coffee, and I raise the discarded, half-eaten cheese stick next to the stack of books to my left. We clink them all together with a quiet *thunk* and a chorus of giggles.

Grace bumps her shoulder into Charlotte's. "Now tell us everything, Charlotte. We need to know about you and Sam before we find out from the rest of the town."

chapter thirty-four

On Friday afternoon, Corinne finally calls Emmett and our dad.

The conversation, at first, is very emotional and productive. Our dad muffles heartwarming words through what sounds like tears on the other line. I can see the relief that soars down Corinne's body when he tells her that he's happy she's safe and spending time with me. Emmett tells Corinne how much she's missed at the office and how worried everyone there is for her, which only makes Corinne's shoulders crunch into her neck and wince at the reminder of her life back home.

When they ask why she's staying with me and Corinne tells them both that she and Mac are getting a divorce, the conversation turns for the worse.

"What the hell do you mean, Cor? Are you going crazy?" Emmett's anger stabs at us through the little holes of Corinne's phone speaker.

"We haven't been happy together in a long while," Corinne replies, not a hint of sadness laced in her tone. If I hadn't spent this week with her, I would think she is lying. But she hasn't spoken of Mac at all, and she has seemed more relaxed and content these past few days than I've ever seen her before.

"So you just decided to uproot your life and disappear off the face of the planet in the middle of the night just because you're *unhappy*?" Emmett scoffs. "You can't just leave your job and clients behind. You have responsibilities, Corinne. God, it's like I don't even know who you are anymore."

"I don't know who I am, Emmett. Stop making me feel like my feelings about my own life don't matter, because they do." Corinne rolls her eyes, even though he can't see her. "I quit on my clients before I even left, and I directed them to Wesley and Eric. They have been attorneys for longer than I have, so I know they would be in good hands."

"Are you going through a midlife crisis? Is that what this is? Do you need help or something?"

"Emmett," our dad warns, "don't talk to her that way."

"Maybe it is a midlife crisis, but who cares?" Corinne says. "I'm finally happy now, Emmett. You don't have to worry about me."

"Of course I have to worry about you!" Emmett screams. "You think moving to a nowhere town in the middle of the East coast with Holland is going to magically make you feel better again? Are you just going to live off your savings?" He scoffs on his line of the call, and there's a sound of a door shutting closed. "And don't even get me started on Holland. What is she even doing these days? Still playing pretend journalist? Traveling to random places in the world and interviewing people for that sad magazine that no one reads?"

"Emmett!" My dad snaps again, sharper this time, but Emmett barrels on, twisting the knife that is puncturing through my chest.

"She hardly makes any money, Corinne. How is this your big solution? You're basing your entire *fresh start* on someone who thinks writing about anything she sees in a foreign place makes her interesting."

Corinne shifts beside me. "That's not fair," she says quietly, and her dejected tone makes my heart pinch, for choosing to not defend both me and herself.

"What's not fair is watching you throw away your future because you're clinging to some fantasy life with a sister who's stuck in make-believe."

A tear tumbles down my cheek. He doesn't even know what I'm doing here in Saltmere, let alone what I've spent my entire journalist career doing by *traveling to random places*. He doesn't believe that what I'm doing matters. *Why am I shocked?* He's never been supportive, never has given me the chance to prove that sharing stories of people with different lifestyles and backgrounds *does* matter. That giving a voice to the overlooked corners of the world is worth something. That *I'm* worth something.

I swallow hard, blinking against the burn in my eyes. He's not just insulting my job, he's dismissing every late night, every interview, every risk I've ever taken just to *be* here.

I don't pay attention to what is said in the rest of the conversation. My dad raises his voice, but Emmett matches his tone, not caring that I'm also on the line, reflecting on the hurtful words that only neglect everything about me. Corinne begins to shut down next to me on the couch, rocking her body back and forth with her phone trembling in her hands. But I don't listen. I *can't*. I can't listen to the belittlement and dismissive attitude of my own brother. I can't do it anymore, can't pretend to be content with my life when my own family can't see the importance in what I do.

When I stand to leave the house with a red, streaked face, the first place I want to stop at is Atlas's. The last time I saw him was Tuesday morning when he stopped by with another two coffee cups from the cafe for me and Corinne, and he told me that he would be going out of town until this afternoon. He didn't tell me why, but I've missed him. I've missed sitting in his truck and listening to the music he knows I like, I've missed him taking me to the beautiful places he knows I'll be excited to write about. I've missed him caring about me.

I don't know what we are, but there's no one else I want to be with right now.

"Wait, Holland," Corinne says from the couch behind me, but I don't stop walking towards the front door. I slip on a pair of flip-flops, grab my bag, and slither out the door without looking back.

chapter thirty-five

Atlas answers a second after my first knock.

His eyes scan over my features before his hand wraps around mine and he pulls me towards him. I bury my face in his chest and my tears soak into the material of his shirt, but he doesn't seem to mind when one of his hands splays out on the small of my back while the other shuts the door behind me.

He leads me to his living room and helps me sit down on his couch. He holds me against him, his hand trailing up and down my back until I can calm down. After what feels like a decade's worth of tears have fallen down my face, his fingers tilt my chin up, and he keeps them there, softly brushing his fingertips against the skin of my jaw and my neck.

"What happened?" he asks gently, but his voice is unwavering.

I sniff, swiping at the salty wetness on my cheeks. "It's nothing, really. I don't really know why I'm so upset." I shake my head. "My family has done this before. It's normal for them to make me feel less than them because they've basically done it my entire life. It's pathetic how much I still care about their opinions."

"It's not pathetic, Holland. Your feelings never are. What did they say this time?"

I meet his eyes, careful not to blink to not let anymore tears fall. "This time, it's my brother. He's mad at Corinne for how she's now living her life and decided to rope me in with his insults towards her." I exhale shakily, my voice wobbling despite my effort to hold steady. "He's trying to persuade Corinne into thinking that being here with me is a mistake. That Corinne's just running from her problems." I sniff again, swallowing down the burn that is threatening to rise. "Then he turned it on me. Said I don't make money, that what I do isn't real, and that I'm just playing pretend. The usual comments from Emmett about me."

He stays quiet for a moment, searching back and forth between my irises and rolling his lips together. It's not the type of silence that makes me feel ignored, but rather the kind that feels like he's choosing the right words to say.

"Your brother doesn't get to define your worth," he finally says. "He doesn't see what I see. He hasn't read your articles or watched the way people open up to you like you're the first person who's ever actually listened to them. That's not pretend, Holland. That's powerful."

My breathing falters, and a single tear escapes, racing down my face.

"And if he can't respect that," he continues, "then maybe it's not your job to keep shrinking yourself just to make him comfortable."

My lip trembles. I look over to the window behind the couch, imaginary fire climbing up my face from his words and the reassurance they bring. The sun hovers above the line of the sea. Sailboats cover the surface in the distance, bobbing up and down with the ripples in the water.

"Will you take me somewhere?" I ask, glancing back at him.

He blinks. "Of course, Holland. Anywhere." He stands, then extends his hand out for me to grab, unknowingly tugging me away from the depth of my doubts and leading me back to the haven that is him. When my hand meets his, he squeezes it once before grabbing my flipflops for me and guiding me out the backdoor. We trudge through the grass, passing the endless blank stares of the gnome collection, and walk onto the dock, where another one of Atlas's boats is roped to it. He helps me step in, but I take one last look up at my house. Through the glass of the back door, I can see Corinne looking back at me.

Maybe I should stay with her. I shouldn't have just left like that. She's probably hurting, too.

But she gives me a soft smile and a wave, mouthing the words *I love you* before giving me a thumbs up.

I mouth *I love you too* back to her, meaning every ounce of them. She doesn't look sad like she did just under twenty minutes ago, and I take that as a good sign. I'm hoping our brother's words didn't get to her like they did to me.

Atlas starts up the boat, and in a matter of seconds, the sound of the motor intensifies and the boat slices white streaks through the water. The front end rises up towards the sky, and I let my back slouch against the cushion of the chair, the one next to Atlas's. He smiles at me, and I smile back before angling my head up towards the sky and feeling the warmth and sprinkles of ocean water on my face.

Atlas takes us further and further away from land and civilization, only shifting the direction of the boat westward towards the only island nearby.

"Are we going to the hidden cove? The one with sea glass?" I ask him.

Atlas nods. "Is that alright?"

"Yes," I reply, excitement intertwined in my tone. "I've been looking forward to coming to the cove since I first came to Saltmere."

He tells me that the cove is only accessible at low tide as we get closer to the island, where the entrance for it is a narrow gap in the line of jagged black rocks, half submerged and slick with salt. The boat rocks side to side against the calm waves towards the opposite end of the island, and on the other side of the rocky tower in the center, the world opens up into a secret crescent of shore wrapped in dunes and overhanging greenery. The calls of ospreys circling overhead and the hush of the waves are the only sounds surrounding us.

Atlas ties the boat off to a large rock in the sand before stretching his hand out for me to grab and helping me down. My flipflops land on the grains with a soft *thump*. The sand is hot and soft, untouched by any type of life. Atlas holds my hand as we trek through it towards where the tide has hollowed out a shallow pool inside the dark opening. But my eyes catch on more colors glowing under the surface of the teal, crystal water. Glittering beneath and scattered along the edges of the entrance, chips of what looks like glass reflecting a multitude of hues arrange themselves chaotically. I gasp, turning my head to look at Atlas.

"This is *stunning*," I say in awe, my eyes widening against the rays of the summer sun and my jaw hanging towards the ground at our feet. The entire scene looks like a painting, something that would sell at Grace's art gallery, something that feels too beautiful and primeval to be real. My body lunges forward, pulling Atlas now behind me as I run towards the entrance. The tall tower of rock immediately shields us away from the sun above, and I take off my shoes and dip my toes into the piercing water.

I keep my hand latched together with Atlas's as my eyes travel up and around the inside of the rock. When my gaze lands back on the water around my ankles, I lean down and pick up a piece of the glowing glass. The rock is worn smooth from years and years of waves, and they're thumb-sized and rounded like river stones. This one, specifically, is in a shade that resembles cobalt blue, but there's a number of colors: seafoam green, amber, and lavender.

"There's a rumor that these are all from shipwrecks," Atlas begins, his voice low and coming from right behind my ear. "And some believe that they were left behind by storms that swallowed entire coastal villages. But in the sun," he pauses to gently pull my hand back to the entrance, where the sun beats down on the rock, "they catch fire, flashing like stained glass windows from beneath the water."

"It's beautiful," I whisper, my eyes glued to the tiny slivers and specks of light bouncing off the rock in my palm. "How come no one comes here? It's a shame that no one gets to see this." I gesture with my hand to the entire small island, the hidden cove cradled in its center like a secret.

Atlas squints up at the entrance of the cove. "Yeah, I agree. But I think that's what makes it special."

I glance at him, eyebrows raised. "What do you mean?"

"If everyone knew this existed and came here, it wouldn't necessarily lose its charm, but it wouldn't be a secret, the glass would disappear, the tide pools would get trashed, and someone would probably try to open up a shaved ice stand or something." "I guess that makes sense," I say. "But I was thinking of writing about this place. If more people saw this, they'd fall in love with it. They'd want to visit."

"I get that," Atlas says gently. "It's just, places like this cove here don't survive being loved by too many people, you know?" He clicks his tongue. "This island has been here like this for decades. Untouched and unscathed. Quiet. Full of miracles that no one really notices unless they try to." Folding his arms against his chest, he nudges at a piece of sea glass at his feet. "Once people start coming here with their phones and beach chairs, it stops being like this."

I frown, not because I disagree, but because I know he's right. "So I shouldn't write about this place?"

He shakes his head. "No, I think you should absolutely write about this place. But maybe write it like it's still a secret. Like a place you would only find if you were really looking. Like someone told you in a whisper."

I slip the sea glass in my hand into my pocket. "A secret worth keeping."

"Exactly."

"If everything goes well with my articles, maybe we could organize tours to this place. That way no one can just come here on their own unless they have a boat and know exactly where to go."

Atlas smiles. "I think that's a great idea."

My own smile matches his. "Thank you for bringing me here," I say. "I'm really glad it was you that showed me this place."

"Oh, we aren't done yet," he says, huffing a laugh.

"What do you mean?" I frown.

He doesn't answer me. I watch the back of him walk inside the entrance of the cove. He turns back to me, his smile so wide that I can see his dimples from here. "Come on," he shouts, "we're going swimming."

chapter thirty-six

"I didn't bring a swimming suit," I utter.

"You don't need one," he responds mindlessly, thumbing his shorts and shirt off in less than three seconds. My lips part open and I suck a sharp breath in when my eyes skim over his bare chest and the horizontal and vertical lines that roam over his stomach. I trail over the *v* of his abs that seeps under the waistline of his underwear. He catches me staring and laughs.

"Are you going to swim in your sweats and t-shirt? Or are you going to strip?"

My brain scatters. "Uh," I say, blinking rapidly at him. My underwear is far from being referred to as sexy, and my bra is one of the four bras I still have from my college days. It's maroon and plain, not at all steamy and exciting. *Do I take both of these off too? Is he keeping his briefs on?*

My question is answered when he takes his underwear off, shimming them down his hips and letting them pool with his other clothes at his feet, exposing his bare ass for me. "You better hurry and get naked. I won't be under for very long." Then he saunters off to the edge of the sand, turns his head back at me with an evil grin, and cannibals into the water.

I hurry and undress, unlatching the hooks of my bra and snaking my thong down my legs before joining him. I holler into the air right as I sink into the water. Bubbles rush upwards besides me before I can, and when my head bobbles up out from the surface, Atlas is already looking at me with a wide smile.

"Holy shit, it's freezing!" I chant into the air, my words bouncing off every surface surrounding us. I slick back my hair and swipe at my eyes. My teeth clatter together and my naked body covers itself with goosebumps. My chest rises and falls as I inhale deep breaths to calm my racing heart and force my skin to get used to the chilly temperature of the liquid. Luckily, the cove itself isn't deep and the tips of my toes can touch the rocky ground. But Atlas swarms in closer to me swiftly, wrapping his arms around my back and pulling me into his warm chest.

"This is better," I whisper, studying the droplets of water that trickle down his neck.

"Warmer?"

"Yes," I say. He smiles down at me before pressing a kiss to the corner of my mouth, and my stomach roars to life with butterflies. Our legs dangle and slide against one another occasionally under the water, and I can feel his length press straight against my stomach. My core pulses with an intense and sudden need, but I force it down. For now.

Atlas's hand travels up my spine, and I withhold a shiver. "Where did you go these past few days?" I ask him.

"I went back to Charleston," he replies, his jaw hardening. "To visit my mom's grave."

"Oh." The air in my lungs fails to come out properly. I glance away from him, focusing my attention to the different coloration of the rocks in this cove and blinking away the emotion rising to the back of my eyelids. *You can't cry every time someone mentions their mother, Holland,* I tell myself, but it's no use. Swallowing as hard as I can, I ask, "How did that go?"

"As well as you can imagine, I'm sure." He sighs. "It was her birthday on Wednesday. I visit her on that day every year."

My mom's birthday isn't until October 10th, and I don't think I'll be able to function while I visit her grave. I flick my eyes back up at him, and he's still staring back at me, his gaze soft and comforting even with the sentiment swirling in his irises. "Does it get any easier?" I ask, sniffing. "Visiting her?"

He shakes his head, and all of the hope in my chest sparkling with steadfast light fizzes out. "No," he says. "It doesn't. Not for me. Every time my truck pulls into the cemetery parking lot, my entire body feels weak and I can't seem to breathe normally. But I visit her because it's the only way I can still hear her voice." His head tilts towards the opening of the cove, and I watch little beads of water trickle down his neck. "There's not a day that passes that I wish I could sit in front of her headstone and just talk to her. It's like when I go to that back corner of the cemetery, I can think clearly. I can find some hope and some closure all at once. Hope to continue living in this life without her, closure for the life I thought I would have with her in it. It's quiet there, like the world pauses just long enough for me to feel what I need to feel without it swallowing me whole." He cracks a smile, a dimple on his right cheek popping out. "Maybe none of that makes sense, but it does to me."

"It does," I mutter. "It makes sense to me, too."

He looks back at me. He smiles sadly, an understanding forming between us. Under the water, his fingertips gently and treacherously skim over the skin of my hip bone. With a playful smirk taking over the sadness, he hitches his hands around my thighs and hoists me up to wrap my legs around his middle. His length, long and rock hard, sits right in between my legs, and my breasts flatten against his chest. Cold water splashes around us and my yelp echoes into the opening above us, but that doesn't stop him from brushing his lips over my exposed collarbone.

My eyes flutter shut when he kisses up my neck. "Is this okay?" he asks in a whisper and chills crawl up my skin.

I nod. "Yes." The word comes out in a breath.

"Good." He backs several inches away to trail his finger down my collarbone to the tops of my left breast, his eyes dark as they pour into mine. He slowly sinks his finger lower and lower until he circles my hardened nipple. "What about this?"

My body aches with the need for his finger to keep sliding down my wet skin and into the lips of my pussy. I need him to stop teasing me and bring his tongue down onto my nipple instead of his finger. "Yes," I utter. My hips grind once against his dick nestled perfectly in between my thighs, and his smirk is replaced with a rigid, pained look. I do it again and again until both of his hands grip behind him at my crossed ankles. He pulls me off him but keeps one hand wrapped around my back, keeping me close.

His lips crash into mine, tongues swirling and colliding together in rapid motion. I grip at his hair on the back of his neck, his fingers splay and press deep into my skin above my ass. Gone is the teasing, the soft and slow movements. Now, his free hand is rushing to my pussy, and when he sinks a finger in without any hesitation, I gasp into his mouth.

I break the kiss, letting my head fall back. I moan loudly into the cove. Then I moan into his shoulder, sinking my teeth into his soft skin when his pumps get faster and faster. His touch and the firmness of his hold on me feels like ice to the fire building inside of me, the fire that I never realized was burning me alive before Atlas. The desperation for him to completely consume and devour me floods every other thought in my head, and, god, I don't want it to end. But I don't know if my core can take it anymore.

"I'm already close," I pant. "*Fuck*, don't stop. Please."

The only response I get is him sliding another finger inside me, pumping quicker and quicker until stars dance behind my closed eyelids and I know I can't take anymore without falling over the edge.

My body tenses. I release onto his fingers, my mouth stuck in an *o* shape and I moan his name into the sky. I hardly feel him slither his fingers out from me, and I keep my eyes closed to force my lungs to fall back to their normal breathing rhythm. I only open them again when he kisses me softly.

The act flickers me back to life.

I go to reach for his dick under water, but his hand stops me.

"What?" I ask, dumbfounded. "Why?"

He brings my hand up to kiss the back of it, acting like a true prince charming here. "I just wanted to touch you."

"Okay, and you did," I protest. "I want to touch you now."

"You can, but later. We have to get back to town."

"Why?"

"Dinner." He kisses my nose, then pulls me and my naked body back to the shore and the opening, staying silent while we dress back into our clothes. He lets me use his jacket as a towel while he pulls on the rest of his clothes, and we head back to Saltmere.

chapter thirty-seven

Once on land, Atlas drives us to the diner, but we choose to take the food back to my house. We get enough to share with Corinne, who, when we walk inside the front door, is currently packing all of her belongings back into her suitcases.

"What are you doing?" I ask her, speedwalking to the kitchen table to set down our beverages and beelining it to kneel next to her.

She gives me a sad smile. "I have to go, Hol," she says. She continues packing her clothes in her suitcase, not caring about folding them.

I shake my head. "Go where? You haven't even been here for very long. Why now?"

"Mac called. He's in Chicago for a week and…he wants to talk. I figured it's time for me to stop running from him and actually have a conversation."

"Does this have anything to do with what Emmett was saying on the phone?" I keep shaking my head, and the room begins to spin. I don't want her to leave. She just got here. I just got her in my life; I don't want her to leave and have us go back to how we were.

She sighs. "What he was saying was complete bullshit, and you didn't deserve that. I'm sorry." She stops packing to rest a hand on mine. "But I need to fix this. Not…*fix* things with Mac, necessarily, but just," she pauses, shutting her eyes for a moment before looking back at me, "to say whatever we didn't the first time. I need to make peace. I think I'm in a better place to do that now."

My throat tightens, but I nod. "Closure."

"Yeah. Closure." She squeezes my fingers in her hold. "I don't know how long I'll be gone, but I'd like to come back here." She glances behind me, up to Atlas. "It feels better here." She smiles at me. "With you."

My body tightens. I don't want to think about going back to New York next week. But I nod again anyway, because her reassuring words make me want to cry. "It feels better here for me, too. And I'd love to be close to you, wherever that is."

Atlas kneels next to us, setting all our food down on the carpet. "Let's eat," he says, giving me a gentle grin and a wink.

"Oh my god, *yes*," Corinne says, clapping her hands together. "I'm starving."

chapter thirty-eight

"Thank you for agreeing to meet with me," I say on Saturday morning as I sit down at one of the cafe booths, plopping my laptop, notebook, and pencil pouch all on the booth table chaotically because I left my bag at Atlas's last night. I didn't want to sleep alone in the house after Corinne left. I cried in his arms for at least an hour before sleeping in his arms on his bed.

I press the record button on my phone and set it on the booth seat.

Kurt Gemini sits before me, wearing a black suit and tie, his fingers interlocked on the metal surface. His dark brown hair is combed over to the side, and his face is free from any facial hair. He's giving me a smirk that shows the creases at the corners of his eyes, and his eyes are a dark brown and raking over me, not just at what I'm wearing but as if weighing the smallness of my existence against his.

Kurt gives me a nod and a closed-lip smile. "I was so shocked that the writer from Wanderlight Journeys wanted to interview me, especially when this magazine focuses on exposing the secrets of the towns the writer visits. Isn't that right?"

I tilt my head to the side. I know what he's trying to do, or trying to say. He's leveling the playing field. Expressing in as little words as possible that he understands what I'm trying to get out of this interview. But I've dealt with people like him before. People who are full of skepticism and faux confidence because they know they are doing something entirely, morally and ethically, wrong.

I give him a bright smile. Suddenly, I have obtained the gift of duality. "I mean, I wouldn't say that, necessarily. As a writer for the magazine, I make it my goal to fully understand the towns I visit. I make it my objective to visit the places that hold the history of the town and bring that history back to life. But I do have to say, this is the first place I'm visiting that is on the brink of falling apart and surrendering to a developer, like yourself. A developer who wants to shred that history into as small as possible pieces that will float into nonexistence. So I'm here to find out why."

He laughs, and it boils the blood in my body. He leans in and says, "You sure are brave, Ms. Anderson." He sits back against the booth seat and sighs, then checks the time on the fancy watch on his wrist. "Before I answer any of your questions, we have to wait for–"

He cuts himself off when he flicks his eyes up to something behind me. The door of the building jingles, and I look over my shoulder to the person coming into the cafe, but air is stolen away from me. A familiar man wearing a light gray dress shirt and black trousers strolls in, wearing a smug smile as his piercing blue eyes connect with mine.

Gordon.

"Right on time, Mr. Cho," Kurt says when Gordon gets closer, after he stands up so he can shake Gordon's hand. The two men grin happily at one another while I sit frozen in place, looking at them with wide eyes.

"Please, call me Gordon." Gordon scooches in next to me, and I want to stab him with my pencil. He runs a hand through his black hair, then folds up his sleeves to expose his tawny wrists and manicured fingernails. He turns his head to me, smiling as he puts an arm around my shoulders. "I missed you, Holland. It's so good to see you again."

I shimmy out of his hold, giving him a tight smile that I'm faking. "I can't say the same. What are you doing here?"

"I asked him to be here," Kurt answers. "He works for the magazine too, and I trust Gordon." His gaze cuts to me. "I wanted to ensure that the article written about my company was in good hands."

If I didn't already know about the trouble this man is causing to this town, I would try to not let that comment get to me. I would shake it off, because for any other company, it would make sense for a business owner to be cynical when a journalist wants to write about their establishment. Especially when the article is about a development company. But this is Kurt Gemini we are talking about, who willingly took advantage of the trust of the other business owners in this town and diminished all of their hard work.

So I ignore the dig and narrow my eyes at Gordon. "How do you two know each other?"

My ex-boyfriend, who I trusted with not only my work but also with my heart, gives me a smile that makes me sick to my stomach. "We met two years ago at our end of year ceremonies for all employees and their families. Kurt, here, showed up to talk to–"

"To talk to your mother, Holland," Kurt says, exhaling. When my jaw falls open, he rolls his eyes. "Oh, don't act so naive. She was threatening to ruin my career and my company, all because she was upset over some decisions I made in the past."

"Wait, I didn't know this." Gordon holds up a hand. "You told me you were wanting to talk to Jenny to have an issue written about Gemini Development."

"H-how…how did you know my mom?" I ask Kurt, my chest rising and falling in anticipation. My stomach feels as if it's performing cartwheels over and over again, and I swallow down the lump in my throat as I wait for his response.

Kurt smirks. Then he shrugs. "I would rather not talk about how we knew each other, but instead talk about how she was only seconds away from ruining my entire empire with a few lies she made up before she got sick. God, she was so demanding, don't you think?" he asks, then chuckles. "After all, she's the reason Jenny gave you this job. She was the magazine's main lawyer for quite some time. Poor Jenny was under so much pressure to make sure the company's attorney's daughter got the position she didn't deserve."

The entire room begins to spin, silencing all the distant chatter and coffee machines. I blink and blink, but my heart beats and beats, racing as if my body is seconds away from crossing the finish line after a marathon. My fingers wrap around the edge of the cool table to ground me, to help hold me steady against the weight of Kurt's words. I shake my head, because none of this can be true. My mom didn't help me get this job. She supported me, yes, but she didn't see how much time I spent perfecting my resume after I graduated from Columbia. She wasn't there to see how I spent night after night before my interviewing rehearsing lines as if I was studying to be in a play. She only heard from my own mouth how I was one of the two finalists for this position of a travel journalist. She was in Chicago working while I called her with the news, and she was proud of me.

There's no way she was the lawyer of the company. She told me that she knew *I* could do it, and I did. On my own.

Kurt's lying to get a rise out of me.

Right?

I force myself to laugh. "Is this how you intimidate people you think are below you? You bring in their ex and make up lies about their dead mother?" I toss a thumb at Gordon but don't look at him. "You two would become friends. Both of you are cruel, sick people."

I push on Gordon's upper arm to get him to move so I can leave this booth after gathering all of my things. Thankfully, he complies, but I stop in my tracks when Kurt says, "You and my son make a great pair, Holland. Both of you are scums of the earth that came from women who spent far too much dreaming instead of living in reality."

chapter thirty-nine

My shaking hand forms a fist before knocking on Atlas's door. I know he's back from the warehouse where he had left early this morning to meet a potential customer because his truck is in the driveway. My body doesn't even feel like mine, and the skin of my face is burning and swollen from crying in my car on the way here. In a matter of seconds, the door swings open, and the man I'm falling for stands in the doorway, wearing a white t-shirt and jeans, a red ball cap covering his dark hair. His chin is covered in stubble, but his soft lips are curled down in a frown as his eyes take in my appearance.

"Who hurt you?"

I hiccup as he pulls me inside and tucks me into an embrace. I slam my eyes shut when the side of my cheek smashes against his hard chest. Lately, it feels like all I've done is cry to him. He's becoming my personal safety net.

He puts his hands on my cheeks and rears his head back. He works his jaw aggressively. "What happened?" he asks.

I sigh. I spent the short drive mustering up the confidence to talk about the words Kurt left me with. I search Atlas's eyes. "Are you Kurt Gemini's son?"

Atlas's lips part, and his hold on me loosens. "What?"

"I just met with Kurt to interview him for another article." I look down and fidget with the necklace around my neck. "I didn't even get to ask him any questions about his motives for the town before he brought in Gordon. Apparently, they know each other, and apparently, my mom helped me get my damn job!" I huff a slobbery laugh because, of course, my tears are back. I swing my arms out to my sides. "My mom was supposedly the lawyer for the magazine and helped convince my boss to hire me. Isn't that insane?" I pace the entryway of Atlas's house. "But do you want to know what's more insane than all of that? Kurt Gemini confessing to me that me and his son make a great pair." I stop and turn back to him. "Are you his son?"

I finally look at Atlas's eyes again, and if looks could kill, I would be lit on fire in the middle of this house. He puts his hands on his hips and exhales, swallowing hard. "Yes."

I open my mouth to speak, but Atlas cuts me off. He stares at something behind me, but I can't stop analyzing his body language, can't stop the conclusions rushing through my brain. "I am his son biologically, but I have nothing to do with him. So before you go assume that I am another face behind the fall of this town, let me make that clear. I don't have anything to do with him or Roman or Warren, or anyone else affiliated with that fucking company. Or family."

I take a step closer to him, placing a hand over his chest. "Hey," I say, my voice quiet. He looks down at me, the vein in his neck pulsing chaotically. I bring my hand up to his neck to soothe it. "I wasn't assuming that you had anything to do with Kurt."

Atlas releases a shaky breath. "I'm sorry," he utters. "I know. I'm sorry." He leans down so our foreheads touch.

His arms wrap around my waist. "I just get so angry sometimes when I think about him."

"Can I ask why? I mean, besides what he is doing to Saltmere." I raise my head so I can meet his gaze. "You don't have to tell me. But I just want you to know that I will listen, whenever you're ready."

Atlas leads me to the living room, and we sit down on the couch. He rests his elbows on his knees and rubs his hands together, and I can see all of the emotions, all of the thoughts, processing on his face. I tuck my legs under my thighs and wait for him to build enough courage to tell the stories that I'm sure he's never said out loud before.

"It was just me and my mom growing up," he says, quietly. "We lived in Charleston, just thirty minutes away from my dad and his new family, but I didn't know any of them. My dad never wanted anything to do with me, and that was fine because I had the only parent that I needed. Until she wasn't here anymore.

"My mom died when I was seventeen. She had a stroke, and it took her away in her sleep." He sniffles, and I reach out to grab onto his hand. He smiles towards the ground. "She was so full of life. She is the reason why I love this town, why I moved back here, because she loved the beach and the people. She loved living here. But eventually, when I came along, she had to move us somewhere where she could find a more stable job with more income, because my dad refused to help her.

"They were never married. My mom was the other woman, but she didn't know at the time. My dad's business was brand new at that point, and he was visiting Saltmere to start developing here, but him getting my mom pregnant with me made him move back to Charleston and pretend that my mom didn't exist in his life. But my mom loved him.

Really loved him, so she followed him. She could've gone anywhere. She could've tried to stay in this town. But she chose Charleston because that's where my dad was, and she thought she could try to still be a part of his life, or at least make him be a part of mine. Of course, he denied even knowing her when she showed up at his house after I was born. His wife, Camille, called the police, and because of their status, she was arrested. I don't even know what happened to me then, but she got me again when she was out. From then on, she never tried to talk to my dad again.

"When she died, I couldn't legally live on my own, so I didn't have a choice but to go live with my dad, Camille, and my two brothers. They were only a few months younger than me, and I was forced to go to the same academy as they did. And they made it their duty to make my last few months of high school hell."

Atlas releases my hand to run his through his hair. He scoffs. "It was like they couldn't accept the fact that I technically was the oldest son, and before I came back in the picture, Warren was supposed to become the second chain of command for the company. By this time, Gemini Development was huge. The word got out that my dad had another son, and to save face, my dad announced that I was going to be the second chain of command. And fuck, did that piss off my brothers. They got their football teammates to pick on me. Completely trash my car, the car that was my mom's before she passed. Jump me while I was walking home from school. Accuse me of stealing, cheating, whatever. I only lived with them for five months, but it was the worst five months of my life."

"I'm so sorry," I croak. "That's horrible, Atlas. You didn't deserve any of that."

He's quiet for a few seconds, before his anger returns. "And the worst part of it all was the shit they did at my mom's funeral. I was dating this girl, Madison. She was the only person I thought was on my side. She was the only support I had left. The funeral was during the first week living with my dad, and my brothers didn't even know what I looked like then. Kurt assigned himself to give the eulogy, and I couldn't take the bullshit that was coming out of his mouth, so I went into one of the rooms of the mortuary, just to walk in on Roman fucking my girlfriend. Then Warren showed up and gave me a couple *brotherly* punches to my face, and I broke my nose. And Camille was behind it all, too, so I couldn't even go to a responsible adult. I couldn't go to anyone because the only person that truly cared for me was gone."

"Oh my god, Atlas," I say, out of breath. I can't even process everything that he's been through.

He turns to me and grabs my hand again. His thumb caresses gently over the back of my palm. "Kurt is a horrible person, and so is his family. I…I never want to be like them. That's why I kept my mom's last name because I never want to be associated with them."

"You aren't like them, and you never will be." I tilt my head. "So no one knows that you are Kurt's son?"

"Sam does. But that's it."

"So that's why you don't like Sam," I say, nodding.

"Yeah. I think that he would've exposed my real identity already if he was planning on it, but I still struggle with trusting him. Or anyone, for that matter." He exhales. "I wish I could've been there with you today. I hate that Kurt said all of those things to you. I had no idea about any of that, I swear."

I glance away because my throat begins to sting. *Poor Jenny was under so much pressure to make sure the company's attorney's daughter got the position she didn't deserve.* Kurt's words swirl in my brain and in my stomach, and the notion to cry again springs to light. I want to call Jenny and demand the truth, or more glimpses of it, because what if Kurt wasn't lying and I don't deserve this job?

I've spent so much time just these past few months questioning whether or not I am good enough because of Gordon's excessive edits and commands. I came here to not only prove to others at the company but *myself* that I am more than what Gordon tried to shrink me into. That I do deserve this job, this byline, this life I'm building for myself.

But now, with Kurt's voice echoing in my head and the questions of why Jenny has given me so much grace in this job ringing louder than any reassurance, that old doubt seeps back in, loud and poisonous.

Was Jenny close to my mom too? She had to have been. She never attended the funeral, but maybe she couldn't have left the office for as long as I did. Is that why Jenny let me take so much time from being at the office after my mom's funeral? Not just out of sympathy, but because she was grieving too, in her own silent, hidden way?

"Come here," Atlas says, bringing me out of my thoughts. He tugs me closer to him, and my head rests on his firm chest, and everything, all of the pent-up emotions I have tucked away since the funeral, since I returned to New York, unravels out of me. It's like I have entered through a tunnel to that single day, to that single *second*, that my mom took her last breath in her bed, with my arms wrapped around her. My tears soaked up the top of her hair, and my sobs echoed into her and my dad's bedroom, and I screamed for my dad to unlatch me from her because my arm was falling asleep and my body couldn't stop shaking, but he was at the store picking up her favorite canned soup and a new book for her to read. He wasn't home. No one was, except for me, a daughter and a person that only she could understand, but she was gone, too.

Being in Atlas's arms launches my flailing body back to the moment I called my mom when I got my job at Wanderlight, how I couldn't stop sobbing on the phone with her because she was the only one that cared enough about what I wanted to spend the rest of my life doing. I only called her because I knew she could give me the boost of confidence, the correct dosage of reassurance, that my mind craved for, because her words always were a slice of ecstasy that tossed out any doubt from my mind, until now. I went home to Chicago a week after the good news and launched myself into her embrace, a place that felt like home, like forever.

I don't want to believe Kurt. I don't want to believe that my mom is the reason I am a writer for Wanderlight. It might not matter to others how they got the jobs that they have, but I feel betrayed, solely because I have spent most of my life being the oddball out of my entire family. I don't have the gift of patience or persuasion or persistence like Emmett or Corinne or my mom to become a lawyer, and I don't have the gift of problem-solving or verbal communication or interpreting technology like my dad. I have spent all my life searching for my purpose, constantly questioning why I wasn't smart in all subjects like my older siblings, or why I was struggling to read at all, but once I found my love for writing and began pushing myself to overcome my challenges, I thought I had caught up to them, in some form. I thought that, yes, I might be on a different path than them, but I didn't have to be different from them.

But I didn't get to where I am on my own. I know I don't have the gift of confidence, but any hope that I did catch a tiny scrap of it has withered away after my conversation with Kurt.

Kurt was right about one thing, at least. Atlas and I do make a great pair. Right now, there is no one else I would rather spend my time with, or have hold me as I spiral into a whirlpool of grief and confusion and despair. We both may be lost in this world of cruelty, but we were brought together somehow, and we can hold onto one another and walk over the trails of broken promises and place shields of armor up against the acts of betrayal from our loved ones.

I don't know how much time passes, but Atlas lets me cry in his hold until I fall into darkness, and sleep washes over me.

chapter forty

The morning sun shines brighter on this side of the East Coast. It's better here, in this small town I wish I could stay forever in, because of the way it casts golden light over the man next to me, sipping his coffee without a hint of stress laced over his skin. It strengthens the charm that is already potent, already unyielding, with the way it softens each of his features.

His jaw is sharp and jagged at all times of the day, pulsing as he grinds his teeth together when something weighs heavy on his mind, but right now, with the daffodil shade of the rays casting down on his face, the sun picks out characteristics others overlook and softens them because no shadow can harden him here. Streaks of honey lose themselves in his usual chocolate hair, as if the light itself can't resist lingering. His eyes, when his lips crowd the edges of his mug, meet mine and I can only focus on the freckles that reside inside them because they only appear when he's caught in the sunlight, like the day wants to leave its mark on him.

The more I look at him, the more that sadness pinches my heart. I don't want to leave him, or this town, or this front porch that we sit together on, listening to the hum of the ocean and watching Saltmere awaken with the sun.

"What are you thinking about?" Atlas asks, setting his mug down on the table between us. His slippered feet nudge my bare ones.

I only smile at him, though my eyes are still swollen from the night I spent crying and words feel massive in my throat. I place my mug next to his and stand, trudging the few steps to sit down on his lap. My arms wrap around his neck and my cheek rests on his shoulder, and that's when I finally release the breath stuck in my chest and sink into his tightening hold.

"Are you okay, baby?" he whispers, and his voice vibrates down my body. I'll never not want him to call me *baby*.

"Better now," I reply, my voice weak.

His hand travels up and down under my sweatshirt I'm wearing, his fingers rough against the skin of my back.

"I don't want to leave," I finally say. He doesn't stop his movements, but I feel his bones tighten.

"I don't want you to leave either."

I sigh again, the ache of my mom's lies still lingering like a bruise I can't stop pressing. "I don't think I could've done anything here without you."

He moves me back so he can meet my gaze again. One of his hands cups around my cheek. "I don't want to let you go." His thumb swipes up and down my chin and jaw, and I withhold a shiver. "You make it too easy to forget everything else."

My eyebrows frown. "What's there to forget?"

He doesn't have the chance to answer me before a loud shriek punctures the air down the street.

"Rufus! Rufus, you get back here before I sell you to the circus!"

Atlas groans, forehead dropping to my shoulder. "Patty."

The shrieking continues, closer this time, the sound ricocheting off the neat Saltmere houses like a fire alarm nobody asked for.

We break apart just as Patty barrels into view sprinting down the sidewalk, hair sticking out like it's been through a wind tunnel. She's wearing slippers, one of them bent at the heel, and waving an empty leash in the air.

"My dog's gone rogue!" she announces as soon as she sees us, as though a national emergency is unfolding right outside Atlas's porch. "Little beast slipped the fence, and if that witch Mabel finds him first–"

"Patty Jean Corrington!" A new voice slices in, sharp as the morning air. I glance up the street and spot Mabel herself, gliding down the sidewalk with a Green Basket grocery bag in one hand. Sure enough, a small brown blur trots proudly at her heel.

"Speak of the devil," Atlas mutters under his breath.

Patty whirls, eyes narrowing like a gunslinger in an old western. "You!" She points an accusatory finger. "You stole my dog again!"

Mabel doesn't flinch. She simply lifts her chin, aiming it high into the air on her cracked concrete runway. "Stole? Please. Rufus was wandering into traffic. I saved him. *Again.*" She gives Patty a onceover and smirks. "Not that you deserve him."

Patty gasps so hard I think she might choke on air. "I'll have you know Rufus loves me more than he's ever loved anything, especially you. You're nothing but a nosy old–"

"Ladies," Atlas interrupts, pinching the bridge of his nose like this is a weekly occurrence. With my hand in his, we trot down the porch steps and walk to them. But Patty and Mabel are already circling closer to one another, Rufus sitting in the middle of the sidewalk like a referee waiting to blow the whistle.

I bite the inside of my cheek to keep from laughing, because the last two minutes have turned from Atlas helping me forget the events of yesterday into the Saltmere edition of a duel at seven in the morning.

Patty's finger is still jabbing the air. "You're just jealous Rufus prefers me. He always has."

Mabel sniffs, clutching her grocery bag tighter. "If by prefers you, you mean he bolts every time you leave the gate unlocked, then yes, I suppose he does."

Rufus barks once, as if confirming.

"See!" Patty cries. "He's on my side!"

Mabel bends down, cooing. "Rufus, darling, you nearly got yourself flattened by a Buick. Don't you dare scare me like that again."

The dog trots straight to her, tail wagging like a flag. Patty throws her hands up, scoffing. "Traitor!"

But Patty snickers, and my eyebrows shoot up in surprise. *She just…laughed?* A short, surprised little sound that startles me as much as it seems to startle her.

Mabel pauses mid-pet, eyes narrowing. "Did you just laugh at yourself?"

"Don't get used to it," Patty snaps, but her shoulders shake again. "He's just…he's a menace. Been one since the day my brother brought him to me all those years ago."

Something softens in Mabel's expression, the corners of her mouth tugging upward. "He *is* a menace. You know how many plants I've had to replace because he thinks they taste good?" She laughs. "It's a good thing he's adorable."

They both glance at Rufus then, who's sprawled across the sidewalk with his tongue lolling, completely unbothered by their decades-long war.

Patty sighs. "Maybe he just needs two women to keep him in line."

Mabel arches an eyebrow. "Are you suggesting joint custody?"

Atlas snorts beside me. "Now there's a headline: *Saltmere's Fiercest Rivals Share One Dog.*"

Patty glares at him, but Mabel's smirk grows. She offers Rufus's leash, still dangling uselessly from Patty's hand, back to her rival. Their fingers brush, not warmly, but not with claws either.

"Fine," Mabel says. "We'll try it. But don't you dare feed him those dry biscuits you call food."

Patty's mouth opens to protest, but then she huffs, almost–*almost*–smiling. "We'll see."

And for the first time since I've known them, the two women stand side by side, united in their mutual exasperation with a slobbering dog.

chapter forty-one

Two days go by, and I've called Corinne every single night. It's a new dynamic for us, being apart most of our lives to suddenly living together for a matter of days and now feeling comfortable enough to call daily. We talk about everything, from the clothes she's wearing to how many tourists have started to trickle in from my articles to how the meeting with Mac went.

It went horribly, apparently, but she won't share the details. I only know because the second that she left the restaurant where she was meeting with her ex-husband, she called me with a trembling voice and couldn't stop sniffling.

She's going back to Los Angeles for a while, but she told me that it's mostly a trip to pack up her things and quit her job. She's serious about finding a new adventure for herself–something that will require her moving across the country to be closer to me in New York. It's bittersweet, the feeling of being able to have her in driving distance, wherever she decides to go. But the other half of me can't stop questioning whether or not she's ready to leave behind the life she built for herself. Her old routine, her job, that version of herself in LA. Change looks good on her–brave, even. But I know how grief can disguise itself as reinvention. I just hope that this move isn't her running away, but running towards something. Towards healing, towards finding something she truly wants.

It's now Tuesday, and I wake up on my own couch where Atlas and I slept last night after watching a Marvel movie. It's easy, strangely, being together like this. It's like we've slipped into this quiet routine without really meaning to. He brings over coffee each morning, and I leave both the front and back door unlocked for him. We order in at the diner, sometimes go and sit and talk to Phoebe while we're there and listen to her tell the story of how the place opened just over thirty years ago. Then Atlas and I sit on the back dock and swing our legs in the cold water, doing absolutely nothing. Yet it feels like everything.

He's still asleep, the blanket kicked off and one arm stretched behind him. I watch his chest rise and fall for a long second before quietly pushing myself up from the cushions. As my socked feet hit the carpet, his body jolts, and his hand wraps around my wrist.

"Where are you going?" he asks groggily, his voice rough and jagged. It sends a shiver down my arms.

"I was going to go to the cafe. Bring you coffee this time."

"Wait," he says, one hand rubbing his eyes and the other reaching for his phone on the coffee table. "What time is it?"

"It's a little after eleven."

"Shit."

"What?"

He stands and checks his phone, fingers scrolling on the screen. "Fuck."

I stand too. "What is it? Are you late for something?"

His fingers type something, then he looks down at me, a hint of a smile present. "*We're* late for something."

Atlas doesn't tell me what we are late for, only that I need to wear something nice and be quick to meet him in his truck. The nerves in my stomach float and wobble the entire drive towards Main Street, and they only increase in size every time Atlas refuses to tell me where he's taking me. The town passes by through the window, and I stare at the moving reflection of the truck in the store windows with Oreo purring in my lap. We pass the cafe, then the diner, then the library. Three of my favorite places here.

I whip my head to him. "I think you should know something about me." I force myself to not smile. "I *hate* sitting here in suspense."

Atlas chuckles, bringing his hand over the console to hold mine. "You're fine. I promise, you're going to like where we're going."

We're heading towards the boardwalk, the same one that the festival was on. It looks empty as we get closer to it, and the parking lot only has four cars parked near the entrance. We park next to a minivan and get out. Atlas holds my hand as we walk down on the wooden boards.

"You know I've been here before, right?" I ask him.

He smirks. "Oh, I know. How could I forget? You kissed me here."

I scoff, shooting a pointer finger up towards the clouds. "Um, I'm pretty sure *you* kissed *me*. I was basically coerced up on that stage by Mabel, but it was you that leaned in first. Don't get it twisted, Mr. GPS."

"Ah. We're back to those nicknames."

I nod, smiling. "Yep."

He shakes his head, but tightens his grip on my hand, squeezing it three times. We walk with Oreo trekking next to us towards the edge of the boardwalk and down the creaking, old stairs that lead to the rocky beach below. But my breathing hitches when I see all of my new friends standing around a table with an array of breakfast foods on top, the tablecloth fluttering in the breeze. Charlotte, Grace, Mabel, Ed, Gill, and the rest of the festival board, Dez, Vance, Jessie, and Sebastian wear the same excited expression. Phoebe from the diner stands next to the owner of the cafe, Sandy, and even Patty has planted herself right next to Piper and Sam under flickering string lights that cast a golden glow over all of their smiling faces. The sound of the waves isn't as loud as their loud *surprise!* that they shout at me.

My heart swells in my chest, and I bring my hands to my rosy cheeks once Atlas and I step off the final step. "Oh my god," I say, and when my eyes find Piper's and glance down at the phone she's holding up, I can see my sister's grin and her blue eyes, and my vision becomes blurry.

I feel Atlas's hand on my back as I walk to each of them, embracing them as tightly as I can. "What is all of this for?" I ask when I hug Mabel.

"This is a little thank you for what you've done for us and our little businesses," she says in my ear, but loud enough that everyone hears.

"We are just so grateful that you've helped us all out this past month," I hear Patty say behind me. I let go of Mabel, and Patty rests her hand on my shoulder. She gives me a kiss on the cheek, which I know that her pink lipstick will stain on my skin.

"Seriously. Your article about the festival brought in so many people," Vance begins. "I haven't seen that great of a turnout in years. And the streets of the town don't look so empty anymore, and we have you to thank for that."

I can't stop the tear that trickles down my cheek. I chat with my sister briefly before she has to hang up, then talk to everyone individually, sharing more hugs and tender words that I will never forget. We eat the food that Phoebe brought from the diner and crowd around the small table, and I find myself tucked in between Charlotte and Atlas and sitting across from Jessie and Patty.

We talk about my experience here, about my next article I'm planning to write that will talk about every hidden treasure people can visit in Saltmere. The last article I plan to write for this amazing town. Everyone asks a million questions about mine and Atlas's relationship, which the two of us haven't even discussed, but Atlas answers each one with ease while I lose myself in the feelings of actually having friends. *Real* friends, not the kind that I only see behind office doors in the city and run into in the break room for a quick, meaningless conversation. These people around us are the kind of people who scoot over to make room, who know each other's drink orders and make inside jokes with one another. I feel like I'm a part of their circle, a part of the bond they have with one another, and my cheeks ache from smiling all morning long, but my smile stays plastered on my face even when the party ends and Atlas takes me back home.

chapter forty-two

Atlas guides me through my front door, his hand splayed on the small of my back. I can't stop smiling. I can't stop the euphoria rupturing down my body, can't stop the happiness that courses through my veins and makes everything in this house, everything in my line of sight brighter, better.

"I can't believe you all did that for me," I say, turning my head to look up at Atlas. He's already smiling down at me.

"Believe it, baby," he says. "You and your work deserve to be recognized and appreciated."

I rise to my toes and press a kiss to his cheek. He picks me up, and I chant into the air in surprise. He takes me to my bedroom, where he lays me gently on the mattress before crashing down beside me.

I shower kisses down his neck as I cradle in closer to him. His hands roam under my blouse and over the clasp of my bra, unlatching it before I can blink. I shimmy off my flowy pants and toss them onto the floor. I tug at his belt, unfastening the buckle and sliding it through the holes of his jeans, but when I look up at his face again, his smile is gone.

"What's wrong?" I ask in a whisper.

"I just…" His voice trails off. I see his shoulders deflate. "I'm just grateful that you came here. That I met you."

The corners of my lips rise. I cup his cheek. "I'm grateful that I met you too, Atlas." My thumb rubs over his stubble. "I know it hasn't been long, but I feel like we're connected somehow. I feel like I've known you my entire life. You've not only shown me around this town, but you've shown me a piece of myself that I didn't believe anyone could see." I sigh, the heat of his gaze too unbearable to withstand. My eyes land on his Adam's apple. "I'm happy to be here with you."

He kisses me, then worships my body the way only he knows how to do. Both of us press our naked bodies together and our hands wander over familiar paths, but being intimate and vulnerable like this still feels brand new. We study one another with our fingers that touch the places our bodies love, with our mouths that whisper promises onto our skin in the form of branding kisses. Kisses that expand the language of each other, slow and soft, then quick and messy. It's a beautiful rhythm, losing myself in the hands of Atlas, someone who I never thought I would ever begin to love.

chapter forty-three

When I wake up in the afternoon on Monday, Atlas isn't laying in the sheets next to me, only an imprint of where his body once was. I blink to adjust my sight, and I notice the folded sheet of lined paper. Opening it, I read in Atlas's familiar handwriting:

Had to stop by the warehouse again to meet another customer. I'll be back around five with some food from the diner.

-A

Smiling to myself, my head falls back onto the pillow that smells just like Atlas's soap and cologne. My eyes flutter shut, and I inhale deeply into the covers. Yesterday, at the party the people of this town threw for me, I never felt more seen, more appreciated, and it's all because of the man I can see myself falling for, can see myself being with if I just had more time. I only have a few days left here. And before yesterday, I had just interviewed Kurt and got revealed a truth I didn't know could break me as much as it did. I rub over my eyelids and exhale as my brain begins to circle and tumble over the events that flash back in my mind like a movie.

Betrayal hums through my bones and sings through my bloodstream, a cruel lullaby I can't seem to silence, even after being with Atlas. He washed away the resentment forming in my body when I needed it the most, helped distract me from the hurt absorbing my mind until I couldn't remember any of it for a brief moment of time, but it's all rushing back to me now that I'm alone. It's inching closer and closer to my heart and bubbling up my throat in the form of burning tears that I am tired of shedding. I don't want to think this way, to reimagine the relationship I had with my mom, to reconsider all of the work I've done for myself.

Did Gordon know about my mom's *help* the entire time we were together? And *why* did he have to show up with Kurt at all?

I didn't even get the chance to interview Kurt. I didn't ask him any questions that would guide me towards finding out his hidden agendas for Saltmere.

But there's one last person that can give me the information I need.

The time on my phone on the nightstand reads just a little after one. *Plenty of time.* Swiping off the covers, I shoot off from the bed, slip on a pair of sweats and a shirt that I've left here, and race out the back door.

Once inside my house, I lock the back door behind me and saunter to my bedroom. I pass Corinne's open door on my way. I pluck my phone out of my pocket and slide up on my notifications, reading the text that she sent me this morning that says:

`Currently sweating through my fifth tank top and questioning every decision that led me to own 23 throw pillows. Also just found a bra from 2016 under my couch. Pray for me.`

If my mood didn't consist of self-doubt and deception right now, I would laugh at that message. But I forward another text before tossing my phone on my bed and tugging all of my clothes off to change into something more presentable. I opt for a pair of jeans and a buttoned shirt I stole from my sister and head out the front door, throwing a leg over my bike and pedaling towards town.

The breeze blows my messy hair back behind my shoulders, my bangs waving in every direction on my forehead as I head towards the parking lot of the boardwalk.

Roman Gemini leans on the end of his truck, appearing just like the first time I met him–minus the booze laying at his feet and the clear indication that he is drunk. He wears a smirk and a ballcap that I know Atlas has a matching one in his closet. Up close, I can see just how much they resemble one another. They have the same jawline, the same hazel shade of eyes. The same crooked nose that perfectly fits in well with the rest of their sharp features. The same hair color, the same tall and burly frame. *God, they really are brothers.*

"Thanks for meeting me on such a short notice," I say to him, leaning my bike gently on the ground and brushing my hair back.

"You caught me at a great time, actually," he says. "I just got done meeting with Grace at the gallery and was about to head back to Charleston."

"Grace?" My eyebrows bundle together. "Why?"

"Don't worry," Roman responds, swiping a hand through the air between us. "Nothing's going to happen to her gallery. I'm making sure of it."

I frown, suspicious. "How?"

"I know what my dad's plans are." He shrugs. "Isn't that why you want to meet with me?"

My eyes go round. My text to him didn't specify the details as to why I wanted to meet with him today. I figured that he would assume it was about Atlas, given that Atlas has been a persistent and ideal topic of interest for him both times I've talked to Roman.

"Yes," I say, standing my ground. "I didn't get to ask your dad any questions during our interview when I met with him yesterday. There was–" I huff a breath, "a little misunderstanding at the cafe during our meeting time."

Roman tosses his head up towards the clouds, his laughter loud and obnoxious. "Yeah, I heard about that. Your ex was thirsty for a little bit of cash. And that bit about my dad bringing up your mom? Cruel, but expected."

"Wait." I pull back. "Kurt paid Gordon to show up yesterday?"

"Of course." Roman nods like this is normal and that *I'm* the crazy one here. "That's typical behavior for my dad. Paying people under the table–sometimes literally– just to prove a point. And his point yesterday was that he didn't want to feel like his business was being investigated by the town's journalist."

"What does he have to hide, though? What is he planning on doing?"

I risk a glance in the slit of my bag, just to make sure my recorder is recording. It is. I would write all of this down, but Roman isn't waiting for me to catch up.

Roman takes off his hat and pulls at his hair, shifting his gaze to the rocky ground. "God, I could get in so much trouble for this," he mutters.

I wait for him, not wanting to push anything. The silence stretches between us until the weight of it finally tips him over.

"He's not just buying Saltmere," he says. "He's clearing the entire east side. For his own private resort, spa, golf course, gated marina–the whole nine yards." His shoulders deflate. "He's been buying properties under shell companies for well over a year now. Small businesses, private homes, even half of the beaches. All of it's going to get paved over."

"What?" I blink, jaw falling. "That's protected land–"

"Was," Roman interjects. "He bribed a guy in the zoning department to reclassify it as 'underutilized' land. Once it's reclassified, it can be rezoned for commercial development. He's already got fake environmental impact reports drawn up."

Chills crawl up my skin. "All of this is illegal, Roman."

Roman throws out a humorless laugh. "It's classic Kurt Gemini, Holland. The man doesn't just bend the rules. He rewrites them with a stolen pen."

I open my mouth, but Roman continues, his voice sharper than before. "You want to know the real dirt on my dad? Ten years ago, back when he tried to do business in the next town over, Greystone, he got caught up doing almost the exact same thing. He bulldozed a neighborhood that he claimed was abandoned, but people were still living there. Elderly tenants. Families. He shoved them out without any warning, any type of compensation. One of them, an older gentleman, died of heatstroke trying to move his stuff out on eviction day."

I gasp, my stomach twisting. "Why didn't anyone stop him?"

"They tried," Roman replies. "But by the time the lawsuits caught up, he'd already flipped the land and moved on. Settled everything quietly and paid off judges. That's just how he and his company works. Fast, dirty, and done before the damage fully sinks in."

"And what? Saltmere is his next casualty?" I'm in shock, but Roman seems to think that this is inevitable.

Roman nods, guilt swiping over his features. "Except this time, it's worse. He's already started hiring contractors, and none of them are local. He doesn't want anyone in Saltmere knowing what's coming. Once summer's over, he plans to start demolition."

The back of my neck prickles.

"He doesn't like that your entire reason for being in Saltmere is to uptick the tourist interest in Saltmere. He doesn't want anyone to catch on to his motives. So, he panicked when you wanted to interview him. All he wants to do is control the narrative."

"And you and your brother are his sidekicks."

Roman shoves a finger up in the air, shaking his head. "No, that's where you're wrong." He leans in closer, tapping on my bag with the same finger. "You can stop recording this part."

I frown and take a step back. "What?"

"Come on, Holland. I know you're recording this conversation. And I'm okay with that. You are welcome to use everything I just told you in your next article. But I want to say something off the record." Slowly, I reach into my bag and click off my recorder. "Okay, it's off."

An evil smile plasters on his face. "I'm taking him down, Holland. From the inside. Every shady deal, every shell company, every fake permit he's pushed through. I've been keeping records. Emails, bank transfers, contracts with signatures he thinks my brother and I haven't seen. I've been building a case for months. And I can give it all to you."

My lips part, and I blink rapidly to make sure I'm hearing this right.

"I play the dumb son, the party boy, the guy who doesn't care about anything," he continues. "And my dad believes it. That's his biggest mistake. He thinks no one around him is smart enough to be a threat." He takes a step closer to me. "But you? You could be the thing that finally tips his entire empire, everything he's built, over. I just needed to make sure you were actually in this. That you wanted to burn it all down."

"You want to sabotage your own father."

Roman nods. "He doesn't deserve a legacy. He deserves a headline." He takes a step backwards to lean on his truck. "I want to warn you, though, Holland. You're a problem now, and my dad doesn't like problems. Especially not ones with press passes. I want you to stick with Atlas and be careful. Publish the article about the company when you leave Saltmere so Kurt can't find you immediately. And take Atlas with you."

chapter forty-four

I rush back to my house, head straight to the table, and open my laptop. I press play on my recorder and type everything that Roman told me, not hesitating to not leave out any vital information about Gemini Development. I even write down everything about how Kurt and his family have treated Atlas, his *secret* son, his entire life–even though I don't plan on using *all* of those details. I wouldn't do that to Atlas. My phone pings next to me with an email from an unfamiliar handle, and when I click on it, there are endless amounts of documents about Kurt's *under the table* business attached. I open every single one and type all of the data onto my document.

Gemini Development won't be able to recover after I expose all of this.

Hours pass by swiftly by the time I finish transferring everything over and organize my article. I don't have to submit this article until at least Monday, when I'll be back in New York, sitting behind my office desk and missing the life I have here in Saltmere. But adrenaline is coursing through my bones right now, blocking away the sadness that I know will crash into me in a matter of hours.

I jolt in my chair when there's a knock on the door. I check the time on my phone that reads it's almost five o'clock, when Atlas should be back from the warehouse.

Smiling with excitement, I jog down the entry hall and whip open the door, but it's not Atlas standing on the other side.

It's Gordon.

"What are you doing here?" I ask, frowning. "How did you find where I'm staying?"

The corners of Gordon's lips rise, but it's not a genuine smile that he has on his features. Instead, guilt is washing over his face. "I might've asked Kurt."

My stomach falters. "How the hell does he know?"

Gordon shrugs. "I have no idea." He scratches the back of his jet-black hair, rocking back and forth on his feet. He looks nervous, an emotion I never thought I would see on Gordon Cho. "Can I come in? I'd like to talk to you."

I suck my teeth. "No." I start to shut the door, but Gordon's stretched out hand stops me. "Please, Holland. I'm sorry for what Kurt said. I didn't know what he was going to talk about when he contacted me to come to this town." His hands shoot up in the air. "I swear."

"It doesn't matter, Gordon. I don't have anything to say to you."

"It'll only be a minute, I promise. I just want to apologize, and then I'll be out of your life."

That sounds tempting. But we work for the same company, so that might be impossible. I sigh as I relent. "Fine, but only for a minute. I have plans tonight."

I don't, not really, but Atlas should be returning any second now.

Gordon slips through the door in front of me, and I shut it behind him before following him to the table. I slide my laptop away from us, but that's the first thing Gordon's eyes catch on. "What are you working on now?"

"That's something between me and my editor."

Gordon's shoulders deflate. His brown eyes go soft when they land on me, and he gives me a sad smile. "That's fair. I'm glad you are working with someone who cares about your work."

My eyebrows skyrocket to my hairline. "Did you just admit that you never cared?"

He winces. "No, I did. *Do*. Sorry." He sighs. "Damn, I'm already fucking this up." His gaze lands on my computer again. "I think you are an amazing writer, and I'm sorry for not seeing that. I've talked to Jenny, and she helped me see how, like, terrible of a person I am. I shouldn't have sent you that message a few weeks ago. To be honest, I only reached out because I missed you. Your article that week really was amazing. All of them are."

I cross my arms, skepticism still running through my body, but I try to not let it show on my face. "Thank you."

He tries to smile again, but it looks off. "So, you're dating someone new. Atlas, right?"

"Yeah, Atlas. He should be here soon, actually."

"Ah. That's great, Holland." His lips fall into a line. "Really, I'm sorry. And I'm sorry for not coming to your mom's funeral, and for hiding the information about your mom being the lawyer for Wanderlight."

"So you knew the entire time, then?"

He nods. "Everyone knows, but we were told by your mom and Jenny to keep it a secret from you so you didn't get the idea that you didn't deserve this job. But–" Gordon takes a step closer, placing his hands on my upper arms. My body tenses under his touch. "I know you deserve to be a writer at Wanderlight. You are incredibly talented, and everyone knows that. The other journalists, the editors, and all of the people you get to meet on your assignments.

Don't let this information about your mom ruin your confidence."

I fake a smile. "Thanks, Gordon," I say through my clenched teeth. I just want him to leave this house and this town. "I appreciate your apology."

"Of course. I mean it." He, thankfully, takes the hint and takes a step towards the door, dropping his hands from my arms. "And I think you should publish the article about Kurt and his company. That son of a bitch deserves to go down. If I knew what he was doing here, I would've never responded to his messages for me to visit."

I huff a surprised laugh. "Yeah, that's something we can actually agree on."

He smirks. "That's a first," he jokes. His arms widen to his sides, gesturing for a hug. I freeze, my eyes flickering back and forth between his stretched-out arms before landing back on his face. I blink at him before giving in, wrapping only one arm around his waist for approximately two seconds before stepping away awkwardly.

I put my hands behind my back and put a tight grin on my face. "Safe travels."

"Oh, before I go, do you have any bottles of water?" He tosses a thumb back towards the front door. "I'm planning on getting back to New York tonight and this town is so hot that it might as well be sitting directly on the sun."

I turn my back to him and walk a few steps to the fridge and retrieve a bottle from the top shelf, then grab him two others. It's a long drive back to New York. And, because I can't help it, I reach into the cupboard beside the fridge and grab a couple granola bars from the box Corinne bought from the grocery the other day. When I turn around, Gordon is standing in front of my laptop with a happy smile on his face.

"Thanks," he says, grabbing all of the items from my hands. He walks out the front door to his car parked on the side of the street with a simple wave in my direction, perfectly timed with Atlas walking from his driveway to mine.

Both Gordon and I look over at Atlas, but Gordon proceeds to wave at him and get inside the driver's side. By the time Atlas makes it to my porch, Gordon's fancy car is pulling out of the neighborhood.

"Hi," I say to the man before me as he steps up the steps.

"Hi, baby," he whispers, wrapping his arms around my waist and hoisting me up. I giggle, and as he sets me down, he says in my ear, "What was he doing here?"

"Apologizing, actually."

Atlas's eyes widen in shock. "Really?"

I nod. "Yeah, I'm surprised, too. He said he felt bad for how your dad talked to me yesterday."

"Of course, someone else always has to take the blame for my dad's actions." Atlas rolls his eyes. But his annoyance is gone in a blink of an eye when he interlaces our hands together. "Come on, we're going back to my place. I have dinner from the diner for us. And don't worry, I got extra for Oreo. I'm not about to face those judgmental cat eyes without offering him some."

My head falls back in a laugh. "He is a harsh critic," I joke, then rise to my tiptoes and press a kiss to his cheek. "Always taking care of us, Mr. Directions."

Atlas smirks before lowering his lips to mine in a soft, tender kiss. "Always for you, Holland."

chapter forty-five

On Tuesday morning, Atlas and I visit the infamous, *haunted* lighthouse.

The wooden bridge underneath us creaks and rattles in the breeze with each step we take towards the lighthouse. The setting sun reflects on the marshy water on either side of us and onto the wispy clouds and condensation trails from airplanes above.

Just a few yards away, I can see an older, run down shack–presumably Peter Ivins's home. Full of *guard* dogs. Overgrown weeds completely surround the front porch, and some stand as tall as the house itself. The roof sags in the middle, patched here and there with mismatched shingles, and there are weathered down slabs of wood that board up the two windows near the paint chipped front door.

As we walk closer to the house, dogs begin to bark. Dogs, plural, as in probably around five or so, and they chant and wail so loudly that I step closer to Atlas and use him as a shield, in case they begin to chase us. Our hands are latched together at our sides, and I squeeze his hand hard each time a dog barks, which is our anthem the entirety of our stroll towards the lighthouse.

The lighthouse stands tall at the end of the wooden path, hundreds of feet into the air. Its bold red and white stripes twist up the length of the tower, and the top glass encased lantern room acts like a mirror against the sun. It's beautiful, the way the cylindrical obelisk cuts the sky vertically in half and behaves as an eye of a storm for the birds that circle around it. It looks at peace, residing against the shore of the endless Atlantic, and not at all haunted.

But we aren't inside yet.

I pull my camera out of my bag and take as many pictures as I can so I can forward them to Selena when I get back to my house.

The house I only have one more night in.

I shake my head to force those thoughts to leave. Right now, I have the man that I am falling for leading me to my last destination in Saltmere, the place I have been waiting to explore since my first days in this town. Right now, I feel anticipation filtering through my veins over what I will be able to see at the top of the tower and the memories I will be able to make with Atlas standing at my side.

Right now, I follow Atlas to the door at the base of the tower and to the spiral staircase, one hand still intertwined with his and the other snapping pictures of the interior. The air inside smells of salt, rust, and musty stone. The walls are made of painted white brick with small, square windows scattering all the way up. At the base of the tower, the floor is a black and white checkered pattern, with one single lounging chair tucked against the wall of the staircase. There are endless amounts of spray paint graffiti on the brick walls, ranging from illegible, sloppy curse words to drawings of shapes and stick figures. But the sight that actually scares me is the dozens of fingernail scratch marks that scatter all over the small room.

I can feel chills grow on my spine and on the backs of my arms, and it's not because of the draft wind that is flowing around us. "This place really is creepy," I whisper.

"Just stay close to me," Atlas responds, giving me a firm nod.

Our footsteps echo on each step we take on the stairs. My eyes travel all around, but my ears perk up when I hear distant singing from below us. An angelic voice carols like a princess up the tower, and I inhale sharply. My body stiffens, but Atlas keeps us moving up the stairs, completely unfazed. Or pretending to be.

He doesn't seem like he needs a break once we get to step seventy-two, but he forces me to stop and helps me catch my breath when he hears me wheezing for air. My agitated state makes it difficult for me to calm down. I lean on his shoulder out the window that overlooks the rocky shoreline, watching the water curl in over itself in white, calming waves.

We finally get to the lantern room. We enter through the narrow doorway, and my jaw is immediately falling towards the floor when I step inside. The ocean feels like miles away from up here. The Fresnel lens structure in the shape of a crystal beehive sits in the center of the room, with a narrow walkway under the window panels surrounding it. The structure is large and tall, taller than Atlas and as wide as a car. Because of the setting sun, light catches on the prisms and scatters flecks of rainbows against the surfaces of the room.

On the only wall made of brick, next to the door, there is a single painting hung in a gold frame. It's a portrait of a woman, with dark brown hair chopped to her shoulders, her bangs swept over her pale, freckled face. She's smiling, her lips a vibrant shade of pink and the wrinkles near her vivid green eyes deepening with the elated emotion taking over every feature of her face. She has a hand cupping around her right cheek, but it's not her own. It belongs to someone else, with rich, tan skin. But the woman's face looks so similar.

It's like I'm looking into a mirror.

It's…my mom.

chapter forty-six

"What–" I begin, taking a step closer to the art. A stinging sensation crawls up my throat, and I don't swallow it down as my eyes wander over every feature that this woman and I share, every piece of her skin that I wish I could touch with my own two hands.

I snap my head to Atlas, a million questions wanting to jump off from the tip of my tongue, but I start with, "Did you know this was here? This painting?"

He blinks a dozen times. Takes a deep breath. Then says, "Yes."

I point a shaky finger to the painting. "Do you know who this is?"

"Yes."

The air from my lungs fails to come out. "This is my mom, Atlas. This is a painting of her face."

"I know."

A tear escapes down my cheek, and I am not sure why. *What does this all mean? How did Atlas know my mom?* I shake my head. I mean, his dad knew my mom. But the entire tower feels as if it is spinning. I clamp my eyes shut, pressing my fingers to my temples. "I know she visited this town but did…did she paint this? Is this her work?"

I feel and hear Atlas step closer to me, and he puts his hands on my fingers and gently removes them from the sides of my head. I open my eyes, and he presses a kiss to both of my palms. "Your mom didn't paint this one. My mom did."

I blink and blink at him. My lips part, and I slide my hands out from his hold on them and tilt my head. "I'm sorry, what?"

"Our moms were friends. They knew each other."

I huff a breathy laugh and swipe at the air between us. "You're hilarious, Atlas." I shake my head. "You sound crazy. There's no way our moms knew each other. How would that even be possible?"

"She loved the ocean, didn't she?"

He doesn't let me answer, and I don't think I would if I could. He trails a finger over my cheeks, swiping at the stream of tears there, but I flinch. He doesn't seem to notice, or he pretends not to. "Before my mom died, she told me about this woman she met in this town one summer in her early twenties. My mom lived here, and the woman–your mom–was visiting what was supposed to be her boyfriend's family, but she found out that he was cheating on her the first day she was here. Found him with Sam's mom, Aubrey, and that man, Sam's dad? That's the man your mom supposedly was engaged to at the time."

I shake my head. None of this is making any sense. "I don't think you have the right person, Atlas. My mom wasn't engaged when she came to Saltmere."

"She was. She left him that night, but she decided to stay in the town for the rest of the summer. Our moms met at the art gallery. My mom was a painter, and even though Kurt abandoned her pregnant with nothing but a soon-to-be child to take care of on her own, she never stopped trying to sell her work at the gallery. Your mom bought one of her paintings, and they became friends. Good friends, in fact. They spent the entire three months together sharing life stories and dreams of how their lives were supposed to go. Your mom said that her parents were sending her to law school in Chicago, and that they wouldn't, *couldn't*, support someone who wanted to waste their life being a painter. My mom explained how shitty of a person my dad was, *is*, for leaving her while she was pregnant. They bonded over how they wished they could escape the people that only brought them down.

"Our moms began to paint together, under the names of Lila Voss and Marina Calder, and soon, the gallery owner at the time, Esme, would sell out of all of their work, back when Saltmere actually had tourists and people that actually cared. Esme never stopped asking for everything they completed, both of their combined pieces and their individual pieces. Once the summer was over, and your mom had to go back to Chicago, Esme decided to keep the last of their two paintings, and those are the ones we saw together a month ago.

"Your mom was there when I was born in August, the day before she had to go back to Chicago and start law school. My mom painted this painting," he pauses to point back at the wall, "right before she passed away when I was seventeen. My mom didn't know where your mom was in her life, since they didn't stay in touch at all, but she knew your mom loved the ocean. So she painted her face and hung it in a place where your mom would always be able to see the thing she loved the most."

I can't see clearly. Salty clouds of tears have crowded on the edge of my eyelids, just seconds away from pooling over and tumbling down my face. Boiling hot anger presses deep onto my chest, seeping into my heart, then spreads into every cell. I take a step back, out of his hold. "You knew this entire time? You knew that our moms were friends?" My voice doesn't even sound like mine. I blink once, and a tear falls down my cheeks. "You knew about all of this and you didn't think to tell me sooner?"

He tilts his head to the side, his eyes squinting in confusion. "You're upset?"

"Of course I'm upset, Atlas!" My lips quiver, but I continue, feeling the hot emotion in every part of my body–my shaking hands, my aching legs, my shattering heart. "I'm always finding out secrets about my mom from other people. And you know how much I miss her. You let me talk about her endlessly, let me cry in your arms about her, and you even asked me questions as if you didn't already fucking know all about her!"

He recoils at my words, but I don't care. My body feels as if it is overheating. My face is on fire, and I am getting sweaty everywhere. I pace around the suddenly too small room, then lean against the railing at the base of the windows and look straight out at the neverending water. My shoulders won't stop trembling, and my tears splatter on my sandals after they fall.

"I'm sorry for not telling you sooner," Atlas says after a while. His voice is quiet. "You're right. I should've said something. I should've told–"

"Is that why you were so suddenly interested in me a month ago? Because you realized who I was? Who I was related to?"

"Mabel told me your full name and said that you were a writer, so I looked you up. But that picture of you and Gordon wasn't the only picture I saw on your profile. I saw you with your family as well, and I recognized your mom immediately. I looked her up after, then found out she passed, but I had already been such a dick to you. I felt so guilty."

I scoff and face him. "What about now?"

"What do you mean?"

"Do you feel guilty for misleading me? For making me fall for you? Why did you feel the need to go from being so rude to me to asking me out? From basically telling me to screw off to wanting to do everything we did together these past few weeks?"

He risks a step closer, and I lean my back against the glass, as if that will help me get farther away from him. He exhales, running a hand down his face. "I might have not told you what I knew, but my intentions for us have always been clear. I shouldn't have acted like that at first, but–"

"But once you realized that our mothers were once close, you felt the need to make it your goal to be with me, right?" I roll my eyes. "Your intentions haven't been clear, Atlas. Why do you want to be with me? Is it because of our moms' past? What if I wasn't the person I am, and we weren't connected like we are, would you still want to be with me?"

He hesitates, and that is all it takes for me to want to leave. I step forward towards the door to the staircase, but he grabs onto my wrist and turns me around.

The vein in his neck pulses like crazy. "You know that I struggle trusting people, Holland. It's difficult for me to make friends. It's hard for me to believe that they wouldn't expose who I really am. Who I am related to."

"You can't just assume that everyone is a horrible person like your dad, Atlas. I'm not your dad, and I wasn't before you put all the puzzle pieces together."

"I know you aren't like him. I know. I'm sorry for assuming the worst. But can you blame me? You heard it yourself what my dad and his wife did to me when I had to move in with him for a year. What my mom, even after she was already dead, had to go through? What my brothers, who I had never met at the time, said about me? About who I really am? I can't help but not be trusting to people I haven't met."

My chest feels like caving in on itself. I huff a fake laugh, then swallow and shake my head. "I'm sorry that you have been through the things you have. I really am. But I wish you never found out who I really was, Atlas. I wish I took your advice and not bothered you on that first night. I wish I spent this summer alone."

If I look hard enough, I think he has his own tears crowding his eyes. But my brain is clearly playing tricks on me in this wounding state of mind. "You don't mean that, Holland. You *can't* mean that."

No, I don't think I mean it. But I don't even feel like myself right now. I am so angry, so hurt, so betrayed that he kept this from me, and that if our moms didn't once know each other, we probably wouldn't even be together right now. Because who I am and what I do, *alone*, isn't enough. My goals and morals and accomplishments are not *enough.*

Why am I not good enough on my own? I've heard it from my family all my life, and I can see it on my dad's and Emmett's faces whenever I see them. Hell, I heard it just a few days ago from Emmett himself. My mom was the only one that believed in me, but even she helped me get to where I am today. Would I even be as great of a writer without her help in getting me my job?

I don't have the gift of confidence, but I thought that I was getting better at it while being in this town. Obviously, Kurt diminished my progress when he told me about the truth to my mom and by bringing Gordon for that short, pointless amount of time, but I had been living off of Jenny's faith in me to help this town and Atlas's and Mabel's and even Corinne's encouraging words that I really did believe that I was making a difference here. I think I was starting to believe in myself and who I am. But now, doubt is planting like a seed and is spreading like wildfire in my veins.

"Hol–" His voice fractures into pieces, and the soles of his feet slide against the floor in a swift movement only to close the distance growing between us. But the seconds tick down and the string that used to tug us together withers apart. "Please, don't go. Please." His shoulders shiver. "Please– I'm sorry. I'm so sorry." He deflates. "Don't leave me. I just started to feel like you're mine."

I shake my head, the tears trickling down my cheeks tumbling faster than I can think.

So I run. I run so fast out the door and down the stairs that not even the ghosts of this lighthouse can catch up with me, let alone Atlas. I sprint down the wooden pathway until I make it to the empty street, where I find the bus stop. As if knowing I'm desperate to escape, the town bus shows up before Atlas's truck tires crunch onto the pavement of the road behind me.

chapter forty-seven

I have dried tears stuck on my face when I hear my phone ring on the dresser next to my bed. It's Jenny calling.

"Hi, hon! Did I wake you up again?"

"Yes, but it's alright."

There's a beat of silence. "Are you okay?"

"Yep!" I say, too cheerily. "What's up?"

"I just wanted to let you know that I loved this new article you sent in. I meant to call you earlier this evening, but my meetings ran very late. Ariana forwarded your work to me because she was shocked at everything you wrote and knew I would love it. It really exposed the secrets of Gemini Development, and I loved that you didn't even hesitate to share all the dark details regarding Kurt Gemini's son, Atlas. I mean, how did you do it? How did you get all of this insider information? I'm asking for a friend, obviously."

"Wait, what?" I sit up in the bed. "What are you talking about?"

"So modest, as always, Holland. But seriously, did you meet with someone who hates Kurt or something? I know you actually interviewed Kurt, but there is no way you got all of this information from him."

"What?" Holding the phone in my hand, I jog to the living room to get my laptop and whip it open. The bright screen shines a cone of light onto my face, and as my eyes narrow and scan the document of everything regarding

Gemini Development and my sent email with every single detail I wrote down about Kurt Gemini's life to Ariana, my heart plummets.

"We're planning on publishing this article early," Jenny continues through the speaker. "Tomorrow morning, actually. The faster we get this information out to the public, the faster Kurt and Gemini Development can be stopped. He won't want to continue with his plans with all of the press in his face. I give it a day before news crews flood Saltmere's streets trying to find him."

No, no, no. Fuck!

Everything, from the documents Roman emailed me to all of Atlas's past memories he told me in confidence, is now in Ariana's, and Jenny's, hands. *I never sent any of this! The article wasn't ready!*

I wasn't planning on including the dark parts of Atlas's past in this article. I was planning on leaving his name completely out of my writing, just like he wanted. I haven't even spoken to him about anything I learned about his dad's company from Roman.

"Wait, Jenny–"

"You are incredible, Holland. I'm grateful we have you here at Wanderlight. I'll let you get back to bed. 'Night!"

The call ends.

Atlas is going to be furious with me. I might not be happy with him right now, but he *never* has deserved to have all of his secrets exposed like this. *What have I done? How did all of this get sent to Ariana?*

My fingers press hard into my closed eyelids, the pressure so forceful that stars blink back to me in the darkness. I *know* I haven't willingly sent any email to Ariana since my article last week. After meeting with Roman, I sat down at the table and typed up all my notes onto the document–

Gordon. Gordon came over and interrupted me.

I think you should publish the article about Kurt and his company. That son of a bitch deserves to go down.

He was standing in front of my laptop while I was getting him snacks and water. *Did he do this while I wasn't looking?*

My jaw clenches as I pick up my phone from the kitchen table. I don't care that it's almost midnight; I press on his contact and hold my device up to my ear, but the call goes straight to voicemail. I try again. And again. No answer.

Just as I bring the phone down, it pings with a new text.

Gordon: `Yes, I sent Ariana everything. Don't hate me.`

I already do! I want to scream at him. I don't think I actually hate him, but my increasing anger is only making my brain scramble in all different directions, and he just admitted that he did snoop onto my computer when I had my back turned and submitted a messy, incomplete article that was nowhere near ready for the public to read.

Slipping on my flip-flops, I sprint out the back door, my feet sliding on the freshly-watered grass of Atlas's back lawn. I knock on the glass window of his door rapidly, my chest rising and falling from anticipation and lack of exercise. I knock again when I don't hear any movement on the other side, then shift to where I know is the window of Atlas's bedroom, pounding my fist onto the glass so hard that it rattles the closed blinds on the other side. *Wake up, Atlas. Please. Wake up!*

I have to warn him of what the magazine is going to publish, to apologize for mishandling his trust and for storming off earlier today without fully hearing him out. I'm still upset that he kept his knowledge of my mom a secret from me this entire time, but that problem seems so little right now, so far out of a logical scope of rationality. Right now, all I care about is knocking on this damn window until Atlas answers and I can explain everything.

But he never answers. I run to the front door where I try ringing the doorbell like a lunatic, my finger turning pale with every push on the button. I turn my head to his driveway, and his truck is gone. *He's not even home.*

My chest caves as I walk back to my house, my mind swirling and my heart racing. There has to be something I can do to stop the article from going out to the public. As soon as my feet step inside the living room, an idea sparks. *If I get back to the city early enough, I can stop the article from being published.*

My head snaps to the time staring back at me in the darkness on the stovetop, reading that it's twenty minutes past midnight. I'll have to leave right now if I want to make it to the office in time.

Another thirty minutes passes before everything in the house is packed up and in my car. I take one last glance at the house, the house that I only lived in for a month but my soul seemed to recognize the second I walked through the door all those weeks ago. It's strange how quickly this house and this town have imprinted on me, how these walls and the cheerful faces of the residents became my closest friends while I was here. I have loved all of the places I've been sent to, but this town is different. I found a life I want to continue living, friendships I don't want to leave behind. *Someone* I don't want to leave behind.

I shift my gaze away just as a tear rolls down my cheek, and before I know it, I'm driving away from the town that feels like home and inching closer and closer to the life in the city I'm not sure I want to return to.

chapter forty-eight

I can barely keep my eyes open by the time I walk through the sliding doors of the skyscraper and step inside the elevator. My finger presses on the eleventh floor button, and I rest my head back on the cool metal wall as the doors close and the box moves upwards. My foot taps against the tile floor, and my fists open and close at my sides.

I'm running on fumes and gas station coffee, the kind that tastes like melted cardboard. It was the only thing that kept me upright somewhere around hour six.

The elevator dings. I jolt forward like I'm being pulled by a string, dragging my heavy limbs into the hallway lined with familiar frame covers and outdated potted plants with yellow hanging leaves. I walk straight to Jenny's open door at the end of the hall, the sound of my sandals tapping on the tile floors mixing in with the chaotic chatter surrounding the office.

Jenny's black hair is pulled tightly into a high bun. Her gray pantsuit doesn't have a single wrinkle on it, and her ruby red lipstick is still perfectly glossy, even with the lipstick stain printed on the coffee cup next to her mouse. She types and types away on the keyboard, her bright pink fingernails that contrast her deep brown skin dancing over the keys intensely.

When I knock twice, her neck cranks upwards, startled. "Holland. Jesus, what are you doing here so early?"

She looks at the watch on her wrist. "I wasn't expecting to see you until Monday." Her gaze travels down my entire body. "God, did you drive all night?"

"I need you to hold the story."

She frowns. "What?"

"Please," I say. My voice comes out more rugged than I intend. "Please. Don't publish the article yet."

She leans back in her chair. "It's solid work, Holland. There are clear pieces of evidence that deserve to be shown to the public."

"Maybe, but the material will hurt someone I care about, so if you could just wait–"

"It's already out, Holland."

My entire body goes numb. "What?"

"It was published an hour ago." She stands, stepping around her desk to put her hands on my shoulders. "It went up earlier than we scheduled, remember? I told you that over the phone." Her frown deepens. "I thought you understood."

The air fails to go through my lungs.

Jenny gives me a sympathetic smile. "It's a great article, Holland. I know you have a heart of gold, but you don't have to feel bad for what's going to happen to Kurt or his company. What you wrote, all of that information you gathered, will only help bring justice to those people he screwed over." She taps my shoulders before dropping her hands. "You should be proud."

I nod, because that's what I'm supposed to do. Because Jenny doesn't understand what this now means, how much harm is now done. She doesn't know who this article affects. She doesn't know that the pit forming in my stomach isn't because of my feelings towards what's going to happen to Kurt or Roman or any other Gemini employees; it's because of Atlas.

I press my lips together. "Right. Of course."

Jenny's smile widens. "Go home. Get some much needed rest, and I'll see you on Monday. Sounds good?" She snickers. "You've been working too hard. You look like a ghost."

I try to laugh, but it's forced. "Yeah."

She turns around, walks back to her chair, and sits down, resuming her typing. I walk out of her office in autopilot mode, only listening to my heartbeat pounding in my ears. Face after face passes by me as I saunter towards the elevator, their smiles too bright and cheery.

My phone buzzes in my pocket once I step alone back in the elevator. My heart plummets with horror, too afraid of who could be texting me, of what the message could say.

With shaky hands, I slip my device out.

Dad: `Hi, Holland. I'm in the city and was wondering if you were back yet. I'd like to talk.`

chapter forty-nine

My apartment feels foreign and bare when I step inside it. The last roommate I had, Lauren, moved out right before I left for Saltmere, and the apartment looks like it's been holding its breath ever since, waiting for someone to occupy the space. The air is stale. There are a few dishes left in the sink, left forgotten like the old books on the shelves near the dusty windowsill. The only light pouring into the living room and kitchen is the sunlight peeking in through the closed blinds.

I drop my keys in the bowl on the table near the door with a sigh, then drag my suitcase inside. The wheels squeak against the hardwood floor like it's protesting against coming back home, and I don't blame it. I don't want to be here either. It's lonely and dark, dampened by no monumental memories because I'm not here enough to make them.

I stand and stare at the place, my eyes roaming to the old and holey couch that my very first roommate, Elena, left behind. There's not a single picture frame on the television stand in front of it, not a single decoration to help bring this place to life. I look at the kitchen. There are no sage green cupboards, no hand painted coffee mugs. No fresh flowers in a vase in the center of the table.

This isn't home to me. I've never thought of it to be, never thought I would have rented out this apartment for this long. I'm not here long enough before I'm sent on another assignment, but standing here, looking at this lifeless, vacant space makes me want to get back in my car and drive the nine hours back to Saltmere.

That town felt like home.

I check my phone, where I see a message from Corinne:

`Call me after you meet with him, okay? You got this, Hol.`

My phone pings in my hand again, and when I read the message, I want to chuck it out the window. I should be happy that my dad wants to meet in person. He's never come to visit me before, doesn't even know where my apartment is located or even what the magazine's name is. But he wants to meet at the coffee shop below my building and *talk*, and there's nothing I dread more at this moment. I'm tired. I'm exhausted. Mentally and physically. I just want to sleep and cry and pray to whoever is listening above that Atlas won't read the article.

He won't answer my calls, but hopefully he chooses to not read this story of mine.

An hour later, I'm sitting in the farthest booth in the cafe that I can't stop comparing to Velvet Bean. The people aren't as friendly, the floors don't creak as loud, and the walls aren't covered with paintings of the mountains and ocean in bright colors. Every customer is dressed in pantsuits and stern expressions with a briefcase crowding their fancy shoes.

The door jingles as a tall man walks inside, his silver speckled hair combed over to the side. His red t-shirt is tucked into a pair of tan cargo shorts, and his black sneakers squeak on the floor after his gaze connects with mine and he strolls over to my table.

I freeze. My fingers grip on the edge of the mug in front of me, and my stomach drops to the floor.

"Holland," my dad says, exasperated, like he's out of breath from running to get here. He takes a seat across from me. His bright blue eyes trail over my face, reading the weariness plastered on it. "You don't look so good."

I sigh. "Thanks, Dad," I say flatly. "You look exactly the same."

He shakes his head, shutting his eyes closed for a second before opening them again. "Sorry, that came off wrong. I just meant that you look tired."

"Yeah, well, I drove back here all night long." I glance down at my coffee, trying to collect myself. "Why are you here?"

He exhales slowly, then forces a smile. "I want to be closer with you. I haven't been able to stop thinking about you after that phone call with Emmett."

My eyebrows skyrocket, but then I scoff. "That's funny. You used to go entire days without saying more than three words to me. If that." I'm being bitter, but I can't help it. I'm running on less than two hours of sleep.

He flinches, but he doesn't deny it. "I know," he says. "I was there, but I wasn't…there. Not really. Not for you."

I turn my head to look out the window. The sunlight bounces off a car door outside, too bright for this conversation. "You were a great father for Corinne and Emmett. You went to every event. Every science fair and award ceremony. You called them brilliant. You said that they were following perfectly in Mom's footsteps like you wanted."

"I remember," he admits. He nods slowly. "And I regret that. I made you feel that because you didn't bring home straight A's or a medal of some sort, you weren't worth as much. And god, Holland, that's not true. That was never true."

"It felt like it," I retort. "You made me feel like I was always a disappointment you didn't know what to do with."

His frown deepens. "I thought I was being fair. Letting you figure things out on your own, in your own way. But in reality, I was just avoiding the hard part. Getting to know you. Understanding you."

A long, treacherous moment of silence passes by before he speaks again. He scratches the back of his head. "I, uh, found out that you have dyslexia. The night your mother passed, before I left the two of you back at home so I could run to the store for her."

I try to breathe normally, but my chest and throat burn.

"That morning, she told me that I should try to talk to you. Try to improve our relationship. And, no, I'm not saying all of this because it's the wish she has for me from her deathbed." He gives me a soft smile. "She told me about your challenges with reading and writing growing up and about your diagnosis. And it all hit me like a brick. There were so many signs, but I didn't connect the dots. Your mother was there for you, and I'm grateful that she was, but why didn't you tell me?"

"Because I didn't think you'd care," I say. "Because when I was eleven and crying at the dinner table over a book report, you told me to stop being lazy and 'use my brain'. I figured that told me everything I needed to know about you."

He rubs a hand over his face and nods, breaking eye contact. "I failed you," he says, voice ragged and staring at the leftover crumbles on the table. "Not because you weren't smart. Because I couldn't see past my own idea of what smart looked like. And I'm sorry. For every time I made you feel less than. For not protecting the parts of you I didn't understand. For being a ghost of a father."

He leans forward, blue irises sliding into my brown ones. "You're not broken, Holland. You never were. You just needed someone to meet you where you were. And I was too blind to do it."

I stare at him, the ache in my chest pulsing sharp and slow.

"I don't know if I can forgive you. At least, not yet." The honesty slips off of my tongue in a soft tone. "But I think I want to try."

He nods. "I'll be there for you, Holland, for the rest of my time. And if you ever want to tell me more, about the magazine or Saltmere or even what you had for breakfast in the morning, I'll listen. *Really* listen."

He sounds so earnest that I think I believe him. But actions speak louder than words. "Okay." I swallow. "I'd like that."

chapter fifty

The week passes by without a word from anyone from Saltmere, even after the article about the coves, the lighthouse, the meadow and treehouse, the tulip field, and the old flower garden was published. And I don't blame them. I might've exposed everything Kurt has done, but I left without saying goodbye. I left everything and everyone I loved there.

Dark, summer storm clouds cover the entirety of the sky, and rain beats down the windows of the building. It's perfect weather for how I'm feeling and how much this week has drained me.

The hours pass by, and when all of my coworkers have left their offices to go home, back to their families and happy lives, I stay glued to my seat. I don't want to go back to my apartment, anyway. There's nothing but loneliness there.

Just as I'm staring blankly at the wall across from me, lost in the quiet hum of the office and the rain outside, the sound of wet footsteps pulls me from my thoughts. My eyes widen and I sit up in my chair when I realize that Atlas is standing in the doorway of my office, holding Oreo in a blanket. His hair is soaked to his forehead and dripping water droplets onto the carpet. His black shirt and denim jeans hug tight against his chest and legs.

I slowly stand from my chair, the wheels rolling noisily behind me. My throat stings, but I swallow down the burning emotion as best as I can. "Wh–what are you doing here?"

He doesn't move, only his chest rising up and down rapidly. "You left without saying goodbye."

I nod, cautiously. "I had to."

"Why?"

I bite my lip. The nerves in my stomach are performing somersaults. "I thought that if I came home in time, I would stop Jenny from publishing the article about your dad."

His eyelids shut, and he breathes deep through his nose, working his jaw.

"But I was too late. I'm sorry," I say weakly. "I'm so sorry. I didn't mean to share the parts of your life you didn't want public. I swear. After I talked to Roman about what Gemini Development was planning on doing to Saltmere, I just wrote everything I knew about Kurt's life down on my laptop. And when Gordon surprised me by coming over that same day, he sent everything to my editor without me realizing." My hands cover my eyes, and I gather all of the remaining composure as best as I can and continue, my voice muffled through my palms. "I promise, Atlas, I didn't mean to share those details. I didn't mean to expose your identity to anyone, especially to the people in Saltmere." My shoulders are shaking. "God, I bet everyone hates you just as much now. I bet they are assuming you are just like your dad. I'm so sorry, Atlas. I'm so sor–"

"Holland."

His deep, low voice comes from directly above me. I part my fingers and peek through the opening up at him. Oreo is now resting on the chair in the corner. With his gentle, calming touch, he lowers my hands from my face, holding onto them at our sides.

My eyes flick up to his hazel irises, then to his parting lips. "I'm not mad at you for that, baby."

I withhold a shudder, blinking quickly to erase the blurriness crowding my eyelids. "Did you read the article, though? Everyone knows now, Atlas. Everyone knows that you are a Gemini."

He shrugs. "I read it. And I loved it."

I pull back. "*What?*"

"I'm not mad that everyone knows who I am, where I come from. I know who I am, and so does the town. Thanks to you." He pauses to bring a hand up and swipe a piece of my hair behind my ear. "Thanks to you, people actually care about me. People who don't assume I'm just like Kurt Gemini, people who want to talk to me in the grocery store aisles and come buy my boats. People care about me *because* of you. Before you came to Saltmere, I purposefully chose to distance myself from everyone. I was so scared that they would judge me once they found out how I was related to the very man wanting to ruin everything the town stood on. But you came along, with your weird graphic tees and your determination to do good for Saltmere, and I knew right then that I wanted to shine just as much as you already did."

A tear travels down my face. "Atlas."

"I was a dick to you in the beginning, and I'm so sorry for that. Some of it was because I didn't want you to try and be friendly to me, but most of it was because I knew I would become addicted to you. You are like a beacon, Holland. Your kindness drew me in, hooked me by a finger and led me out of the darkness I thought I was content in. I didn't realize just how lost I was before you moved in next door. And I promise, Holland, that had nothing to do with our moms' connection in their past." He pauses, squeezing my hands.

"It was all you," he says in a whisper. "Your stubborn hope, the way you see beauty in everything around you. The way you continue to look at me like I matter, like I'm worth knowing–it undoes me every time. *You.* Not anyone else. No one in this universe has ever made me feel the way you do, has made me feel like I belong. And you are the only person that can take credit for that." His shoulders fall. "I'm sorry for not making it clear about my intentions. But I know that I'm falling for you, Holland, and I just want to be yours. I want to be someone you can trust, someone you can feel safe and seen with." He exhales shakily. "I just want to be with you."

My heart pounds in my chest, and another tear streams down my cheeks. He brings one of my hands to his cold lips, kissing my skin gently. Quietly, he says, "But only if you let me."

My throat burns.

"If you need time, I'll wait. If you want to shove me out of this office, out of this building, out of this *city*, I'll understand. But I had to come and tell you the truth. I needed you to hear it, and maybe it's too soon, but I don't care. I couldn't let another day pass without telling you that I'm falling in love with you, Holland."

His voice cracks on my name, and he drops my hands. He takes a step backwards, as if he's giving me space to make a decision. But his words float and dance around in the silence coursing between us, our gazes locked and filled with everything we've said and everything we haven't. Both fear and hope intertwine in his eyes, fragile and flickering. He's handed his heart out on the line for me without any armor to protect it. But still, he waits for my answer, body trembling from the cold and lips rolled together.

I let another tear cascade down my cheeks. "I'm falling in love with you too, Atlas."

I close the remaining distance between us and lunge into him, wrapping my arms around his neck. I can't help it. I couldn't wait for him to assume any longer that I don't want him.

He's everything I need, everything that strengthens my very existence and reminds me of my purpose. He's done that the entire time I've known him, minus our very first interaction. But I think that's something we can laugh about one day.

I kiss him, long and hard, desperate to feel his lips on mine and his fingers threading on both the back of my head and the small of my back. My own hands cup his cheeks to pull him even closer to me.

"So *that's* why you didn't want the article published," a familiar voice says from the doorway of my office.

Atlas and I both look at Jenny leaning against the frame, arms folded. She takes a step inside as a smile widens on her red lips. She helps herself by sinking onto the edge of my desk and crossing her ankles together. "It all makes sense now. You fell for the son of the enemy."

I wince, but Atlas chuckles, rubbing both of my arms. "I think it's kind of romantic," he says, turning his head to look down at me. "Tragic family history, next door neighbors, a tiny bit of fake dating that never once was fake, and invisible string tying us together. Honestly, we should've seen it coming."

My cheeks hurt from smiling so hard. "Yeah, we should've."

epilogue

A Year Later

Atlas

I hold the latest issue of Wanderlight Journeys in one hand and Oreo in my other as I walk back up the steps of the porch of our house, smiling down at it like a lovesick fool. On the cover, Holland stands in front of Grace's art gallery with her beautiful, wide smile on her face and she's holding her mom's completed painting, the same one that the two of us got to see in the back room a year ago today.

Her being on the cover with a special piece of Saltmere in the background is a full circle moment for her. After her assignment to this town that we both call home now, she was assigned to visit multiple towns on the East Coast to highlight different art galleries to help bring more people to them. We roadtripped together to each destination, and as we hit our last location, Jenny promoted Holland to features editor, a title that means she can still chase stories, but she gets to decide which ones. No more weekly deadlines–just honest, human stories that she loves. She now gets to explore wherever she wants *and* gets her own issues once a month. She does still work closely with Ariana, but she has the option to edit her own work as well.

I'm so fucking proud of her.

And because of the article that Gordon sent forward without Holland's permission, my business is flourishing, too. People, even those outside of Saltmere, were quick to connect the dots about my real identity and the boat company, and I have been swamped with special orders from customers all over the country. I couldn't be more grateful, even if I want to still throttle Gordon.

But because of that rush to publish that article, my dad is now in prison, serving a sentence that he should've gotten years ago.

I open the front door of what used to be Mabel's house that we officially purchased from her a couple months after Holland returned from New York. We are renting out my house to Corinne, who vowed to stay in Saltmere just to be close to her sister.

The woman I love is sitting at her usual chair at the kitchen table, her face glued to her laptop screen and her fingers typing away on the keyboard. I lower to my knees to set Oreo down and he jumps out of my hold, scurrying away towards the laundry room where I know he will take a nap in his favorite basket full of clothes. With two hands, I hold the magazine and wrap it over Holland's head and in front of her face. She jumps in her seat before leaning her head back against my chest.

But when she realizes what I'm holding, she leans forward. "What…how do you have this?"

"I asked Jenny for an early copy."

"But," she peers up at me, "this issue doesn't come out for another couple weeks. There's no way Ariana had time to go over every article in this issue. I sent everything to her two weeks ago. I *just* took this photo for the cover." A line forms on her forehead when her eyebrows crease together. "How did you get this?"

I shrug. "I have my ways." I tug at the chair closest to her and take a seat, placing the magazine in between us on the table. We flip through the pages together, and I listen and love the small gasps and contented sighs that come out of Holland's mouth every time I turn the page and her eyes roam over the content. She points to every picture she took of each gallery and some of the artwork for sale there that's on the pages, telling me information I already know because I was there with her. But I can't help but stare at her in awe as the smile on her face widens and the dimples on the sides of her cheeks deepen with every word that comes out of her pretty mouth because she's amazing and so, so incredibly talented, and she's adorable when she's excited.

When we get to the final page, the nerves in my stomach strengthen. I glance over at Holland and watch her head tilt slightly and her lips fall into a line. Her eyes squint and she brings the magazine closer to her face.

"I didn't write this," she says quietly, her eyes dancing over the words that *I* wrote.

I asked Jenny if I could have just two pages of the issue, and when she said that she couldn't do that, she offered an alternative. An early, personalized issue of the magazine that's just for the two of us.

The feature is titled, "The Girl Who Sees Everything", and the first lines read:

I fell in love with a woman who photographs everything but herself.

Her camera catches sunrises and rusted hinges and the shimmer of light through pieces of sea glass. But she never turns the lenses to herself. She doesn't know what she looks like when she's locked in wonder. She doesn't see the way her brows furrow right before she presses the capture button, or how she whispers "got it" under her breath like it's a secret.

This is what I've seen for the last year. This is the story I need to tell.

Holland doesn't speak for a long time. She flips the page slowly after she finishes reading it, and then she gasps again, louder this time. On the next page, there are multiple photos of her as she's taking pictures of whatever's in front of her. The rows of tulips in the tulip field, the line of the horizon and the calm ocean waves, the array of blinking stars above the two of us. Full-bleed photographs of Holland, taken without her noticing. Some are framed from behind her shoulder, catching her silhouette against the golden light. In the very last one, her hair's blowing wild across her face as she laughs, mid-click.

She slowly turns her head up to look at me. Her eyes are glossy. "You did this?"

I nod.

She sniffles before wrapping her arms around my neck, pulling me into her. I feel her tears tumble down my neck.

She pulls her head up, locking our gazes together, then leans in. "Oh, Gemini," she utters against my lips. It's her newest nickname for me, and I don't mind at all. Because when my last name comes from her lips, it doesn't sound like a burden. It doesn't sound like pressure or history or scandal. It sounds like mine, like something I can be proud of if she's the one saying it.

"I love you," she continues, pressing a kiss to the corner of my lips. "So, so much. Thank you for this." She kisses me gently, then smiles with watery eyes before she turns back to the magazine, looking at herself on the cover.

I reach for her camera on the table as quietly as I can and snap a picture.

THE END

~~~~
~~~~

acknowledgements

First, I want to thank my husband, Jorge, who has been my safe place from the very beginning. Thank you for believing in me while I step into this journey I've dreamed of since I was a little girl. Thank you for listening to my wild ideas, celebrating my wins, and lifting me up when I doubted myself. Without your constant reassurance, I don't think I would've gained the courage to try to spill my words onto the page for everyone to read. I am so grateful for you!

Second, I want to thank the girls I've worked with at The Book Box. I will forever be grateful for each of your friendships and the way you have cheered me along in every single way.

Thank you to my family for teaching me the value of stories and hard work, and for always reminding me that my dreams were worth chasing.

Thank you to my editor, Katherine, and my cover designer, Madison, for caring about this project just as much as I did. Your enthusiasm to work with me and get this book to where it is now is something I will cherish forever!

Finally, thank you to every single reader who has picked up this book and giving me the time to share something so dear to my heart. The fact that you are holding my words in your hands means more to me than I could ever express. You are the reason these pages exist, and I am honored to share this journey with you.

Made in the USA
Coppell, TX
02 March 2026

72700138R00187